MOLOCH'S CHILDREN

DAVID A. RILEY

Parallel Universe Publications

First serialised in *Filthy Creations* published by Roger Pile
2013 as *Sendings*
First book version published by
Parallel Universe Publications 2015
David A. Riley © 2015

ISBN: 978-0-9932888-1-4
Parallel Universe Publications, 130 Union Road,
Oswaldtwistle, Lancashire, BB5 3DR, UK

For Linden

PROLOGUE

Teb crouched over his glass of beer. He glanced up at the clock above the bar. A quarter to ten, and already the sky was solid black through the dappled windows of the pub. He looked back at his beer as three dart players, two farm labourers and the son of a local grocer, burst out laughing at a murmured joke. Another ten minutes, Teb thought through the explosion of mirth, and he'd finish his pint. By that time Cathgart, the head gamekeeper at the Fentons' estate, would be parking up outside the Hare and Hounds at the opposite end of the village. Leaving plenty of time for a few hours poaching. Teb smiled. Though times were hard, at least the prices they paid in London for freshly killed pheasant were satisfactorily high. Very satisfactorily high, he thought to himself with a feeling of contentment. Earned from his last nocturnal visit to the estate, a thick bundle of five-pound notes in an elastic band still burned a hole in his trouser pocket - a solidly reassuring bundle he hoped he'd double tonight.

He smiled slyly as he sipped his beer. His callused hands tingled with anticipation. Even if the money he regularly earned from poaching hadn't been as good as it was he would still have been tempted. The tense exhilaration was more than enough to justify the risks he ran, though whether it was the risks that excited him so much as the sheer satisfaction of 'getting one over' on the smug owners of the estate, he did not know. Probably both were part of it, he thought.

Wiping his fingers across the bristles on his jaw, Teb glanced around the bar, wondering with cynical amusement how many of the others in here would have the nerve for it. It suited his narrow egotism to think he was the only man here who would have dared, especially when he looked at the self-satisfied faces of the middle-aged couples at most of the tables.

"How goes things, Teb?"

Round-shouldered and seedy, Arthur Ramsgrave peeled himself from the bar with an oily exuberance and swayed towards him, a half empty glass of beer in one hand and a dirty, disreputable-looking pipe in the other.

Though Teb had seen him earlier, he had done his best to ignore the Liverpudlian exile, even though he was aware that Arthur had repeatedly glanced at him during the night, trying to catch his eye. Teb squirmed irritably. Arthur - whose local nickname was Arthur Tittlemouse - was a notorious gossip. Rumour had it he'd been forced to leave his native city years ago because one of its more violent criminal gangs suspected he'd given information to the police about some of their members. Whether he still had the ear of the police, Teb didn't know, but he didn't want to run any unnecessary risks either. In any case he couldn't stand the man. Arthur's hands and face had a nasty, greasy look to them, and his eyes were yellow and too close set, like a ferret's.

A sick ferret's.

"What d'yer want?" Teb asked belligerently.

Arthur tapped his sleeve with the tips of his nicotine-stained fingers.

"Now is there any need for that?" he asked in a plaintive tone that grated with Teb. "I only asked a civil question, like, didn't I?"

"Why don't yer go an' ask yer *civil* questions o' someone else in 'ere, 'cause I don't want to know." Teb noisily emptied his glass in one gulp.

Arthur gazed about the bar for a moment as if put off. Its beamed ceiling was all but hidden by the cloud of cigarette smoke that had built up during the evening. Lower down, it covered everything with a pungent blur.

"I hear someone's been at it again at the big estate," Arthur said, finally. He looked back at Teb - calm and studious, like a well-seasoned gambler studying the odds.

"At what again?" Teb made a stab at sounding disinterested.

"What d'you think? Someone's been havin' a go at the pheasant. So I've heard."

Teb gazed at his emptied glass.

"Are they doin' anythin' about it?" he asked eventually, as off-handedly as he could manage.

Arthur shrugged.

"They're watchin' the area. There's only so many ways in and out o' the estate - as you well know." Arthur tapped his sleeve again, even though he had gained Teb's interest already. "But there's still one route they'll not be watchin'."

Teb looked up from his beer glass, ignoring the urge to caution that twinged inside him.

"An' which is that?"

A confidential smile lurked across the Liverpudlian's lips as he wet them with his tongue.

"They'll not be watchin' the woods around Elm Tree House, will they?"

Teb nodded his agreement. That, at least, was true, he thought. No one was likely to go through that dark patch of land, especially at night. The house was ugly enough, almost derelict now, but the woods were even worse: overgrown and wild, they were a nightmarish jungle, well matched to the tales that had grown about them. Legends, folklore, old wives' tales, a load of ridiculous nonsense, Teb knew, as at home in the country at night by himself as he was in his pokey little cottage. The darkness held no hidden fears for Teb. He'd have been no good as a poacher if it did.

A suspicion crept into his mind as he finished ruminating about the place. He stared hard at Arthur.

"Why did yer come o'er to tell me this?" he said. "Why should I be interested?"

Arthur leaned closer till Teb could smell the thick odour of his breath.

"Come off it, Teb. I knows as well as you do who's been havin' a go. I'm not as blind as the rest o' the buggers in 'ere. I know what's goin' on."

"And I s'ppose yer know what folk have to say about you as well, eh?"

"Folks can say what they like. Just think on this: a wise bird doesn't shite in its own nest. No one in Endon can point a finger at me and say I've got 'em in trouble. Now is there or isn't there?"

"So?"

"Just think on this as me doin' you a favour, that's all. If you find what I've said's been useful to you - a show of appreciation would be nice afterwards. You know what I mean?"

"I get your drift," Teb muttered. He watched the man carefully for a moment, then reached out and took hold of his tie, gripping the material in his strong fingers. He pulled on it hard with a deliberate, calculated, brutal slowness, till Arthur's face was inches from his own. "If I get caught going through those woods," Teb whispered, "if the cops or the gamekeepers are out there, waiting for me, all set up, I'll know what sneaky little bastard arranged it... won't I?"

"Nothin's been set up. There'll be no one there, I promise."

"There'd better not be, for your sake, 'cause I could be just as good at dealin' with sneaky little bastards whose mouths are too big as I am at dealin' with pheasants. D'yer follow that, Arthur?"

Teb let go of his tie and the Liverpudlian pushed himself back, his cheeks flushed pink as he loosened his collar and smiled nervously.

"You've nothin' to worry about, Teb. I told you. I never shit in my own nest."

"Yer'd better not do, Arthur, or it'll be the last time yer shit - ever."

Arthur glanced round the bar.

"Would you like another drink?" he asked.

Teb banged his glass down on the table between them.

"Yer can get me one tomorrow. It's time I was off." He stared hard into Arthur's jaundiced eyes, his brows darkening. "Remember what I said. Anythin' goes wrong I'll know who to blame. Won't I?"

Arthur made as if to pat Teb's arm in reassurance, but his fingers held back when he looked at the poacher's face.

"You'll be all right, Teb. I like you. I've always liked you. I've never done anythin' to harm someone I liked. Never."

"Yer'd better not," Teb muttered. He climbed to his feet, glanced once more at the man, then lumbered heavily towards the door. The warm air outside was comfortingly fresh after the smoke-filled atmosphere of the pub, and Teb breathed in lungfuls of it to clear his brain, before striding to a clump of bushes on the far side of the road. He'd left a canvas bag in the grass behind it. Inside were the tools he'd need for the night's work. A quick check showed no one had disturbed it. He swung the bag over his shoulder, looked both ways down the cobblestone street, then headed out over the hump backed bridge by the pub and strode towards the woods. For a while, at least, he would be safe on this road. Deep ditches filled with grass and weeds lay on either side; it would only take him a second to hide inside them if he saw any sign of the police. Beyond the ditches there was usually only a wooden fence or a low, dry stone wall, neither of which would hold him back for more than a moment if he had to make a dash for it. Teb knew the ways through the fields and woodlands around here far better than most people -

certainly much better than any of the police who were likely to be lurking about the place in wait for him. The local bobby stationed in the village - and the only one of them who might have known the district as well as he did - was Andy Fisher. But Andy wasn't far off retirement now and wouldn't be much use scrambling through hedgerows in the dark. It took him most of his time nowadays to mount the saddle of his bicycle. As for any of the younger policemen who might have been brought in from the main police station at Fenley, they'd only get themselves lost in this area at night once they were off the main roads. Teb smiled to himself as his boots crunched on the gritted road in the gloom.

An almost cloudless night, the sky was ablaze with stars. Teb was glad the moon was no more than a sliver at this time of the month. Although he had no appreciation for the prowess of the police in hunting him down, he had greater respect for Cathgart and the other gamekeepers on the estate. Some of them had almost caught him in the past. Because of this he had already decided to take Arthur's advice, despite the qualms he felt about him. It was an inarguable fact that the woods around Elm Tree House were the least likely route anyone would ever expect him to take to the estate. Superstitious fears of the place were too strong. Teb spat into the ditch beside the lane for good luck. Others might be put off by what they had heard about it. Not him. He'd spent too much time out at night by himself over the past thirty years to be put off by a few wild tales. He knew there was nothing to be frightened of in the woods at night. Nothing worse, at any rate, than a few gamekeepers and the police.

Three quarters of a mile further on from the village the woods were considerably thicker beyond the hedgerow. The darkness between the trees was so dense, in fact, that Teb doubted if even at midday much light could penetrate the dense masses of leaves to hit the forest floor. Silhouetted against the stars above the black treetops, no more than a hundred yards away, loomed the roof of Elm Tree House. It was a tall building, grey where moonlight washed across the slates of its roof. It was more than ten years since anyone lived there, and For Sale signs from an estate agent in Fenley had acquired a mouldy, forgotten look to them which Teb was sure would put off any potential buyers even more than the dilapidated state of the house itself. The building was an imposing edifice. Hundreds of years old, it was three floors high in parts, with tall, almost stately windows. Teb had always been impressed by its ornate ugliness, from the stone figures stood about the edge of its roof to the dried-up fountain in the drive.

The wrought-iron gates at the start of the tar-macadam drive beneath the trees were padlocked, but Teb merely squeezed through a gap in the railings alongside, where several uprights had rusted and fallen in over the years. He landed with a thud on the clumps of grass that sparingly covered the bare earth on the other side.

As he threaded his way through the trees, he supposed it would have been a wiser course of action to lie low for the time being till things had had time to cool down, but he had too many debts and too many promises to fulfil to be able to allow himself a luxury like that. Besides, there was always the added thrill of being able to pull off a trick like this right under their own noses. Teb's grin deepened into a self-satisfied smirk, which lingered about his mouth even when he drew nearer the house, despite the chill that seemed to fill the air as he walked across the drive. The trees immediately next to the house had a gaunt, unhealthy look to them that contrasted with the lush vegetation elsewhere about Endon. As he skirted the dismal building, he noticed the grass looked grey and thin, as if stricken by some kind of disease. He glanced up at the unlit windows high above him, tall and thin in the stonework. None of their grimy panes had been broken, which was proof enough of a sort, he supposed, that none of the local children had felt brave enough to come here since the owners left the place. He felt at the thick, vein-like growths of ivy that had overrun its walls.

With a grunt of disgust, Teb turned from the house. The Fentons' estate was close by now. Pausing to unfasten the bag over his shoulder, he took out the pieces of walnut and metal that made up his shotgun. His practised fingers soon fixed them together in the gloom. He reached for a cardboard box at the bottom of the bag, picked out a couple of shells and loaded the gun in readiness, though he cautiously kept the breach broken.

He tucked the gun under his arm to set off, when he suddenly stiffened. Not far away he heard the unmistakable crack of a breaking twig.

Teb's eyes narrowed as he stared into the gloom in the direction the sound had come from.

At any other time, in any other place he might have shouted to ask who it was, but only an idiot would have done anything like that when he was out at night with a bag full of poaching equipment and a loaded shot gun. And Teb, for all he might have been hard pressed to spell much more than half a dozen words correctly, was no idiot.

He scanned the area for the slightest movement, his breathing stilled.

Something rustled through the leaves, and a tall, thin shape emerged from the darkness. It appeared to be staring at him, and Teb felt his flesh start to crawl with nausea, as if he'd slipped into a burrow full of slugs. The intensity of his nausea astonished him. What was it? What could it be that sickened him so much, even though he couldn't make out any details as yet in the gloom? Superstitious fears rose with a force he would have thought himself incapable of feeling earlier.

With an attempt at resolution, Teb snapped the shot gun shut, the sharp sound of metal slotting into place reassuring him as he aimed the gun at the shape.

"Who are yer?" His voice betrayed his growing nervousness, despite the resurgence of some kind of courage the gun had given him. He hooked his finger round one of the triggers. "Yer've five seconds to speak afore I let yer have a bellyful of shot." He steadied his aim. "Four seconds!" Sweat trickled down his forehead like an ice-cold beetle. "Three!" He pressed the stock to his shoulder. "Two!" He paused one second, then two seconds more - then fired. The gun went off with a thunderous crash in the unnatural silence of the woods. Even through the ringing echoes that drummed through his ears he still heard the pellets thrash through the leaves of the bush at which he'd been aiming, shredding them - and the figure in front of them - in an instant.

Teb stared, transfixed with sudden, disbelieving panic as the figure swayed, then moved towards him. For a moment he expected it to fall - or cry out at least in some sort of pain. Then its face moved out of the shadows into the dim twilight of the clearing, and Teb felt his throat contract as he struggled with a silent scream of despair before a crashing, thudding, pumping darkness exploded through his brain.

11

The early morning mists had left the road into Endon slippery with dew as Walter Barlow took his milk van along it at a steady fifteen miles an hour. At this time of the day he had learned long ago it wasn't wise to go any faster. You never knew when some stray animal, probably a sheep, with a lamb in tow, would appear round a bend in the road. Although he knew he shouldn't swerve to avoid one, instinct had taken over last time and cost him half his load when the van tipped into the ditch.

Nice and steady. That was the trick. Nice and steady. There was no need to hurry. Not in a village like Endon, anyway.

Walter whistled to himself while he drove, feeling cheerful at the fine weather the morning promised for the rest of the day. The sun was already shining bright above the trees.

His whistling died when he caught sight of a man stagger out into the road ahead of him. Despite his dishevelled appearance, Walter recognized him. He'd seen Teb often enough over the years in the Squire's Arms, though he'd rarely if ever exchanged more than a couple of words with him.

Walter slammed on the brakes and parked.

"What's up, Teb? What's the matter?"

Walter climbed out of the van as Teb collapsed in the middle of the road, groaning. Racing to the man, Walter reached out and rolled him over, cradling his head in one arm as he tried to make out what was wrong with him. Walter grimaced as he looked at the Teb's distorted face. There was a horrible twitch down the side of one cheek that seemed to pulse with a life of its own, as the man struggled to mumble something; his eyes rolled uncontrollably, full of fear.

"Easy now. Easy," Walter said, soothingly. "What is it? What's wrong? What's happened to you?"

But there was no sense to be got from him.

Not yet.

Nor for many months to come.

CHAPTER 1
APRIL, 1992

Morgan Davies stooped over the breakfast table and peered at the letter his wife had left out for him, propped against the marmalade. It was in an unopened envelope, handwritten, postmarked Fenley. Oliver - Oliver Atcheson - that was who must have sent it to him, Morgan realized. A grin of pleasure, tinged only by a slight feeling of apprehension, spread across his lips as he reached out for the envelope and slit it open with the unused butter knife. It was ages since he'd heard from Oliver, and Morgan wondered how his friend was now. Oliver had left for Spain during the winter to recuperate from the nervous breakdown he'd suffered after the violent death of his wife. Morgan unfolded the letter in front of him. He'd only received one letter from Oliver since he returned to England, and that was to say he had decided to settle in Fenley, where he was buying an old house he'd been told about, and that it was in need of renovation. He'd sold the home he'd shared with Louise before he set out for Spain. No doubt the memories it contained had been too painful for a man of Oliver's nature. Now, it appeared, as Morgan read through the letter, Oliver had carried out his plans, and enough of the renovations had been completed on the house he'd purchased to make it "fit for habitation".

"I'd be delighted," the letter read, "if you and Winnie would come here to spend the week-end - or, perhaps, even longer, if business commitments permit (I know how demanding that damned firm of yours is on your time, Oliver!). You'll love it here, as I'm sure will Winnie, who always told me how much she delights in the countryside."

Morgan laid the letter to one side and ate his breakfast. The weather was unusually fine for April at the moment and things were slack at work; perhaps he could take a week off, he thought, though it might be better, he added to himself, to spend a week-end first at Oliver's to test it out. His friend was a born Romantic, and what he might think of as "fit for habitation" would probably not meet with Winnie's far more demanding standards. He gazed around the meticulously neat breakfast room, with its large Welsh dresser, rustic pottery, and the earthenware vases of freshly cut daffodils from the garden. Oliver would consider a cowshed fit for habitation once the cows had been removed - but Winnie would have decidedly other views about that, Morgan admitted to himself with a mischievous smile of amusement.

After thinking the matter over, he decided to wait till tonight when Winnie returned home from the florists she ran in town. Then, maybe, he would suggest visiting Oliver by himself for a couple of days. If the place passed muster, they could both pay Oliver a longer visit later on. He could tell Oliver that Winnie was too busy at the moment to spare any time away from her shop, which he knew was not really untrue, what with two of her part-timers ill with flu and her order books filled with Spring weddings.

Morgan sipped his coffee, satisfied he had worked things out quite well. It would be better, in any case, he ruminated further, if he saw Oliver by himself first if only to find out how well he had recovered in Spain. A historical novelist, it was ages now since Oliver last had anything published, and Morgan had already begun to wonder why he was spending untold thousands on renovating an old, dilapidated house miles from any decent town. He didn't think it spoke much for the stability of his friend's mind, though he hoped what doubts he had were unfounded and that he would find Oliver fit and well again and deep into writing his next novel.

By tea his half-formed plan had sorted itself out in his head and Morgan found he was able to make his wife see his point of view.

Winnie touched her greying hair when he'd finished.

"No doubt he'll have filled the house with some ghastly old suits of rusting armour," she said, "all of them fakes, of course. And not a care in the world about it."

Ghastly old suits of rusting armour, Morgan thought, would perhaps quite appropriately fit in with Oliver's ghastly old historical novels, but he left this unsaid, since Winnie had a soft spot for them.

"Well, one of us will have to go and see him," Morgan said. "I can spare a couple of days during the next few weeks, if you're sure you'll be able to cope till I get back."

Winnie glanced at him in disapproval.

"*I* can cope, Morgan. It's you I'll be worried about." Her frown broke into an affectionate smile. "I hope Oliver's all right again. It was worrying after Louise's death. I really thought he would end up in an institution. I really did."

As did Morgan, though he did not say so.

"He's a bit of an eccentric. Always was."

"As was Louise, of course," Winnie added. "Two peas in a pod."

"Which probably explains why he fell to pieces after her death. They needed each other more than most couples, perhaps, because of their peculiarities."

It was an old game, this affectionate dissection of their oldest and dearest friends, though they had not indulged in it since Louise's death eighteen months ago. At the time it had seemed inconceivable that Louise Atcheson should have been killed in a pointless motorway accident. It was little wonder Oliver had started to behave even more peculiarly. Over a period of time these peculiarities, though, had begun to become progressively worse. Morgan remembered the frightful mess Oliver eventually got himself in, his house cluttered with dirty dishes, half filled with uneaten food, his face unshaven, his eyes darting from side to side as if he was frightened of something he could only see out of the corner of his eyes, like phantom snakes or spiders. The empty whisky bottles littered about his house more than explained the state he was in, though when he'd sobered up it didn't take much to convince him of the need to see a doctor. This in turn had led to a prescription for Valium and advice to take a long, carefree rest. A vacation in Spain for the winter had been an ideal solution, when the holiday resorts were at their quietest, though Oliver had typically said he'd take the opportunity while he was there to explore some of Spain's historical landmarks. That, though, was the surest sign, so far as Morgan was concerned, that the old Oliver they had known for so long was still there.

"I'll write tonight," Morgan said. "Perhaps I should suggest visiting him the week after next? That would give me time to get everything in order at work."

CHAPTER 2

"'Ere, what the fuckin' 'ell's this?"

Harry Sykes, foreman in charge of the labourers, looked across the floor of the cellar at the burly twenty-year-old. Bobby Henderson had only been taken on by Mortimer, Gilbraith and Pike, the firm they worked for, a month ago, and already had shown himself to be even thicker and more work-shy than the usual flotsam and jetsam they hired these days. Harry gave a grimace of exasperation, already sick of this job at Elm Tree House, in particular the work they had been doing this week in the cellar. Despite the string of electric lights they'd hooked to the ceiling, they did little to dispel the dismal shadows that loomed oppressively about the place.

"What's the matter, lad?" Harry's voice grated in the echoes that bounced back almost at once from the distant walls, hidden in the gloom. He climbed to his feet and strode over to him. Bobby was supposed to be sweeping some of the lighter debris - lumps of stone and fallen plaster - into heavy-duty polythene bags, ready to be hauled upstairs and taken away in the firm's skip outside.

"Well?" Harry asked. "What is it? What's 'olding you up? We're behind already, without any more friggin' delays."

He looked over the labourer's shoulders. The powerful light bulb overhead beamed across the cellar floor. The carved inscription uncovered by Bobby's brush on the massive flagstone stood out in the brilliance with an inky clarity. It wasn't this, though, that made Harry Sykes stand and gape like a pole-axed bull, unable for a moment to speak, but an ugly, green foot that terminated, with a stomach-churning abruptness, at a ragged stump no more than an inch above its ankle. As Harry stared incredulously at it, horrified, he was struck by the way in which it looked decayed. Almost twice the size of a normal human foot, it had large, knobbly toes that ended in thick, bird-like talons, long enough to have ripped a man open.

Harry bit back the bile that rose in his throat.

"What is it?" Bobby's voice was almost a squeak, as if it had never broken. The other men, drawn by their reaction, crowded round.

Bill Parkinson's enormous beer belly wobbled before him as he dropped to his knees and hit the foot with his spade. He grinned at Harry with a look of amusement as his blows resounded with an unmistakable metallic clang.

"It's nowt but a lump of brass. That's all it is," he sneered. "Verdigris. That's why it's green. It's covered with it. Always 'appens with brass, 'specially when it's owd like this."

Harry stooped and felt at the foot. His fingers moved across the cold metal as he tried to pick it up, but it was solidly fixed to the ground. He rubbed his fingers across the rough stump above the ankle.

Recovering from his shock, Bobby Henderson took a grip on his brush and began to sweep energetically at the debris piled a few feet away from him. A couple of quick strokes uncovered another foot a yard away from it.

Harry Sykes ran the palm of his hand across his face as he stepped back a pace to gaze at the feet from a distance. Whatever stood on them must have been massive, he realized, though the ceiling didn't look high enough for something so huge to have stood there. Not upright, he thought. It would have been forced to crouch beneath the arched stonework, he realized, as his imagination tried to conjure with the unwelcome images the ugly, predatory feet brought to mind.

"I'm goin' to see the gaffer," he said finally. "I'll find out what we've got to do with these things."

An uneasy movement passed through the men as they followed him.

"We'll all go," Bill Parkinson said as impromptu spokesman for the others. "We'll all go an' see what he's got to say."

Harry looked back at them, tempted for a moment to enforce his authority and order them back to work. It was what he would have normally done without hesitation. But there was an unsettled air about the men that dissuaded him from doing this now. Though none of them had ever liked the place - it was too large and cold for that - there was an atmosphere about it now that disturbed them, almost as if they had strayed towards the edge of a snake pit.

"All right," he muttered, crossly. "If you're goin' to behave like a gaggle of old women. But we've work to do, don't any of you forget that." He turned around, irritated with himself for having let the place get to him, and hurried up the stairs.

CHAPTER 3

When Morgan Davies drew up outside Elm Tree House in the startling heat of a bright afternoon in May, three weeks after receiving the letter from his friend, he was surprised to find the place in turmoil. Piles of rubble were heaped about the drive, alongside plastic bags of refuse, and an enormous half-filled skip. Groups of workmen in dusty overalls were toiling with more bags, which they were heaving out of the front of the house, their faces covered in sweat. A Jaguar XJ6 was parked by the house at the opposite side from the skip, and a short man in a smart, fashionable business suit with Italian-style sunglasses stood beside it. He was talking to a stooped figure dressed in a baggy grey sweater and dirty jeans. Morgan recognized the second man at once as Oliver, though his tall frame seemed even thinner than when they last met. His clothes sagged from him in ugly, almost shapeless folds.

Morgan drove towards them and parked his Orion beside the Jag.

Oliver turned and squinted against the glare from the sun, then waved as Morgan exited his car and strode towards him. They shook hands warmly.

"It's great to see you, Morg." Oliver turned to the man he'd been talking to. "Let me introduce you to Alan Gilbraith - he's in charge of the renovation work I'm having done on the house. Alan, this is an old friend of mine, Morgan Davies."

They shook hands. Gilbraith, Morgan noticed, had a firm, no nonsense grip that belied the soft, well-fed face of the businessman.

"Pleased to meet you," Morgan said as he turned towards the house. The place was surrounded by a haze of dust, white in the sunlight. Vines covered the face of the house, which rose to a crenellated ledge high above them. Its windows were tall, dark and leaded, their small, diamond-shaped panes reflecting the sunlight that shone from above the elms. It was a very old house, almost ancient. That was obvious to Morgan, though the wings that extended on either side were of a different and blatantly inferior style to the main part of the building, and had a nineteenth century look to them, whereas the solid, central part was obviously several hundred years older at least.

"It's been messed about with a bit over the years," Gilbraith said, as if he'd read his mind. He pointed a plump, gold-ringed finger at the dismal wing of the house to their left. Shadows clung about its cracked walls as tenaciously as the ivy that had overrun those at the front. "That abomination was added on in 1830 and is the latest extension, though it's also in the poorest state of repair. Shoddy, gimcrack jerry-building at its worst. We may have to pull it down altogether."

"It only has four rooms in it, and none of them are particularly large," Oliver said. "It wouldn't be much of a loss."

"Except financially," Morgan added.

"There's always that," Oliver said. "Which is why I might leave it for the time being. At the worst it'll collapse of its own accord. And none of the rooms will be used. If that happens, I'll see about having the wall patched up where it stood."

Alan Gilbraith shook his head.

"It's a bad policy," he said. "You'd save money in the long run if you acted now."

"I'd save money if I had it to start with," Oliver said. "The work has cost me a small fortune already. If I hadn't got the place for a song I wouldn't have been able to afford what's been carried out so far. There are limits, though. And we're near them now. I'll see what my bank manager will agree to, but I'm not optimistic."

"How's the writing coming along?" Morgan asked.

Oliver smiled. "It's coming along fine. I've a book off at my publisher's now, which should clear most of my overdraft in the next few months. I'm part way through a second, though I need some further research before I can finish it." He glanced at Gilbraith. "Maybe next year I'll get more work done on this place," he said. "I'll have to apply the brakes for the time being, though. When the work's been finished in the cellar, we'll have to call it a day."

Gilbraith nodded soberly, his eyes inscrutable behind his solid black sunglasses.

"I'll chase the men up to get that completed for you as soon as possible," he said, "what with all the delays we had last week."

Oliver grinned. "Don't apologize for that," he said. "I'm more than delighted at what your men found. That makes up for any delays."

"What was that?" Morgan asked. "A cache of gold?"

"I wouldn't be worrying about getting the work finished if it was," Oliver said. "I'll show you later, when the men have gone."

Gilbraith glanced at his watch. "They should be wrapping up any time now," he said. "I'll have a word with Sykes so they can tidy things up before they leave. By the middle of next week, they should have finished in the cellar. Then we'll be able to leave you in peace." He shook hands with Morgan again and marched off to the men about the front of the house, a short, solid, immaculately clad figure who stood out in vivid contrast to the roughly-dressed workman he called to him.

"An efficient man," Oliver commented as they watched him. Gilbraith spoke briefly to the workman, then waved back at Oliver and returned to his car.

"They'll be finished and away within half an hour," Gilbraith called. "I'll see you again Monday morning. Think again about what we've been talking about. I mean what I say. It'll cost you less to have the work completed now than to let those wings collapse."

"I'll think about it," Oliver said. "No promises, though."

Gilbraith waved at them again, then climbed into his car.

"He's right, of course," Oliver said to Morgan as the big car drove away. "But..." He spread his hands in a gesture of helplessness.

Morgan hoped his friend hadn't been throwing away good money after bad. The elms that crowded about the house had a dispiriting look to them that he strongly disliked - they were too tall and too silent. There wasn't even any bird song to enliven them, he realized. Not a single bird could be seen anywhere, though he'd seen plenty on his way here.

"Now, Oliver, what was this mysterious thing that was found here?" he asked, taking a firm grip of his friend's arm as they walked to the house.

"We'll wait till the workmen have finished in the cellar first, then I'll take you to see it," Oliver said. "In the meantime, I'll give you a guided tour of the house."

He led the way through the entrance past a solid, wooden door, standing open wide on its huge, black hinges.

"It's the original door," Oliver said as they walked past. He rapped its oak panels with his knuckles. "It could almost stand up to a siege," he said proudly. "They made things to last in the old days."

"How old is it?" Morgan asked, impressed by the spacious, stone-paved hallway, with its smooth walls. Several low doorways led off, while a broad staircase led to an overhead gallery lined with doors.

"This is the oldest part of the house still standing," Oliver said. "Built in 1658 for Sir Robert Tollbridge. As Gilbraith mentioned, the wings on either side were later additions, and far inferior to this part of it. So far as I can gather the additions were never used very much and were derelict much earlier than the rest of the building. They were originally entered through doorways knocked through either side of the house, but these were bricked up years ago. The only way into them now, curiously enough, is from outside."

They paused at the foot of the stairs. Though broad, the steps were uneven and badly worn over the years, and the wood looked slippery.

"I presume we take our time going up," Morgan said as he took a grip on the thick, decoratively-carved banister rail for support.

"I've slipped on them once or twice," Oliver admitted as he led the way up. At the top he pointed along the gallery. There was an arched doorway at either end and three smaller doors in between. "These are all bedrooms," he said. "The door at the far end leads into a corridor down the side of the house to the front. It extends all along the house. The first room there is - or was - a library of sorts, then opens out into a dining room. The large windows at the front of the house give it ample light. I'll show you."

Their feet clattered loudly on bare floorboards of polished oak as they walked down the gallery. Oliver glanced over the railings into the reception hall below and felt himself begin to warm to the house. It *was* impressive, Goddamn it, he thought to himself. Too impressive to have been left like it was all these years. Too impressive by far.

The panelled corridor through the doorway at the end stretched out before them, brilliantly lit by the massive leaded windows along it. The walls were bare, though Morgan could imagine how they would have looked when hung with paintings - probably portraits of the family that originally owned the house. He breathed in the smell of old plaster and wood that pervaded it.

Oliver opened a door at the end.

"This was the library," he said as they entered a long, narrow room. It looked bare and Spartan without the packed bookshelves it once contained. Morgan glanced through the windows down at the drive, where the last of the workmen were stacking their tools by the skip.

"The next room is much more impressive," Oliver interrupted, as he strode on and opened a further door at the end. The room beyond was longer but no wider than the library and contained a plain but splendid table that extended almost the full length, perhaps twenty feet or more of solid oak. A number of wooden chairs stood at the table, mainly at one end. Dark patches marred the wooden panelling on the inside wall, where pictures had been hung in the past. The broad view from the windows drew Morgan's eyes once more, and he gazed at the elms that flooded his field of vision beyond the drive.

"Quite a dining room, uh?" Oliver said, as he sat at the head of the table and beamed down it, his historian's imagination no doubt filling it with visitants from the past, Morgan thought, knowing his friend.

"How do you get up to the next floor?" Morgan asked as he remembered the row of smaller windows above the ones he was looking through now.

"When we turned right from the gallery, you turn left instead and there's a staircase to the next floor. Only the rooms on this floor have been seen to, though. Those above us have lower ceilings and were probably intended for the servants - small and cluttered with all kinds of junk and an unimaginable amount of dust and dead insects. Talk about cleaning the Aegean stables! That's another job for Gilbraith's men, I suppose, but only when I've the money for another week's work out of them. Till then they can stay as they are."

"I should think you've more rooms than you can cope with as it is," Morgan said. "This is a very large house. Too large for a man to feel at ease in by himself, I would have thought."

"Perhaps," Oliver said, his hands resting flat on the table. He gazed down its well-polished length for a moment, lost in thought. Abruptly he stood up and strode to the windows. He peered down at the drive and nodded. Morgan saw the workmen had gone now; the drive was deserted, apart from the half-filled skip.

"Perhaps we can have a look at the cellar, and I'll show you what they found," Oliver said.

They returned to the reception hall back the way they had come.

"The door to the bathroom and W.C. is by the stairs to the top floor," Oliver said as they passed it on their way to the gallery.

Back in the reception hall, Oliver produced a set of keys and unlocked one of the doors at the back. This led to a large, square-shaped room that looked out onto the grounds at the rear of the house through a set of barred windows. All it contained was a diesel generator and drums of fuel.

"This supplies the electricity for the house," Oliver said. "Though I eventually intend having it moved into the cellar," he went on. He pointed to a low, timber door. It had a heavy old-fashioned lock with the key still in it. Oliver turned it and gave the door a tug to pull it open. He flicked a switch on the wall inside and a series of light bulbs, hooked along wires strung from the ceiling, came on.

"We might need a torch as well," Oliver said as he reached beside the door for one.

The cellar steps were made of stone and dipped in the middle where they had been worn away over the years.

"This part is even older than the rest of the house," Oliver called over his shoulder as he led the way down, "perhaps even older than the house itself." A musty smell of neglect filled the air, earthy and rotten, and Morgan began to regret having expressed any interest at all in whatever it was they had found here. He dusted off the sleeve of his golf club blazer where it brushed against the walls alongside. Scabrous lumps of old fungus covered them like the marks of an awful disease. He drew his lips back tight against his teeth as the dankness became even worse as they went down the stairs into the cellar, till the walls opened out into an echoing black space that seemed vast, low ceilinged and hollow, like an enormous underground cavern.

Morgan looked at the ceiling, where the line of light bulbs continued overhead. Beyond them loomed a thick, impenetrable darkness that seemed to go on and on forever. Massive stone pillars stood here and there as further support for the ceiling, which had the appearance of having been carved out of the natural rock. The pillars dripped with slime that had collected and dried into a bluish-grey crust about their bases. The paving stones across the floor had been swept clean and were free of debris in the area Morgan could see, apart from several piles of plastic bags and some brushes and spades.

"Next week the men should have finished here," Oliver said as he switched on the torch and shone it beyond the area lit by the electric lights. Its beam picked out further pillars and nets of cobwebs festooned in the distance. "I was told this was too much of a health hazard as it was, so I had to have it cleaned out. If you think it smells bad now, you should have come here before." He wrinkled his nose with mock nausea.

"How old are these cellars?" Morgan asked, puzzled at the elaborate style of the pillars. They were round and massive, well cut and surprisingly ornate. He wondered if they were Corinthian, as he scraped at his memory for what bits of architectural knowledge he'd collected over the years.

"According to Gilbraith these date from Roman times and may have formed part of a pagan temple. Later, a Christian monastery was built on top of it, using the cellar as its foundations, though this too fell into disuse and was a ruin by the time the main part of the house was built. I was more than impressed by all of this already," Oliver said as he led them further into the cellar, "but when some of the workmen came across this..." They stopped at a ringed-off area about which a number of steel rods had been wedged between the paving stones and a length of rope fastened between them. In the light from the light bulbs overhead Morgan stared at the feet. Most of the verdigris that had disfigured them had been cleaned off since Bobby Henderson discovered them, and the ancient brass gleamed in the lamplight.

Oliver stepped over the rope and pointed at the stumps above the ankles.

"Whatever stood on these was hacked off. The marks are rough and crude."

Noticing a line of carved letters in the paving stones close to the feet, Morgan asked what they said.

"They're in Latin of a sort. Army Latin, I think," Oliver said. "They refer to the Sumerian god, Moloch. If these feet are those of an idol dedicated to him - which they probably are - then

24

terrible things must've happened here in the dim, distant past - some very terrible things indeed," he added pedantically. "Idols of Moloch were made of brass," he explained, "just like these feet." He paused significantly. "The belly of the idol would be hollow, with an opening at the front. Inside was a furnace, and sacrifices, usually live animals, but sometimes humans, particularly babies, were flung into its fiery heart."

"And the Romans brought this worship to Endon?" Morgan asked.

"Some, presumably, though it will have been in secret, since the Romans were never keen on human sacrifices. After all, look what they did to the Druids for carrying out sacrifices like this in their infamous wicker cages."

"So this was a secret Roman temple to Moloch?" Morgan said.

"Built for a cult that probably emigrated here from the eastern end of the Empire. How long it lasted I don't know, but eventually it either fell into disuse or was disbanded - perhaps discovered by the authorities and purged - and hundreds of years later a monastery was built on top of what remained of its ruins."

"And that too fell into ruins?"

"Yes," Oliver said. "Though the monastery didn't last long. It had gone, anyway, long before the Dissolution - long gone and forgotten."

Morgan shook his head in bewilderment.

"And you want to live here, alone, with this place under you?" He wondered how much his friend had really recovered in Spain, or was this just a sign that things were far from right with him yet? He had an idea what Winnie's opinion would be when she heard about it.

"I don't intend to live here alone," Oliver said. "Though this," he went on, with a nod at the remains of the idol, "wouldn't put me off if I did. Since Louise's death I've felt lonely enough without wishing to seclude myself away like a hermit in an isolated house the size of this. It's going to be an artistic colony. I've already been in touch with a number of people I know: artists, writers, poets - Tom Paxley the sculptor, Lorrieman, Hazel Metcalfe, Jack Meadows, people like that. There's been a lot of interest in the plan - a place where artists can come and go, staying for as long as they like, working here, discussing things, exchanging ideas, away from the hue and cry of modern, commercial life. It's what I've dreamed of for years - long before Louise's death. We'd both discussed it. We'd planned to do it one day. In doing it now I'm not only carrying out my plans, but hers as well." His eyes had grown bright with enthusiasm while he spoke, and Morgan felt himself drawn to the excitement of his friend's plans.

"Come on," Oliver said, "let's return upstairs for a bite to eat. Then I'll tell you more about this project. I'm sure you'll see that I haven't cracked up when I've explained it to you."

CHAPTER 4

"Hullo, Winnie, it's Morgan. Can you hear me all right?" Morgan pressed the telephone close to his ear in an attempt to cut out the noise from the pub, but a booming juke box and an enthusiastic game of pool were almost too much.

Faintly he made out her reply.

"Yes, everything's all right," Morgan said. "I couldn't ring you from the house. Oliver's not had a phone connected yet - I know, that's crackers, but he's spending most of what money he's got on having the place renovated - yes, there's still a lot of work needed on it - no, dear, no, not quite a cow shed, though it does have a touch of the barn about it, in size, anyway." He smiled to himself as he thought of the hacked-off feet of Moloch in the cellar. He decided not to mention them yet, not when explanations would be blurred or buried in the noise from the pub.

"What was that, sweetheart?" he asked. "What does he want the place for?" He laughed to himself, partly intoxicated by Oliver's firebrand enthusiasm for the project and partly by the three halves of bitter they'd refreshed themselves with in the pub. "You'll not credit it, Winn, but Oliver wants to set up some kind of artistic colony in the house - yes, that's right. It seems it was a pet project of his and Louise's, and he wants to complete it now as a kind of memorial to her. He's even arranged for Jack Meadows - you've heard of him, haven't you? - to do a portrait of Louise to be hung in the reception hall. That's right. Yes. Look, the pips have just gone. I'll phone you tomorrow to let you know when I'll be back. Till then, sweetheart, I love you. Good-bye."

He hung the phone up gratefully. He hated noise, but never so much as when he was trying to talk through it over a phone. Carefully he made his way back through the people thronged about the bar and headed for the table he and Oliver had secured for themselves by the open door. A breeze wafted through it, dispelling some of the sticky heat inside the pub. Oliver's face was flushed as he drank his beer.

"Well?" he said as Morgan sat beside him. "Is everything all right?"

"Fine - fine," Morgan said. He lifted his glass and took a drink. "She's a bit of a worrier is Winn," Morgan added.

"I know that all right," Oliver said with a smile. He finished his drink. "Would you like another?"

"Why not?"

While Oliver wound his way to the bar, Morgan took time to study some of his friend's new neighbours. Most were well dressed and obviously prosperous. Several of the younger men wore La Coste T-shirts, their alligator labels standing out on their chests like a tribal badge, while three middle-aged men nearby in suits stood talking about an agricultural show in Leeds, in between puffs at half-corona cigars. Morgan was glad he'd taken time after they'd had a simple tea of whole-meal bread, matured cheese and pickles in the partially modernized kitchen at Oliver's house, to change into a clean pair of slacks and a polo neck. Oliver still wore the same baggy sweater and jeans. But, for all the sloppiness of his dress, he seemed cheerful enough. And the tan he'd developed in Spain had certainly given him the outward appearance of health. Morgan's hoped it was more than skin deep, though the exuberance Oliver displayed whenever he was talking about his project for the house had an over energetic quality to it that somehow failed to seem right to Morgan, as if something he couldn't quite work out yet was missing.

"When did you plan to set up this colony?" Morgan asked when Oliver returned with their drinks.

Oliver scratched the side of his nose for moment in thought.

"That depends on a few things. Several of the people I've approached are keen to come, even offering to help clean the place up. We might have a go at the rooms on the top floor if they mean what they say. It's only junk and filth up there - nothing structurally wrong with it. The rafters and roof have already been seen to, as have the floorboards, though they weren't too bad anyway, considering the length of time the house was empty. With any luck, I suppose we can start within the next two months. Tom Paxley's coming in a week or so with his wife. He says he'd like to start a sculpture he's been commissioned to do. I've told him he can use one of the downstairs rooms at the back as a studio. He's a strong brute of a man and won't mind a bit of hard work in lifting the heavier stuff on the top floor. In fact he's looking forward to it, he says."

When they'd finished their round of drinks, they decided to call it a night. The air was invigoratingly warm when they strolled out of the pub to Morgan's car.

Morgan took his time driving back, with the windows down and the early evening scents of hedgerow and fields breezing in, though he could not help noticing how gloomier the trees looked as they drew nearer Oliver's house. They towered over them tall and black when Morgan paused at the entrance to the grounds for Oliver to climb out and open the gates. Morgan glanced into the dark depths of their leaves. They contrasted grimly with the sun-drenched sky beyond. Again he noticed the quietness here, more marked than before after the non-stop birdsong that accompanied them along the road, as great, sweeping flocks of birds scythed back and forth above them. Now the sky shone a deep, iridescent blue above the austere trees, with nothing - no passing birds, no bats, no moths, no movement at all.

Morgan drove through the opened gates, then waited while Oliver shut them. When he'd climbed back in, Morgan said: "Is it always so quiet here?"

Oliver glanced at him for a moment. "It's peaceful, yes," he said. "I like it that way," he added, "though it'll change soon enough when people arrive. You'll grumble at the noise and wonder whatever happened to the peace and quiet we're enjoying now. You mark my words," he said with a grin as they pulled up at the house and climbed out. Beneath the trees shadows reached across the drive, and to Morgan it was as if dusk had abruptly leapt forward. Even the air felt cooler. He shivered as Oliver unlocked the door and they slipped into the hallway.

The cheerfulness of the pub seemed suddenly a hundred miles away.

They spent the rest of the night talking in a partly redecorated room on one side of the front of the house. It was an ample room, with all the original decorative plaster mouldings on the ceiling, while the walls had oak panels. Two large lights from the ceiling soon improved the atmosphere of the room as they sat back in the old armchairs that Oliver had furnished it with. Stacks of books lay piled about the foot of the walls, waiting for shelves to be fixed up, while a long, low, oak table stood to one side of the fire. A silver tray lay on it, and several bottles of spirits and a cluster of crystal tumblers. Two of the tumblers were soon in their hands, half-filled with single malt whisky as they stretched their legs and leaned back in the chairs. The gloom outside locked away from them here, Morgan had all but forgotten about it till he glanced at one of the large, leaded windows and saw the utter darkness that lay beneath the trees. Even now the sky was still bright, but that didn't seem to make any difference to the woods.

"Have you ever thought of having some of the trees cut down to make more space?" Morgan asked.

Oliver hissed scornfully between his teeth. "Do you have any idea how much that would cost?" he asked in return.

They lapsed into silence, till half an hour later, his glass now empty, Morgan announced he was "bushed" after all the travelling he'd done today.

"I think I'll turn in, if you don't mind, Oliver. What with the fresh air, the beers we had in the village and that whisky of yours, I'm already starting to doze off."

"You know where your room is," Oliver said. "I'll just go round and make sure everything's switched off and the doors are locked, then I think I'll turn in as well."

They said good night, and Morgan crossed the hallway to the stairs. Oliver had given him the second bedroom along the gallery. It was a large room and, considering the short time that Oliver had had to do it up in, quite pleasant. Morgan had already unpacked his suitcase and hung what few spare clothes he'd brought in the large Victorian wardrobe. Dark velvet curtains, matching the ubiquitous panels on the walls, hung at the window. He decided to leave the curtains open to let in some air, and reached to open the window in the hope of dispelling some of the mustiness that still lingered in the room. Now that the sun had set, the narrow stretch of grass that separated the house from the trees was totally lightless. A trickle of moonlight shone across the upper branches of the elms as they swayed in the breeze, but it seemed to stray no further than the very top and served only to emphasize the utter darkness below.

Annoyingly, now that he was ready for bed Morgan felt unable to sleep. He regretted not having brought a book. He'd even neglected to buy a newspaper, and there was no radio or television in the house. An aversion to both was a long-standing "peculiarity" that Oliver used to share with his wife. Morgan strode up and down the thin carpet, too edgy to sleep, let alone lie down in bed. He walked to the window and stared again at

30

the darkness below. It was almost twelve, and the air was still. Even the topmost branches of the elms were motionless against the blazing stars that almost filled the sky. A sudden noise in the darkness below caught his attention, and he craned his neck to see if he could see what had caused it. Perhaps a stray animal, a fox maybe or a badger, had wandered into the grounds and was foraging about the undergrowth. As his eyes slowly adjusted to the darkness, though, Morgan thought he could see something white below his window. It was round or oval in shape, but his eyes appeared to be playing tricks with him in the gloom, since whatever it was seemed to change its shape as he looked, as if it was no more substantial than a puff of smoke. But it stayed too long to be anything as frail as that. Morgan concentrated his eyes on it. For a moment he wondered if it was a face, dim and white, staring up at him. A chill shivered down his spine, and he felt suddenly afraid.

Less tired than before, Morgan drew away from the window and climbed into bed. He lay down beneath the blankets, unable to sleep, his detestation of the woods confirmed.

CHAPTER 5

"Do you often find people prowling the grounds at night?" Morgan asked as he tucked into breakfast the next morning. It was going to be another hot day, and sunlight glowed across the kitchen window.

"What do you mean? Prowlers?" Oliver asked.

"When I went to bed last night I couldn't sleep. I spent a few minutes looking out of the window. I saw what I took to be someone's face staring up at me. Whoever it was must have been creeping through the trees. It could have been a poacher, of course."

Oliver laughed. "Not from what I know of what the locals say about these woods. I doubt there's been a poacher here for the past twenty years, not since a local character called Teb was found here back in the eighties."

"What happened? Was he dead?"

"Nothing so spectacular. He'd had a stroke. Half paralysed, he was unable to speak properly for months afterwards, though he did eventually manage to gabble something about what happened to him. Apparently the local tales and legends about this place must have got to him when he tried to take a short cut or something through the woods to the big estate further on, where he was after some game, and his inflamed imagination brought on the stroke that crippled him."

"Local legends?" Morgan asked, interested. "What kind of legends?"

"Stuff and nonsense. I'll not try and put you off this place by telling you. They're just the type of rustic gobbledygook you'd expect in an out of the way place like this." Oliver laughed to himself and concentrated on his bacon and eggs. However much Morgan tried to persuade him to say any more about what tales there were about Elm Tree House, his friend refused. "Stuff and nonsense," he repeated. "They're not worth going on about, I tell you. Just stuff and nonsense. Ill educated, nonsensical claptrap. Nothing more."

By midday Morgan felt ready for a change of scenery.

"I'll set off home in a couple of hours," he told Oliver. "Perhaps we could spend a bit of time in the Hare and Hounds over a pub lunch and a couple of beers."

Oliver agreed straight away.

When they arrived at the pub, they found it was almost empty.

They ordered a couple of drinks and some cheese sandwiches, then settled at one of the tables. When they'd finished their food, Oliver excused himself and went to the Gents. While he was away Morgan wandered to the bar and ordered another round of drinks. The landlord, a portly, bearded man with a balding head and tinted glasses, asked how he was getting on at Elm Tree House.

"Quite well," Morgan said. "Though it must have been in a poor state before my friend bought it."

"Aye, that'll be the truth of it," the landlord said. He placed the drinks he'd ordered on the bar. "Few of us thought your friend would stick it long. That we didn't."

"I hear it's got a bit of a bad reputation."

The landlord laughed good-naturedly.

"*That* would be putting it mildly. I know no one living hereabouts would have bought the place. Though, fair does, it seems as we were wrong about it. No harm's come to your friend, has it?"

Morgan smiled faintly, not sure. Not sure at all anymore. He could still too vividly recall the nauseating way in which his flesh seemed to creep as he stared at the face in the darkness beneath his bedroom window last night.

Oliver sauntered towards them.

"Has Bob been filling you with all the local horror stories about Elm Tree House?" he asked.

"Now, you know better 'an that," the landlord said, with a grin. "I was just saying to your friend as how what's said about your place must be nothing more than foolishness."

"It certainly must," Oliver said, "since I'm still there and my hair hasn't turned white yet. Not completely, anyway. Though it might if the costs for renovating it rise any more."

"It's been empty for nigh on twenty years, ever since the Murdocks left in such a hurry back in the seventies. It's a wonder the building's fit enough to be renovated at all after all that time."

"I'm curious about these tales about the house," Morgan said. He noticed Oliver's smile freeze.

"Gobbledygook and nonsense, that's all they are. I've told you," Oliver said forcefully, and the landlord looked at him with upraised eyebrows, obviously surprised at his vehemence.

"Harmless old legends. A bit of local colour," the landlord added.

"Maybe they're harmless. Maybe they're not," Oliver said. "Once you plant an idea in someone's head, though, there's no telling where it might lead. Look at what happened to that poacher of yours - Teb. He went to take a short cut through the woods and scared himself half to death."

"He's always said as how something touched him - something hard and brittle and dry. I'll always remember those words. I've heard them often enough when he's in here, drinking. Hard and brittle and dry. That's about as much as any of us have ever got out of him about what happened that night."

"And if his head hadn't been stuffed full of nonsense about ghosts and what-have-you about the place," Oliver went on, "he might not have had that stroke."

The landlord shrugged. "None of us rightly knows what happened that night. Only Teb. And he's said no more than what I've said just now."

"Probably because there's no more to tell, except an over-excited imagination."

The intensity of Oliver's feelings about the subject puzzled Morgan, almost as if his friend was afraid of it. Again he wondered just how well Oliver had recovered from his breakdown. Or had he? There seemed so much about his friend these days that was different it was hard for him to tell. Morgan finished his beer and placed his glass on the bar.

"Does Teb come in these days?" he asked, ignoring the frown from Oliver.

"Now and then," the landlord said. "Though his local's the Squire's Arms down at the other end o' the village. You pass it on your way from your friend's house."

Morgan remembered the crumbling, stone-built inn next to a hump-backed bridge over a river.

"The Squire's Arms? A bit of a rum looking place, isn't it?"

"Keeps a good pint, though," the landlord added, "even if I shouldn't say so," he added with a grin.

Morgan looked at his watch. It was one fifteen.

"I must be off now," he said. "Would you like a lift back to the house?" he asked Oliver, but his friend shook his head.

"Thanks for the offer, but I think I'll walk home today. I could

34

do with some exercise." They shook hands, and the landlord wished him good luck on his journey and hoped to see him again some time. For a moment after he climbed into his car Morgan wondered whether to call in the Squire's Arms to see if Teb was there but decided against it. What would he gain from doing that, he thought to himself, except make his feelings about the old house even worse?

With a sigh of exasperation Morgan started his car and drove off. In another few hours he would be home with Winn. He wondered what he would tell her about his visit.

CHAPTER 6

Over a month had passed since he stayed with Oliver, and Morgan Davies had all but forgotten his worries about the place. The warm, cloudless days of an unusually fine May had advanced into a blistering June, and the fears of that one dark night he spent in Elm Tree House seemed a bad dream, to be ignored and forgotten.

"Oliver's project seems to be getting off the ground at last," Winnie said as they relaxed on the lawn at the back of their house. Bees buzzed inquisitively about the roses along the borders.

Morgan looked up from his Sunday newspaper. Yesterday they had received another letter from Oliver, full of details about the people who were coming to stay at Elm Tree House and how he and the Paxleys had managed to clear most of the rooms on the top floor. According to Oliver he now had enough bedrooms to put up to eighteen people at the house, though he intended to keep this down to no more than a dozen to start with.

"He's worked hard," Morgan said. "I wish him every success."

Winnie glanced at him and lowered her sunglasses, surprised at his lack of enthusiasm.

"I wondered whether we shouldn't pay him a visit, now the place sounds more well ordered than when you stayed," she said.

The letter had roused her curiosity, especially Oliver's remarks about the people he had already interested in his idea for an artistic colony.

"Oliver was always behind the times. He should have founded a commune in the sixties and filled it with hippies."

"And drugs?" Winnie asked disapprovingly. "You don't think they'll be on drugs, do you?" she said, suddenly alarmed.

Morgan laughed. "I shouldn't think so. These are respectable, for the most part middle-aged people, Winnie, not dropouts. Just because they're interested in the arts doesn't automatically mean they'll be into drugs as well."

Winnie joined his laughter. "Of course not," she said, relieved. "Well, Morg," she added, "do you think we should accept his latest invitation or not? I'd rather we went during the summer than later in the year when the weather won't be half so good."

For a moment Morgan remembered the cloying darkness that enclosed the house at night, certain that he agreed with his wife whole-heartedly. Elm Tree House was a place to visit during the summer, when the days were long and the nights agreeably short, not during the autumn and winter. It could be gloomy enough even in the sun, let alone when the weather was dismal too.

"Okay," he said. "I'll write to him. I can spare some time off work in a few weeks. We could both do with a break."

When Morgan came to write to Oliver, he found he was strangely reluctant to start. He stared at the paper for several minutes, deep in thought, and wondered why it was he felt so unwilling to write. Was it because he did not really want to visit the house again? Was he frightened of it? He screwed up his first attempt at a letter and started to write a straightforward, no-nonsense reply, stating that he and Winnie would love to accept his invitation to spend a week with him. That done, he sat back and stared at the wall in front of him. There was a feeling of finality to the letter, of doors being opened, stepped through and shut, and through which he knew they would never return. He shook his head irritably. He was going soft in the head. He picked up an envelope and addressed it to Elm Tree House, folded the letter and sealed it inside. He'd get his secretary to post it for him in the morning at work. With that he dropped the letter in his briefcase and got up.

The sun lay low in a cloudless sky. Winnie still sat on the lawn, reading her latest Catherine Cookson. Her thick brown, slightly greying hair moved as she flicked the pages before her, and he felt worried somehow he could be involving her in something wrong, something they would both regret. Why this was he could not explain, even to himself. "Damn it all," he muttered finally. He turned and made his way into the lounge where he poured himself a whisky and drank it neat. "Damn it all, damn it all, damn it all!"

CHAPTER 7

The unusually fine weather had deteriorated by the time they arrived at Elm Tree House. The sky was overcast, with great towering banks of clouds. Three weeks had passed since Morgan wrote to Oliver and had received an enthusiastic letter of confirmation in reply. As Morgan turned their car up the long drive through the trees, Winnie shivered. She stared at the trees.

"Are they always so bleak and inhospitable?" she asked.

Morgan drew up in front of the house, next to several parked cars, then looked at his wife, disturbed she should feel affected by the place so soon, almost as if it was some sort of premonition.

"So far as I remember, yes," he told her. They climbed out as Oliver opened the front door and greeted them. Behind him stood a solid-looking man in lumberjack shirt and brown, corduroy trousers, stained with paint.

"Winnie! Morgan! It's great to see the two of you here at last," Oliver called out to them. He rushed over and gave Winnie an enthusiastic hug. He turned to the ruddy complexioned man behind him. "Let me introduce Tom Paxley." A woman - short, thin, with dark wavy hair and a pleasant smile - appeared at the door behind them. "And this is Tom's wife, Alicia." They greeted each other cordially. "Tom's been a great help in getting the top floor ready for use," Oliver said. "While Alicia has been a marvel in organizing things, especially the food. They're marvels, both of them. I don't know how Tom managed to find the time over the past few weeks to get any work of his own done, what with all we've been doing on this place, but he has. By God, he has!"

Oliver led them inside, and Morgan was pleased to see Winnie's admiration for the interior of the house as they stepped through the hallway.

"I thought I could give you the same room as before," Oliver said. "It's big enough for the two of you, and even pleasanter now Alicia's had a go at it."

"When are the other's you've invited due to arrive?" Morgan asked.

"Some are already here - Hazel Metcalfe, Howard Brinsley. I'll introduce you to them shortly." Somewhere in one of the rooms at the back of the house a man swore and there was a clatter of wood being knocked to the floor.

"That's another of Howard's canvasses gone west," Oliver said, smiling with amusement. "He goes through four or five of them before he settles down and gets something he can tolerate started."

Tom Paxley grinned hugely, his brown eyes glinting with a lively intelligence.

"If I was as temperamental as Howard your floorboards wouldn't be worth much now," he said.

"With a hundred weight of granite tipped over them, I should think not. Though temperament isn't one of your faults, is it, Tom?"

"Not a Taurean trait," the sculptor said complacently, his broad chest and thick, sinewy forearms more than suggestive of the down-to-earth, stolid bull.

They made their way into the lounge, where Oliver offered his guests a drink.

"Help yourselves," Oliver said. "You too, Tom, Alicia." He poured himself a gin and tonic and strode to the windows at the front of the house. The leaden light only dimly shone through the panes, and his face was lost in shadows. Morgan noticed shelves had now been fixed to the panels and were packed with books, many of them historical textbooks which Oliver used for reference while he was writing his novels. Winnie seated herself on one of the armchairs before the fire and drew her knees in front of her as she sipped a weak martini. Morgan could not help contrasting his wife's elegant but simple suit of pale blue cotton with the threadbare jeans and checked shirt Alicia wore, her sleeves rolled up to her elbows. It wasn't a contrast just of clothes. Alicia's face, so cheerful outwardly, had a deep line of worry, like a folded crease, between her eyes, and there was a dowdy look about her which no amount of make-up - even if she'd worn any, which she didn't - could have hidden. Oliver, he saw, looked better than before, though he still wore a scruffy pair of jeans, and his heavy sweater hung from his shoulders in loose folds, but there was more meat on his face now, and it was obvious the arrival of the others, in particular Alicia in all probability, had led to him eating more regularly.

"Winnie's been curious about this place ever since I visited you in May," Morgan said as he poured himself some whisky and water.

"I hope you're not disappointed," Oliver said, "though the weather today doesn't show the place off to its best advantage."

"It's splendid," Winnie consoled him. Her face, though not beautiful, was delicately pretty for all she was in her late forties, and she knew how to use her eyes. They sparkled as she gazed about the room. "I love old houses," she said, "though Morg never told me how huge this was inside. That gallery inside the hallway made me gasp." She smiled engagingly, and Morgan could tell her earlier qualms had been swept away by the impressive interior of the house. He noticed that Oliver was pleased.

"The two wings on either side are a flaw," Oliver said. "I wish I could afford to have them renovated as well, or pulled down, but I can't. Not yet, anyway."

"I'd have them pulled down if I had any choice in the matter," Tom Paxley said forcefully, a can of lager in one hand. "They're dismal, dreary things. Should never have been built in the first place. They ruin the purity of the original design. Have them pulled down and grassed over. That's the best thing for 'em."

"You don't care for Victorian architecture, I take it?" Morgan asked.

Tom pulled his jaw into a scowl of contemplation.

"Victorian architecture of that sort, no. Emphatically no. But there's good and bad in all schools. And good Victorian architecture is a joy by anyone's standards. But these things, for Christ's sake, no. They were a poor, shoddy job from the start. I've looked at them close up. They're riddled with decay. Riddled with it. If the doorways that originally connected them with the rest of the house hadn't been bricked up you'd be able to smell it now." He snorted in disgust, taking a deep gulp of lager.

Later, after they had unpacked their suitcases, Morgan and Winnie decided to drive into the village. Though the house infatuated Winnie, a quick look through the grounds outside beneath the omnipresent elms was enough to dissuade her from wanting to linger there.

"I don't know about having those wings demolished," she said as they drove. "If I were Oliver, I would be seriously thinking about having a go at those woods. They're intimidating. He'd have more sunlight and a much better view if half those trees were cut down. I don't know how old they are, but they reek of age to me."

Before Morgan could answer, they had arrived at the village. He drew up outside the Squire's Arms. It was not yet twelve and the pub was still shut, but an old man, dressed in a dirty overcoat, slouched by the door, one hand held for support on the wall. His other arm was crooked at an awkward angle, its hand stuffed beneath the open flaps of his coat. Morgan glanced at his half-averted face as they climbed out of their car. He noticed how wrinkled skin was drawn painfully tight across the man's cheeks so that his mouth had a fixed leer. He was certain at once who the man had to be, just as he recognized straight away what was wrong with him.

"Just a second, dear," Morgan said to his wife, "but I wonder of that's Teb - the man I told you about, the one who was struck down by a stroke when he took a short cut past Oliver's house years ago."

"Teb?" Winnie stared at the old man, then looked back at Morgan. "He's had a stroke at some time. That much is obvious. Just as it's obvious why he's in the state he is if he's at the pub as early as this every day. There must be another ten minutes to go before the pub opens."

They strolled down the cobblestone street that meandered pleasantly through the village. A Norman church stood in its own grounds in the centre, close to a general store, a sub-post office, a cottage-like branch of the Midland Bank and a dreary, double-fronted and over-priced antique shop with bed pans and dusty-looking chamber pots in its windows.

Morgan said: "I wonder if it would be any use going back to have a word with Teb."

Winnie glanced at him. "Why? What use would that do? Whatever happened to the poor old man was a long time ago. It can't matter any more, can it? In any case, what's so mysterious about a man having a stroke?"

Morgan shook his head, puzzled as much as to why he should want to find out as to what he expected to be told. "You're probably right," he said. "Besides, if we didn't get to him within the first half hour of opening time, I don't suppose we'd get much sense out of him anyway."

"*If* there's much sense to be got out of him when he's sober," Winnie said.

Morgan shrugged. He led them to the Hare and Hounds,

where he ordered a round of drinks and a couple of ploughman's lunches. The landlord remembered him at once.

"We don't get that many strange faces hereabouts I can easily forget a new one when I see it," Bob said as he pulled a half of bitter. "And this will be your good wife, I presume?"

They took their lunches outside.

"What's troubling you, dear?" Winn asked after they'd silently sat eating for several minutes. "You've been quiet ever since we set out this morning. More than once over the past few weeks I could tell you've not been looking forward to coming here. Is that why you were so keen on getting out for a pub lunch? It's not like you."

Morgan ruminated for a moment, then dabbed at his mouth with a napkin, and said: "There's something about the house I don't like, Winn, though just what I'm not sure. There's something about it - something, perhaps, I don't so much dislike as fear." He stared at her frankly for a moment. "When I came here last time I had trouble getting to sleep. After a while, for want of anything else to do, I went to the window and gazed out. I thought I saw someone looking up at me from below."

"Who?"

Morgan shook his head. "It was too dark. All I could see was a pale blur, like someone's face."

"It could have been your imagination, dear," Winnie said. "You told me yourself you and Oliver went out for a few drinks that night."

"You could be right," he said. "You could be quite right, of course, but..." He shrugged. "I don't know. It's not *just* that either, trivial as it is. You noticed how oppressive those trees are."

"Something that Oliver could rectify. All he needs is to have them cut back to make more space about the house."

Morgan thought for a moment. So far he had not told her what had been found in the cellar, nor about the age of the place or the use to which it had been put at one time. To do that now would look as if he was clutching at straws to justify his feelings about the house - and perhaps he would be. In a sense he wished he could go to Teb by himself and find out what happened all those years ago.

"Everyone else seems happy at the house," Winnie said. "At least, those of Oliver's guests we've met so far have been."

Morgan remembered the deep crease between Alicia Paxley's eyebrows. Then told himself not to be stupid. She'd probably looked like that for years. It was preposterous to think she'd developed that worried look ever since she came to the house. And Tom Paxley showed no signs of worry at all. Morgan stared at his beer. It was his own imagination that was working away at his feelings about the house, he knew. Nothing more.

"Okay," he said. "You win." He smiled, pushed his empty glass away from him and said: "Let's get back to the house. You haven't looked at all of it yet and I'm sure you're impatient to have the chance."

When they got back to Elm Tree House Oliver conducted them on a tour, enthusiastically showing them how much work had been done in the past few weeks to clear out the upper floor.

"Though small, these are adequate enough," he said as he showed them the bedrooms. Dust lingered in the atmosphere and the sunlight that entered through the small windows shone in brilliant beams, highlighting every mote, but the rooms looked cheerful now that their walls had been painted and their floors scrubbed clean. Some already had beds, cupboards and wardrobes installed, ready for use.

"How do you work out the running costs?" Winnie asked as they headed back for the flight of stairs from the top floor to the gallery.

Oliver said: "Everyone who stays here, apart from personal guests like yourselves, of course, shares in the general running of the place - food, electricity, rates, et cetera. When more people are here the costs will be relatively small. Alicia has kept the accounts for me. Before she married Tom she was a bank clerk in Sheffield, so she's excellent at it. She really is."

They returned to the lounge, where they chatted for another hour till Alicia came in and announced that tea was ready.

"I've prepared a hot pot," she said, "since it's rather cold today and we need something to warm us up."

"We eat in the room next to the kitchen," Oliver said, leading them to it. "The dining room upstairs is too far away. All very well when you have a host of underpaid flunkies, but not when we're all volunteers."

The room was large, with two long tables. Bright metal chairs with fabric seats were set at them, three to each side.

43

"A bit utilitarian," Oliver explained, "but we like it that way."

Tom was already there, helping to bring out dishes of hot food from the kitchen. Stood by one of the tables was a short, pale-featured man in his early thirties with a bristly, very black beard and prematurely receding hair, that had left a crescent-shaped patch of bright pink skin on his forehead, almost like a Celtic tonsure.

"Let me introduce Howard Brinsley. We heard him earlier," Oliver joked lightly.

Morgan was relieved to see the tense-looking man smile at the comment.

They shook hands, then Oliver said: "Here's Hazel. *Hazel!* Let me introduce Winnie and Morgan. I told you about them."

The girl who had entered the room was of medium height, with shoulder length, reddish-brown hair that glinted blond in the sunlight. Her fine features had a serene tranquillity about them that impressed Morgan with a sense of calm. She wore no make-up, but unlike Alicia there was nothing dowdy about her, from her white chiffon, wide-sleeved blouse to the stonewashed jeans that clung to her legs. She extended a cool hand to them and said she was pleased to have met them at last.

"Hazel's an excellent poet," Oliver said. "Excellent. I have a couple of her collections in the lounge. If you haven't read any of her stuff you must have a look at them after we've eaten. Really excellent, I can tell you."

Hazel Metcalfe twitched her pale lips as if he was praising her too much, though Morgan noticed she did not appear to be upset at his praise. Far from it. There was a sense of self-collectedness about her that showed all too clearly she knew how good she really was and had no false illusions about it. Winnie, he noticed, smiled the thinnest of smiles as they shook hands.

Morgan wondered how many of the mundane household chores Hazel Metcalfe helped with, unable to imagine her thin white hands grasping hold of a scrubbing brush to work on the floors upstairs like Alicia Paxley.

During the meal talk was vigorous and brisk, with Tom Paxley's full-blooded laughter helping to cheer them all. An excellent raconteur, he knew endless anecdotes about people he knew, and was unscrupulous in what he said about them. Oliver uncorked a large bottle of wine, while Alicia went for some glasses. As they sat back, replete, to drink the chilled Vino Verdi, Winnie asked Howard Brinsley how his painting had progressed today.

"I got it started," he said to a guffaw of amusement from Tom.

"Thank the Devil for that!" the sculptor burst out. "You go through more easels than I do chisels - *and I hammer mine!*"

For all the intensity that was so obviously suppressed within him, Howard seemed to enjoy Tom's comments, as if his temperamentality was a kind of hallmark. Perhaps it was, Morgan thought as he watched them exchange amiable banter. He turned to Hazel Metcalfe. She had only sipped at her wine so far and her glass was almost full.

"Do you find it easier writing here?" Morgan asked.

The girl smiled. When she spoke she had a clear, light voice. "There's a good atmosphere in this house," she said. "I can relax. And I need that in order to write."

"Even when Tom Paxley's hammering away at a sculpture, or Howard - if he'll forgive me for bringing the subject up again - is hurling canvasses about?" Winnie asked, with an arch smile.

But Hazel Metcalfe was not so easily dealt with. She smiled back at Winnie with a disarming frankness.

"They don't disturb me, not here, not in this house. It's so huge anyway, you could almost be alone in it at times, even when everyone is indoors and working. Perhaps *especially* when everyone is indoors and working. Tom's work is good - the solid hammer blows are no more disturbing than the steady sounds of a good, old-fashioned clock. While Howard is silent most of the time. You hardly know he's here once he's got to grips with his painting."

"Surely things won't be quite so peaceful when more guests arrive?" persisted Winnie, unwilling to give ground easily.

"Perhaps not," Hazel conceded. "We'll have to wait and see. But for now it's ideal. For me, anyway. And if I achieve nothing more than what I've been able to write so far I'll consider my stay worthwhile."

"I'm very pleased to hear that, Hazel," Oliver said from the head of the table. "I'm very pleased to hear that indeed."

Tom shook his head, his ruddy complexion even redder now after three and a half large glasses of wine. "It's no more than the truth, Oliver. I've never been able to get on with my work so well

45

as here. Never in my life. You ask Alicia what I was like before."

His wife smiled faintly.

"It was difficult," she said. The tired look that came across her eyes hinted at just how difficult it might have been.

"Unless you've made it, you're on the edge of the precipice all the time," Tom said. "Materials I need in order to work are expensive. Then there's the noise people complain about and the need for room. God, how we struggled with ghastly landlords - and landladies too! – and neighbours who thought nothing of ringing the police every two minutes because of what they called the "racket" I made. God, how we struggled!" He drained his glass of its wine. "And now," he went on, "now I can *really* work."

After they had finished and the plates and cutlery had been cleared away, Oliver led the way into the lounge. He went over to one of the bookshelves and extracted two slim volumes with white dust-jackets and blue lettering printed on them, very neat and elegant. Morgan recognized a photograph of Hazel Metcalfe on the back of one of them as Oliver handed them to him and his wife.

"*Silent Dreams* and *Shades of Twilight*, Crompton Press," Oliver said as they opened the books and slowly leafed through the short, clearly precise poetry inside. "I've had a look at Hazel's latest stuff and it's even better. Mind you, I'm only a hack historical novelist. But I know quality when I see it. As I'm sure you do as well." He waited expectantly.

Winnie looked up first.

"This is good," she admitted, somewhat ruefully, Morgan wondered, impressed by the poems as well.

Hazel glanced at them from one of the armchairs. Don't expect any false modesty there, Morgan thought, then chided himself for being uncharitable.

"Oliver's showing us some of your poetry," he said.

"I hope you like it," Hazel said, and Morgan noticed the veiled laughter in her eyes, as if she had read his thoughts a moment before. He felt his cheeks warm, though he hadn't blushed in years - and hadn't thought he was even capable of it anymore.

"Excellent," he told her. "Really excellent."

"Have you both seen the remains of our pet in the cellar yet?" Tom Paxley asked. Morgan felt the heat drain from his face just as suddenly as it had come.

"Pet?" Winnie looked round at Morgan as if she thought she must have misheard the sculptor's words.

"He means the brass feet of Moloch," Oliver said, teasing her with yet another mystery.

Winnie laughed at them both.

"Come on, now, what are you two talking about?"

"They're both talking about the remains of what Oliver supposes to have been an ancient Roman idol some workmen accidentally discovered in the cellar when they were clearing it out," Morgan said flatly. "It's a pair of brass feet - all that was left when the rest of it was cut away and, presumably, destroyed."

"Moloch?" Winnie said. "I'm not well versed on ancient gods, I'm afraid. Was it Roman?"

"Sumerian," Oliver said.

"An evil, hungry, brass-bellied idol whose insides were a furnace into which live sacrifices, animal and human, were flung," Howard said. "Bel-Marduk, he's sometimes called."

"And that was worshipped here?" Winnie asked, as if unsure she was being tricked or not. "Oliver, you *are* joking, aren't you?"

Oliver shook his head. "Certainly not. Don't blame me for it. Blame the workmen who uncovered its remains. The very fact of its existence was forgotten till now - *if* it was ever widely known, even in Roman times, which I doubt."

Winnie looked at her husband. "And you knew about this?"

Morgan nodded his head.

"Oliver showed me the feet when I came here before. They're in the cellar. In the distant past he said it probably formed part of a secret temple dedicated to its worship."

"And it's been locked away all these years?"

An uncomfortable silence filled the room. Tom coughed. Then laughed.

"At least it's not been in regular use. That's one thing to be said in its favour, uh?" He pulled the ring of a can of lager and there was a loud hiss that broke the mood of introspection.

"Throw me one of those cans, Tom, will you?" Oliver said. He grinned at Winnie as if to say that everything would be all right.

And, for the time being, it was.

*

Morgan and Winnie made love that night in the large, comfortable bed in their room with an intensity neither of them had felt for years. When, finally, they rested, to stare at the darkness of the ceiling, they felt content. Winnie snuggled her head against Morgan's shoulder as he wrapped one arm about her, and they slept.

Day-break came early, with bright sunlight glowing through the curtains. Neither of them had been disturbed during the night after they'd fallen asleep, and all thoughts of prowlers and pagan idols in the cellar were far from their minds. Morgan felt refreshed and revived. He smiled at Winnie as she rolled over and the warm blankets fell from her breasts. Wakening, she opened her eyes and smiled at him. She wrapped her arms about his shoulders, and they hugged.

In a sense it was as if they wanted to hold onto something safe, something that was theirs and theirs alone. Something which both of them felt, somehow, was threatened.

After breakfast Winnie expressed a wish to be shown what remained of the idol. Oliver looked relieved, as if he'd feared its presence might put her off their visit here.

"Certainly," he said. "Perhaps Morgan could show it to you. It's not much of a thing really," he said with a wry grin.

When they reached the cellar, Winnie stared at the feet with a look of disappointment.

"Oliver's right," she said, after a moment's silence, "they don't look much, do they?"

Morgan had to agree with her. They didn't. Set against the vastness of the cellar, they paled into insignificance, though he still felt disturbed at the ugliness of the things. Whoever cast them all those centuries ago had even gone to the trouble of adding intricate details, like networks of wrinkles about the large, misshapen toes.

They only stayed for a few minutes, during which time Winnie glanced at the seemingly endless darkness of the cellar, then they retraced their steps and climbed back to the ground floor. The diesel-powered generator next to the cellar door throbbed reassuringly, untainted by the arcane evil hinted at below. Morgan turned the key in the door behind them with a feeling of relief. After the darkness of the cellar they decided to get a breath of fresh air, though even the warm breeze outside couldn't cope with the gloom beneath the elms, and they soon agreed to head for the road, leaving their car behind at the house to walk the three quarters of a mile to the village. The sun shone brightly through the leaves of the hawthorn and cedar that grew beside the road once they'd passed beyond the edge of the woods around Elm Tree House.

As they neared the village Morgan said: "Has something peculiar about Oliver and the house struck you?"

"What do you mean?" Winnie asked. "His enthusiasm for it?"

"Not that. That would be normal for anyone. After all, it's a magnificent place and he did get it for a ridiculously low price. Even taking into account the costs of renovation so far, he's had a bargain. I'd be enthusiastic, too, in his shoes."

"Then what?" Winnie said. "I haven't noticed anything."

"Neither did I till I thought about it this morning, then it hit me." The hump-backed bridge at the edge of the village came into sight as they turned a bend in the road. A group of children were leaning over it, throwing stones into the river. They whooped with laughter when one of them, reaching out over the wall too far, almost fell in.

They left the road before it reached the bridge and climbed down the grassy slopes to the riverbank. There were a small number of large stones by the river and they sat on two of them. The river gurgled at their feet through piles of pebbles that formed a line of stepping-stones across it.

"You know Oliver pretty well," Morgan said after several minutes. "You know his ways, his habits. Have you known him miss an opportunity to lecture us on the history of some old place or building we came across? It's an obsession with him, isn't it?"

Winnie agreed, remembering too well how irked they had sometimes become at his passion for out of the way historical facts. There wasn't much about the area in which they lived they hadn't been told and re-told several times over, till it was ingrained in their memories

"You must have noticed how little he's told us about the house so far. The bare facts, that's all. Is that the old Oliver we knew?"

Winnie considered it, frowning.

"It could be because of his breakdown," she said, though she sounded doubtful. She looked at Morgan, as if searching his eyes for a clue. "Why do you think this is?"

"I'm not sure, Winn. It's odd, though. It's almost as if he doesn't want to tell us what he knows about the house. And he must know more than he's said so far. I can't believe he's not looked into it. A pre-Christian temple? The ruins of a monastery? A house built back in the seventeenth century that hasn't been lived in for the past twenty years? And why was it left empty so long? Why were the wings blocked up so they couldn't be entered through the house, only from outside? Why did they fall into disuse, to become ruins that are ready to collapse any day?"

"You don't think you're making too much of it all, do you?"

Morgan shook his head. "No, Winn. There's something wrong. I don't know what, but I do know there's something. Why else should Oliver hold back on all this? It's just not like him. Why be silent about it? We should be bored of the subject by now. You know that too."

Winnie had to agree.

"Why should he want to 'hold back', though?"

"I don't know," Morgan said. "That puzzles me too. It's not as if we haven't been close friends. And you can't doubt the warmth of his welcome."

"What should we do about it? Ask him outright?"

"No. If he's evading the subject there may be a reason, at least from his point of view. Perhaps it would be better to make enquiries of our own and see what we find out about the house."

"There's a library in the village. I noticed it yesterday when we drove through," Winnie said. "It's near the church. There might be something there. Some books on local history, perhaps."

"Or we might be able to approach someone locally, like the landlord of the Hare and Hounds. Or even the vicar."

"One of them should know something. I suggest we set off for the library and see what we find out there."

The village library - a sub-branch of the main municipal library in Fenley - was a small, stone-clad building that faced the church beyond a cramped car park almost filled to capacity by a large Toyota estate and a Volvo. It was pleasantly cool inside and had the hushed atmosphere that seemed natural to a library, as if to speak inside it was like sneezing in church. Winnie's high heels clicked loudly across the parquet floor. A young lady, her hair fastened in a bun, was sorting through a tray of reference cards. She looked up at them and smiled.

"Can I help you?"

"We're staying with a friend who's bought a house near the village," Morgan said. "Elm Tree House. You'll know the place."

"I'm not local," she said, "but I know it, yes. I thought it would end up falling down before it was sold."

"Do you have any books about local history that might contain some information – anything - about it?"

"We have," she said, "though if you want to save time you'd be better off having a word with the librarian, Mr Wilkes. He's lived in Fenley all his life and is something of an expert on local history. He knows more than any books I could show you." She nodded towards a grey-haired, elderly-looking man at the far side of the library, flicking through a catalogue by one of the windows. He had a strong but scholarly face and gold-rimmed spectacles that tottered on the brink of falling off the tip of his nose. Every second or two he had to push them back, but they invariably slid to the same precarious position again almost straight away.

"If you'll wait a moment, I'll go and fetch him," the girl said. She stepped from behind the desk and went across the library. She spoke to the librarian and he glanced towards them. For a moment he looked disarmingly to Morgan like the old British comedian Will Haye as he stared from above the top of his glasses at them, and Morgan had to suppress a ridiculous impulse to laugh.

Wilkes put aside the catalogue he'd been leafing through and walked towards them.

"Elm Tree House?" he asked in a quiet, cultured voice that shattered Morgan's image of Will Haye instantly. There was a quick intelligence behind his pale grey eyes as he looked at them enquiringly.

"A friend of ours bought it recently," Morgan said. "I wanted to know if we could find out something about its history."

Wilkes nodded his head. "Oliver Atcheson. I got to know him quite well when he first came here. That would be early March. There was still snow on the ground at the time, though your friend had an impressive tan."

"He'd been holidaying in Spain," Winnie explained tactfully.

"So he told me," Wilkes said. "We talked a lot about history, though I've not seen much of him lately." He thought for a moment. "I hope he's well."

"Very well," Morgan said.

"I'm pleased to hear it. Though I'm surprised you're making enquiries about Elm Tree House. I'd have thought Oliver could have told you all you wanted to know about it himself."

Winnie exchanged glances with Morgan.

"Unless it's a bit of an imposition," Morgan said, "could we invite you for lunch with us in the village? We were thinking of going to the Hare and Hounds for a bite to eat. You could join us as our guest. We'd be very grateful. Perhaps you could tell us something about the house?"

The librarian considered his invitation for a moment, then said: "Your friend has told you nothing about Elm Tree House?" His voice sounded oddly significant.

Morgan said: "No. He's preoccupied at the moment with so many things, what with all the renovation work that's going on."

"I understood that had finished, at least for the time being," Wilkes said.

"Professionally, yes," Morgan said. "But there's still plenty of clearing up to be done. I don't know whether you're aware of the project he has for the house," he added.

"The artists? Your friend did tell me about his plans." He smiled wryly. Turning to his assistant, he said, "I'm going out for lunch. I'll be back in an hour."

*

The landlord of the Hare and Hounds welcomed them like old customers when they walked into the pub.

"And good afternoon to you, Mr Wilkes," he said. "It's not often we see you here before an evenin'."

"That you don't, Bob." Wilkes reached into the inside pocket of his suit and pulled out his wallet. "A pint of my usual, Bob, and whatever my friends would like." He waved aside their protests. When they'd been served, they took their drinks to one of the tables in the beer garden outside.

As soon as they'd settled Wilkes said, "Most of the house your friend has bought was built in the early seventeenth century by Sir Robert Tollbridge. He was a nephew of the third Marquis of Barchester. By reputation a hard man he lived most of his life under a number of clouds for various things, most of them deserved. Why he chose that particular site for the house I don't know. It's always had a bit of a sinister reputation. In the twelfth century a monastery was founded there by an obscure order of monks. It didn't last long. Within a short time the brothers had earned the hostility of the local yeomanry, mainly because of the harshness of their demands and their cruelty. It was claimed they acted more like a band of brigands than a body of men under Holy Orders. Appeals were made to Sir Hugh de Lacy and to the Sheriff at Barchester, and an investigation into their activities followed. So much can be gleaned from various chronicles written at the time and from Adrian Weeke's *The Fenley Wanderer*, a well researched book published in the nineteen thirties. Suspicions were raised that the monks had turned to darker practices. What these were, I don't know, but whatever the investigation uncovered about what was going on at the monastery was bad enough for it to be razed to the ground and for every monk to be hanged till, it was said, not a single tree in the woods thereabouts was without its burden. For the Abbot a grimmer fate was reserved. He was hung, drawn and quartered, his remains left in an iron cage to be hung to rot in the village square."

Morgan shot a quick glance at his wife to see if she had seen the connection between the monks' deviation from their faith and the idol of Moloch found in the cellar. Was this what Sir Hugh de Lacy and the Sheriff found when they investigated the abbey? Had it been put back to its original use? That would explain why the abbey was destroyed and why measures were taken against the monks. It seemed incredible that Christian monks could have been perverted to things like that, but not impossible, he knew.

"Strangely enough," the librarian said after a drink of his beer, "it's said a storm blew up on the night of the Abbot's execution. The sky grew so black nothing could be seen. Winds howled, thunder crashed through the heavens, and for hour after hour the storm raged on. When day-break came, the Abbot's remains had gone. No trace was ever found of them."

"Were any explanations offered for this?" Morgan asked.

"There's a quaint woodcut in Weeke's book showing a horned devil plucking the Abbot's body from its cage, perhaps to carry it off to Hell. If there's any basis of truth in the disappearance, though, I imagine it more likely one of the brothers managed to escape the holocaust and used the darkness of the storm to steal away what was left of the Abbot." Wilkes drank some more of his beer and said: "Local legends of a thin creature that haunts Elm Tree Wood have persisted for centuries, said to be the Abbot's ghost. A 'twig-shinned phantom' is how the thing is often described."

"So our friend's bought himself a haunted house," Winnie said.

The librarian shook his head.

"No ghosts have ever been claimed to haunt the house. The grounds, yes, but not the house. Built, as I've said, in the seventeenth century, it has a peculiarity about it which might interest you, though it wasn't unusual at the time, when superstition was stronger than now. People in those days often tried to guard their homes against the supernatural when building them. One superstition has it that a demonic spirit cannot enter through a misshapen door or window frame. As a result, every door and window in the original part of the house is misshapen. It seems Sir Robert Tollbridge intended to prevent any harmful supernatural force from entering his home. Which could make you wonder, I suppose, if this was why the Victorian wings, which wouldn't have had this built into them, so quickly fell into disuse. From what information there is these wings were hardly ever used, and the doors into them were bricked up less than a year after they were built. And no subsequent owner ever went to the trouble of having them opened again. In fact, for most of the last century, just as for most of this, the house has been empty."

"Did any of the people who bought the house stay long?" Winnie asked.

Wilkes shook his head. "So far as I can gather, no. The last people to buy it, the Murdocks, only managed a few months before they left. Once they'd gone, they never revisited the place. It was put in the hands of an estate agent, where it remained till Oliver bought it this year."

Morgan considered what the librarian had told them for a few minutes while they finished their drinks. Afterwards, he went to the bar to order something to eat and a fresh round of drinks, then slowly returned, deep in thought.

"This house," he said, "have there ever been any deaths

connected with it?"

"As I've said," Wilkes replied, "the house has never had anything said about it. All the tales concern the grounds, which are said to be haunted. There is the 'twig-shinned phantom', I've already mentioned. And some would have it on certain nights the bodies of the monks who were hung from the trees can still be seen, writhing in their death throes. There have been a few incidents concerning the woods. The most recent, of course, was Teb, though that's a dubious tale, and could be accounted for naturally. You know this story, don't you?"

Morgan said that they did. "I think we saw him waiting by the door of the Squire's Arms."

"That will be him. He never lingers far from that place. It will be the death of him yet. As I say, what happened to him could be explained quite naturally. After all, it's not unusual for people to have strokes. And his imagination and the onset of the stroke could have supplied whatever else he thought happened to him that night."

Morgan agreed.

"Other tales go back some time, since few locals ever venture there, certainly at night, and the place has only occasionally, and for brief periods, been inhabited. Of those few occasions, violent incidents have been reported taking place in the grounds. There were even a few deaths, most of them unaccounted for. The worst I can bring to mind was the murder of the youngest daughter of Hugh Montgomery, who bought the house in the nineteenth century. She was found one night almost ripped to shreds beneath the trees. No one was ever charged with the murder, and the Montgomerys left the house days after the incident. Mrs Montgomery underwent therapy for months afterwards in a clinic in Switzerland. The last death was in 1926. One of the gamekeepers from the big estate wandered into the woods in search of a poacher who was thought to have made his escape in that direction - though whether he did or not is anyone's guess. The gamekeeper, a big, burly fellow in the prime of life, was found with his throat ripped open as if by a mad dog."

"No wonder it has a bad reputation," Winnie said. She looked at her husband. "Yet, knowing this, Oliver is still living in that horrible place?"

"Perhaps he doesn't take these tales too seriously," Morgan suggested.

"These aren't just tales," Wilkes said. "These and many incidents of violence can be verified by looking up the appropriate records made at the time. They're not legends, passed down by word of mouth, distorted and exaggerated over the years. They are verifiable fact."

The Davies returned to Elm Tree House later that afternoon in a subdued frame of mind. Neither of them knew how much weight to place on the incidents Wilkes had described to them.

Winnie stared at the large, grey trunks of the elms as they walked along the drive. The darkness beneath them seemed claustrophobic and dense - unnaturally dense, as if something more than just shadows accounted for it. The warmth of the sun seemed cut off from them and she shivered, clutching at Morgan's arm as if for comfort, though that was not her nature at all. Morgan knew they would look at the house and the grounds around it differently from now on, that neither of them would ever again feel at ease in the place.

Oliver was busy typing up the final draft of his latest novel when they arrived back to the house. The others seemed preoccupied with their various literary or artistic activities, and there was a studious atmosphere about the place that could have been attractive had it not been for what they had found out about it.

They wandered into the kitchen, where they found Alicia preparing tea.

"Hi, there," she said when she saw them come in. "Have you had a good time? The weather's been beautiful today, hasn't it?" She looked at them with a carefree expression on her face, marred only by the crease between her eyes. It was hard to imagine that anything terrible could be wrong with the house or its environs when she could look like she did after having spent more than a month here, and Morgan wondered if they were allowing their imaginations to override their commonsense.

"Where did you get to today?" Alicia asked as she put the final touches to a large fruit pie, before carrying it to the oven.

"We went into the village," Winnie said. She told her about meeting the librarian. "Have you heard any of these tales?" she asked when she'd finished.

Alicia carried on with her cooking while Winnie spoke, and she did not pause even now. She brushed a hand through her hair before bending down for a bag of flour in one of the units by the oven.

"I've heard some of them," she said incuriously. "You're bound to do eventually. The locals hold this place in dread, bless 'em." She smiled at the silliness of it all. "But Tom and me, we don't hold with that kind of thing. We like to keep our feet firmly on the ground, Tom especially. You won't find him worrying his head about ghosts and things that go bump in the night, especially about some medieval monks." She laughed at the notion and shook her head dismissively.

"You don't feel concerned what happened here in the past?" Winnie asked. "Even the murders?"

"If people worried about every act of violence that has ever taken place there wouldn't be many places left to live, now would there?" Alicia said with firm practicality, her brown eyes stolidly unimpressed by what she'd heard. "In any case, nothing's ever happened inside the house, has it? Even in the tales they tell you about it in the village."

Morgan thought about the misshapen door and window frames that Wilkes had mentioned to them, but the idea seemed too ludicrous to mention, especially to someone as practically minded as Alicia. She would wonder what he was talking about and why he was taking whimsical stuff like that seriously.

When Oliver had finished typing for the day, Morgan wandered into the lounge and mentioned meeting Wilkes.

"You've met him, haven't you," he said.

Oliver chuckled. "I've met him all right. I talked to him quite a bit when I came here. But he's such a ridiculously superstitious old buzzard. How he harped and harped about this place! You'd have thought it was one of the gateways to Hell."

"It hasn't exactly had a peaceful past, has it?" Morgan said.

Oliver snorted derisively. "It's all right now. That's all I need to know about it. I've lived here long enough to know, unlike Wilkes. D'you know, he wouldn't even come here to take a look at the place when I invited him? That's how superstitious the man is. Oh, he knows its history all right - *from books* - but he's never set foot inside the place to see what it's like for himself. *Pah!* I can't put up with it. That's why I haven't seen him recently.

In the end he annoyed me with his tales and legends." Oliver stood up and paced about the room, too agitated to sit down again. Flinging his arms open wide in a flamboyant gesture, he said: "He's like so many people, blinded by their own preconceptions. They don't look at things as they are, but at what they expect them to be."

Morgan was surprised at the heat of Oliver's feelings. He knew it would be pointless to argue, though. Nothing he could say would change Oliver's attitude towards the house. And perhaps he was right. God damn it, of course he was right. Why shouldn't he be? Why should there be anything in all those things that Wilkes had told them? Why should there be anything wrong with this house or the woods surrounding it?

Yet Morgan knew he wasn't sure. With a feeling that went deeper than reasoning, he knew there could be something wrong with this place. He could feel it like a tumour working inside him. But he knew there was nothing he could say to Oliver that would alter his opinions, that the most he could achieve by attempting it would be to create a rift in their friendship.

He shrugged and let the subject die, while Oliver went on to tell him something about the novel he was working on. Half an hour later Alicia popped in to tell them tea was ready. As they went in to join the others in the dining room, Winnie looked at Morgan with an expression of curiosity, but he shook his head at her. She shrugged and sat down beside him at the table. Despite Tom Paxley's non-stop good humour and irrepressible anecdotes, neither of them felt the same as they did the night before, as if somehow they were sealed off from the others by a feeling of gloom. Morgan noticed that Oliver glanced at them once or twice during the meal with a look of curiosity on his face, and he knew this change had not passed his attention.

CHAPTER 8

Nevil Wilkes was in a pensive mood when he returned home from the library. He walked the quarter mile to his house without seeing anything he passed. It was almost with a feeling of surprise when he realized he was home and that his wife, Marian, was calling to him. Four years younger than Nevil, Marian Wilkes was a short, stocky woman with grey hair and a round, suntanned face. She recognized the look on her husband's face straight away when she saw him, and she knew what it was that had caused it.

"It's that house again, isn't it?" she said as they walked into their house together. "Is it?"

Nevil gave his wife a hug.

"I've been talking to two friends of Oliver Atcheson. They're staying with him for a few days and were asking about history of the house."

"Did you tell them what you know?"

"I told them what was recorded about it and what has gone on at that site in the past. They didn't seem surprised."

"Do you think Atcheson sent them to find out what you know?" she asked. They walked into the lounge, where Nevil stretched back gratefully in his favourite armchair by the window. He looked at his wife thoughtfully. A smile played about his lips.

"You needn't worry," he said to her. "I'm certain they were genuine."

"But will they tell Atcheson what you said?"

He shook his head slowly. "I don't know," he said. "Maybe. I didn't swear them to silence or any nonsense like that. But there's no harm in that, is there? I didn't tell them anything they couldn't have found out for themselves given time. I didn't tell them anymore than that." He sighed. "Though I wish I could. I honestly wish that I could."

CHAPTER 9

When everyone had finished eating that night, Morgan and Winnie decided to have another look in the village. Oliver looked over curiously for a moment when they mentioned this, and Morgan wondered whether he was going to say more about the librarian, perhaps a last-ditch effort to dissuade them from seeing him again, but he held back - *visibly* held back - from doing so, though the sour expression on his face was eloquent enough.

For all the suspicions Oliver might have had about their intentions, they had decided, in fact, to seek out Teb at the Squire's Arms, not Nevil Wilkes. Morgan knew they had probably found out all they could for the time being from the librarian.

They took their car, and with it a much-needed sense of freedom - of escape. When they drew up outside the Squire's Arms a short while later they saw the pub doors were already open and several farm labourers were stood outside, drinking their pints in the sun

It was a much smaller place than the Hare and Hounds, and older. Faded prints were hung about the smoke-stained walls, and narrow, blackened, wooden beams spanned the ceiling. A strong smell of beer, slightly yeasty and stale, filled the squat, L-shaped room, around the edge of which were hard wooden benches, while the stools at the bar were scarred and wobbly. More scars covered the scratched surface of the bar itself, which was so sticky with spilled beer that Morgan fastidiously refrained from letting the sleeves of his blazer anywhere near.

They ordered a couple of drinks, then Morgan asked the landlord if Teb was in tonight.

"Yull find 'im down there in the window," the man said, a half-smoked cigarette stuck to his lower lip while he spoke.

At the far end of the room Morgan made out an alcove. Wooden walls enclosed it on two sides and there was a bench-like table inside and three chairs. An old man in a dirty overcoat sat hunched over the table, staring at a glass of beer in front of him.

"I'll have another beer," Morgan said. "Give me a pint of whatever it is he drinks."

60

The landlord laughed sarcastically. "'E'd drink the slops from the bucket if you offered them." He pulled a pint of bitter, though.

Morgan paid him and carried their drinks to the alcove. Winnie walked dubiously behind him. She hadn't set foot in a place like this since in her teens, slumming it with her friends round the Barbary Coast in Blackburn.

"Good evening," Morgan said to the old man. He placed the beer next to the one he was already drinking. "Do you mind if we join you?"

Teb looked up and stared. Morgan felt shocked at the way in which half the man's face was stretched across his skull, pulled tight by a spasm that had never, over the long years since his stroke, relaxed its awful grip. One eye squinted blindly, and there was a vicious sneer on his lips that made Morgan think for an instant he was about to snarl abuse in reply. But the only response was a muttered: "No, yer can sit if yer likes."

Gingerly they inched their way into the alcove, seating themselves across from him. Winnie clutched her gin and tried to keep a friendly smile on her face, though the thick odour of unwashed clothes and sweat that reeked from the old man was almost too much for her.

Morgan sipped his own beer while Teb took long, slow swallows of his. When he'd finished the one he'd been drinking Teb reached for the one Morgan had given him.

"Thanks," he murmured as his thick, brown hand closed in on the glass and he raised it to his lips.

"You're welcome," Morgan said, with a forced grin.

Teb drank, then placed the half-drained glass back on the table. His good eye twinkled in scrutiny of Morgan for a moment.

"Did you want somethin'?" he asked; a look of curiosity crept across the unmarred half of his face.

"Maybe," Morgan said, uncertain how to ask him. "We were curious about certain parts of this place you know very well."

"Certain parts?" A thin trickle of saliva dripped from the twisted side of his mouth. Teb reached up and wiped it away with an impatient gesture. "I knows plenty o' parts 'ereabouts. Plenty. There ain't 'ardly a bit o' countryside I didn't know when I were younger, afore..." (His gnarled fingers felt the twisted muscles of his cheek.) "...afore this," he went on, his voice

61

sounding vague, as if he was losing himself in thought.

Morgan glanced at his wife, then looked back again at the old man.

"We were told you used to be something of a poacher."

Teb's eye darkened with concentration.

"A poacher? Aye, I were a poacher once. Best there were. Best there were in these parts anyways." He straightened up. "Then this 'appened."

"Was that at Elm Tree House?" Morgan said.

The old man's head jerked upright; the muscles in his neck seemed to quiver.

"Elm Tree House," he said in a mutter. "It were there. Waitin'. Waitin' for me. Knew I'd be comin'. It knew, God blast it! It were waitin' for me, waitin' in the dark all 'ard an' dry an' brittle."

"What was?" Morgan asked. "What was this thing that was hard and dry and brittle?"

Teb shook his head.

"No one wants to know. They laugh at me be'ind me back. Think I don't notice. Think I'm darft. Think when this 'appened," (He touched his face again) "think it got my mind as well. But it didn't, yer knows. It didn't get me there. It didn't. Not completely, it didn't."

"We'd like to know," Winnie said earnestly.

Teb looked at her for the first time.

"No one wants to know," he told her. "No one." He shook his head. "It were 'orrible." He shuddered as if the years since it happened had done nothing to lessen its impact. "It were white, like bones, an' scratchy. 'Ard an' dry an' brittle. Long fingers, it 'ad, like uncut nails. Empty sockets where its eyes should 'a' been." He shuddered again. "No one wants to know that. No one. They laugh at yer when yer tell 'em. Say yer've 'ad yer brains affected. But they weren't." His hand reached for Morgan's, and Morgan felt the brown fingers tighten about his with unexpected strength. "They think I'm thrippence short. I'm not, yer know. I saw it. Others must've seen it too. I think it got 'em. Killed 'em. The bugger damn near killed me. But it didn't." He stared at his beer and shook his head. A deep sob shuddered from deep inside his chest. "Though I sometimes wish it 'ad."

Morgan signalled to Winnie silently, then said: "We'll buy you another beer, then we'll be off."

62

He stood up to go to the bar when the old man suddenly tightened his grip once more about his hand.

"I saw it, yer know. I really saw it. It were real. As real as you or me. All white an' bony an' rotten."

Morgan prized his fingers free.

"We believe you, old fellow." He stepped back and nodded to the landlord. "Another pint of bitter for our friend." He passed him the money, then took hold of Winnie's arm as they left, the close atmosphere of the pub too cloying and stale suddenly.

Outside, they walked towards the bridge. They leaned against it and gazed at the water as it rushed across the pebbles below. The air was fresh and clean, with the scent of new mown grass.

"What did you make of that?" Winnie asked.

Morgan considered for a moment, then shrugged. "I don't know," he confessed. "Perhaps his mind was affected by the stroke. It must have been one Hell of a bad one to have left him like that. Probably damn near killed him."

"And left him with a nightmare that's stuck in his mind ever since."

"That's one explanation," Morgan said. "It's probably the most logical one, after all. Let's face it, what's the alternative? That he really was attacked by some devilish creature straight out of *Night of the Living Dead*? Come on! This is our friend's house we're talking about."

"This is Elm Tree House we're talking about. And a friend who seems hardly like the man we've known for the best part of our lives anymore."

Morgan nodded. "Perhaps there's something in what Teb said. He's obviously too befuddled, though, for us to place much faith in what he says."

"No matter how much or how little faith we put in it, there's something wrong with Elm Tree House. Something bad. And I don't want to stay there a minute longer than we need to. I don't care if no one else realizes there's something wrong with it. Or even if they swear that everything is all right. Because you know as well as I do, there is something wrong."

Morgan agreed with her. "Though why the others seem unaffected, I don't know. It's not as if they're unimaginative. Quite the opposite, obviously."

"Perhaps too much the opposite," Winnie suggested.

"Perhaps," Morgan echoed doubtfully, though it had worried him more than once that it seemed as if it was only he and Winnie who found the place uncomfortable. "I wonder how much the others know."

On their way back to the house they decided to make their excuses the next day and leave. One more night there was as much as either of them wanted to spend.

They found the others sitting in the lounge when they returned, listening to a Shostakovich symphony on the stereo. Winnie sniffed in distaste. She had never been able to abide Shostakovich, whose music sounded like dirges to her ear. Fortunately, the record had been turned over and was nearing the end. Tom Paxley passed Morgan a can of lager while Winnie helped herself to another gin and tonic.

"Did you see Nevil Wilkes?" Oliver asked when the music had finished, and he put the record in its sleeve.

Morgan said: "No, as it happens, though we weren't looking for him. We went to the Squire's Arms."

"The Squire's Arms?" Tom Paxley asked. "Isn't that where that damn fool poacher hangs about?" He looked over at Oliver. "You know who I mean. Teb? Or something as ridiculous."

"You've not been to see that old reprobate, have you, Morgan?" Oliver sighed with mock exasperation. "Wilkes has got to you, hasn't he? Wilkes and his ghosts and ghouls and God knows what else!"

"I've only met Wilkes a couple of times," Tom said, "so I shouldn't say too much about him, but in all honesty the man's a fool. He really is. God, how he tried to stuff my head full of nonsense when we first came here and I didn't know him better!"

"He's a crank," Oliver said. "Nothing but an interfering, stupid old crank. And as for you, Morgan, going out of your way to see this Teb character, well, I'm surprised at you. And you Winnie too. I can't imagine what's got into you both."

Again Morgan wondered at his friend's reaction. It was as if he was afraid they might find out something he was desperately trying to keep secret. But what? There was nothing they'd discovered so far that could explain it.

"We were curious, that's all, Oliver," Winnie said, her voice the epitome of calm commonsense. Morgan envied her. "The way you're reacting, I could almost believe you were trying to keep something from us. Which I know would be ridiculous, especially since we've heard nothing that could possibly affect you."

"It's this house," Tom said. "Oliver's so infernally proud of it, he can't bear the thought of people being put off by the kind of scurrilous tales told about it in the village, especially when we know what utter insufferable nonsense they are. Is that right, Oliver?"

Mollified, Oliver said that it probably was. "After all," he said less truculently, "it *is* a damn fine house, isn't it?"

The conversation turned to other things as Hazel Metcalfe entered the room with several sheets of poetry she'd been working on over the day.

"I wondered whether you might be interested in seeing them," she said to Winnie, as she sat beside her.

The night passed peacefully on.

CHAPTER 10

It was several hours since it had gone dark and everyone within Elm Tree House was in bed. There was a heavy silence. An oppressive silence. A silence that felt ready to burst as Morgan and Winnie lay in bed, neither of them able to sleep.

Eventually Morgan looked at his bedside alarm clock on the chest of drawers beside him. It was two o'clock. He breathed out slowly in a vain attempt to lull himself to sleep as he turned his gaze to the open window, an impulse to get out of bed and walk over to it burning inside him, though at the same time he felt alarmed at the prospect, as if he knew, with a grim certainty, what he would see.

"Can't you sleep?" Winnie asked. Her voice sounded weary.

"Not a hope, sweetheart." The impulse to get up and look out of the window grew stronger as he spoke, as if his words had cut through the restraints that held him back, though the dread remained just as strong.

"What's wrong?"

"It must be the air. It's too close. I feel as if I'm going to suffocate in here." Which was halfway true. It did feel close. Horribly close. Slowly, he pushed the blankets from him and swung his legs out of bed.

"Where are you going?"

"Just to see if I can get some fresh air at the window, that's all." He approached it slowly, his legs feeling weak. As he reached out for the casement to steady himself, he leaned out. The warm air outside was still. Expectant. He breathed in slowly, conscious of the space separating him from the ground barely twenty feet below. As he turned his eyes downwards a cold wind blew into his face. He felt his breath catch in his throat, and he wanted to step back and look away from the darkness. He had to.

He had to!

He choked back a cry and tightened his grip on the casement, as if he was afraid of falling out of the window if he didn't.

"What's the matter? Are you ill?"

Then he saw what he had been looking at for the past few seconds without realizing what he'd seen. Dead white, like freshly picked bone, it stared up at him, gazing at his eyes, distinct in the darkness, yet his eyes were unable to make it out as clearly as he knew he should be able to do, as if a haze surrounded it. It stared at him, *straight into his eyes.* Boring into and through them and into his brain. He cried out as he threw himself back from the window.

"*Morgan!*"

Winnie was beside him on the floor even before he realized he had fallen.

"What happened? Are you all right?" He felt her hand cradle his head and he tried to get up, then lay back again as a feeling of nausea swept over him. "Take it easy," Winnie urged him comfortingly. "You gave yourself a nasty crack on the end of the bed when you hurled yourself back into the room. There's a spot of blood in your hair."

Morgan closed his eyes for a moment till the nausea began to subside and he began to feel all right again. Gingerly he felt across the back of his head. A lump the size of the proverbial egg was starting to swell, and he could feel a patch of stickiness which he knew was blood.

"That must've been some crack," he said. Winnie helped him sit upright on the floor.

"It was," she told him. "Would you like some water?"

"I think I'd better. And a couple of aspirin. I can feel a headache starting already." He climbed onto the edge of the bed while Winnie went out of the room. He felt calmer now after the shock of seeing whatever it was outside, and even felt as if he was strong enough to go back and look again. But before he could Winnie returned with a glass of water.

"Take these," she said, handing him a couple of pills.

When he'd finished, Winnie said: "What happened? What made you jump back like that? Was it something you saw?"

"Or thought I saw," Morgan said, no longer certain. He told her about the white face that looked up at him. "It was like what I saw when I stayed here before." He shuddered. "God, it frightened me though. *How* it frightened me!" He grinned wryly, as if it was a joke, but Winnie knew him too well to be taken in. And she could tell how frightened he really was by the look in his eyes. She glanced at the open window.

"Should we both look?" she asked. "To see if you really did see something there?"

At the prospect of going back Morgan felt the dread from

earlier come back, but worse. Far worse. He did not want to see that face again. Nor did he want Winnie to see it either. He clasped her hand.

"Perhaps it would be better if we got back in bed and cleared out of this place in the morning. Goddamn Oliver if he wants to live here. He can come and visit *us* next time. And the time after that."

"You *are* frightened, aren't you?" Winnie said.

"I saw it," Morgan told her simply. "And I don't want to see it again."

Winnie reached up and turned off the light and they climbed into bed. Eventually, despite the traumas of the night, they slept, and it was not till the sun had risen above the trees they awoke.

CHAPTER 11

Nevil Wilkes left home every day for the library at 8.45. Despite the worry that nagged at him after his meeting yesterday with Morgan and Winnie Davies, and their talk about Elm Tree House, he adhered to his normal routine. Two scrambled eggs and a slice of bacon, lightly grilled, with a cup of black, unsweetened coffee for breakfast with his wife, a quick look at the *Guardian*, then a stroll around the garden to see how his beloved flowers were doing.

"The fuchsia are coming on nicely," he said to his wife when he returned indoors to pick up his jacket and keys.

Marian kissed him, as she invariably did when he went out to work. It was only a fifteen-minute walk from where they lived to the library, and he seldom used their car except when the weather was bad. When it was a day like today, with a cloudless sky and a sun that would be blazing by noon, he looked forward to the stroll through the village, when he could casually exchange small talk with whoever he met.

"Good morning, Mr Wilkes," Fanny Didsbury called on her early morning trip to the shop. She lived alone with her aged sister, Amanda, in a large house that had once belonged to their parents. "Have they sent any more Mills and Boon?" she asked expectantly. As she always did. She went through more than a dozen romantic novels every month, and it was a constant struggle to keep pace with her. The village library only stocked a limited number of books and it depended on supplies on loan from the library in Fenley for variety.

"If they haven't arrived this morning I'll be sure to get on the phone straight away. You can rely on that, Fanny," he assured her with a wave. Although it was easy enough to deal with her during the summer, when winter came, especially when the village was snowbound - which it was for at least a week every year - then he had problems. Not even the worst snowdrifts could keep Fanny Didsbury away from the library, nor appease her insatiable appetite for more and more books. If he had his wits about him he usually ensured he got a larger than normal stock for her before the bad weather started, though his constant fear was that even the library at Fenley was one day going to run short of titles for her.

As he strode down the main street past the Hare and Hounds, he saw the landlord, Bob Hopkins, sat out in the beer garden, sunning himself in a pair of cotton shorts that did nothing to hide the bulge of his well-stocked stomach.

"Good morning, Mr Wilkes," Bob called with the formal cordiality they had playfully built up over the years.

"Good morning to you, Mr Hopkins." Nevil paused as the sun's heat beat on his head. It would be a scorcher today and no mistake, he thought to himself; he felt momentarily envious of Bob as he watched him lazily reading through the sports pages of *The Sun*. "Did you see anything more of those people I came in with yesterday?"

Bob shook his head as he laid his paper to one side. "No, they didn't come in last night, though I heard someone saw them in the Squire's Arms earlier on. Seems they were talking to Teb of all people."

"Thanks," Nevil called to him as he continued on his way, deep in thought, interested that the Davies should have sought out Teb. He wondered what they had found out about the house that they should have been driven to carry their enquiries to Teb. More than idle curiosity lay behind it, he was sure. Much more than that.

He crossed the road and reached into his pocket for the library keys. He paused for a moment at the door, shaded by the lintel. A large van pulled up in the street behind him with a squeal of brakes. He heard its door open.

"Mr Wilkes!"

It was a hard voice, self-confident and deep. He turned, recognizing Tom Paxley, though it was several weeks since he last saw him.

"Have you come to see me about something?" Nevil asked, uncertainly. There was a hard glint in the man's eyes that jarred oddly with the transfixed smile on his face. Forewarned, Nevil hesitated a moment, then stepped back. As he did so, the larger man rushed forwards, and Nevil felt the sculptor's hands grip his throat. Hard fingers tightened painfully into his neck, and he felt himself being choked. He struggled to breathe but couldn't. In disbelief he stared at the florid face in front of his, certain the man intended to strangle him. Paxley's strong, white teeth ground together in a snarl of effort as he tightened his grip.

"You talk too much," Tom said, his voice grating. "You talk too much for the good of your health."

Suddenly the sculptor relaxed his grip, and Nevil breathed in agonizingly as Tom moved his hands to the librarian's lapels and hurled him sideways along the front of the library. Nevil tried to save himself, but spots still spun before his eyes and he couldn't counteract the brutal violence of the shove. He fell full length on the floor, grazing his hands on the rough concrete paving stones. His glasses fell from his nose and he felt his head hit the wall. Through the blur the loss of his glasses had left him in he saw Paxley stride towards him again. A huge hand reached down and grasped his shirt, jerking his face upwards.

"Anymore loose talk out of you and you'll suffer. Do you understand? This is *my* way of dealing with people like you. Count yourself lucky, because there are those who would prefer to use other ways, ways that aren't so easy to control - ways that would leave you crippled - or dead." With a casual push he sent the librarian sprawling again, then spun on his heel and strode back to the van.

Shaken, feeling suddenly sick, with a strong urge to heave his breakfast violently against the wall, Nevil crawled onto his knees as the van started with a loud roar and drove away.

CHAPTER 12

"Why, for God's sake? Why?" Oliver Atcheson cried in exasperation. For fifteen minutes at least he had argued and argued against the Davies' decision to leave. "I can't understand you anymore. I really can't. It's unbelievable that you should let your imaginations put you off this place. Do you hear anyone else here complain about it? Has Tom or Alicia or Howard or Hazel told you they've ever seen anything prowling outside this house? Have they?" He wiped his forehead and strode away from them back to the window.

"I'm sorry, Oliver," Morgan said, an edge of hardness roughening his voice, "but we've made our decision and intend sticking to it. Whether anyone else has seen anything or not, I don't really care. *I* saw something. I'm certain of that. And I'm not staying another night."

"Winnie? Can't you talk any sense into him?" Oliver appealed in desperation.

"I stand by every word that Morgan says," she insisted. "We're going as soon as we've packed our bags."

"And did *you* see anything?"

"Morgan did. That's good enough for me, Oliver."

"But, God damn it -"

"Oliver! We've decided. We're leaving. We haven't broken our friendship with you, and you'll be more than welcome to stay with us anytime you like, just as you have in the past. But we will not stay another night in this place."

"You're mad, the pair of you," Oliver moaned. He turned away from them. "You're mad. Like Wilkes." He looked at them again. "It's all his fault. If he hadn't filled your heads with nonsense -"

"Wilkes didn't fill our heads with anything, Oliver," Morgan snapped. Oliver's over-reaction and the growing heat of his language were beginning to get under his skin. "If you want to retain our friendship, you'll let it drop," he said. "What we've decided is nothing personal against you."

"You just can't stand staying in my house, that's all, isn't it?" He stared at them scornfully for a moment.

Tom Paxley looked over from the sofa. There was an aura of menace in his burly form which Morgan had never noticed before, and he bristled against it.

"Come on, Winnie," Morgan said. "I think we've had enough of this. It's time to pack our things and get started." He glanced at Oliver. "I'm sorry you've taken it like this, Oliver. I really am. But that's your choice. And this is ours."

Hazel Metcalfe entered the room as they left to go to their bedroom. She smiled at them as they passed. It was a smile that struck Morgan as odd, as if someone had just confirmed something for her, something she had insisted upon before and had just had proven right. They exchanged greetings and continued on their way to the stairs.

"She looks like the cat that just got the cream," Winnie said when they were out of earshot.

"I thought you and her were starting to make friends," Morgan said as they climbed to the gallery. The door to the lounge was firmly shut behind them.

"Because she chose to show me some of her recent poems?" Winnie asked, with a laugh. "Hardly! I don't know why she did it, to be honest, Morg. The ones I looked at in those anthologies were all right, but those she showed me last night! They were dark, mystical things, not at all like the others. And such an undercurrent of violence in them!" She shuddered. "If they are what this place has inspired her to write then we're well shut of it."

When they'd packed their bags in the back of their car, they bade farewell to Oliver. Their friend was still morose. But Tom Paxley strode out with them and gripped Morgan's hand in a strong clasp, shaking it vigorously.

"I hope we get the chance to meet you again," he said with conviction.

Morgan said: "Maybe. But you know my feelings about this place. They haven't changed since I spoke with Oliver, and I don't think they'll change in the future."

"Who knows?" Tom said with cool complacency. He grinned. "Who knows?"

Winnie lowered the window on her side of the car as they drove off. Gusts of air blew in, tousling her hair, and she ran her fingers through it, as if to clean it. She smiled at Morgan with a look of relief as he slowed at the gate, then drove onto the road.

"Do you feel better now?" he asked.

"Better? I never thought I'd ever feel such intense relief at leaving a house."

Morgan pressed down on the accelerator as they went down the road. The hedgerow rushed by on either side. It was as if they had made their escape, though neither of them had been under constraint. Morgan smiled at the ridiculous notion. Then screamed. A man stepped out from the hedgerow in their path. Too late to avoid hitting him, Morgan instinctively tried to swerve to one side, but the figure, as if intent on suicide, kept pace with them, and he had to turn even more. Too much, he realized an instant before the car collided with the hedgerow and was thrust into the air on its side. Winnie cried out as he glimpsed her throw her hands before her face; the windscreen shattered into thousands of tiny fragments in front of her as the car lurched to a sudden halt.

Morgan coughed, tasting blood in his mouth. Shocked and nauseous, he felt for the buckle of his seat belt to free himself. He fell heavily against the door beneath him and groaned. His chest felt as if someone had kicked him in the ribs with a heavy hobnailed boot. He looked up at Winnie.

"Are you all right?"

There was a tremor in his voice, and he knew he was close to passing out. Winnie raised one hand and he saw her nod. Her face was grey, and he thought she must have passed out when they crashed. He pulled himself to his feet, then reached up to help his wife from her seat. Carefully he managed to get her to the ground. As she clung onto the instrument panel for support, he clasped her legs, then lowered her inch by inch. Once she had squeezed through the broken windscreen, they made their way across the road, then slumped onto the grass.

Minutes passed before either of them felt able to look up. When they did, Winnie asked where the man had gone.

"We must have hit him," she said. "We couldn't have missed."

But they were alone. There was no one, dead or alive, anywhere in sight as far as they could see in both directions.

Morgan forced himself up, though his legs felt stiff, and they ached in every joint. He looked round the car, but there was no one there. Where could he have gone? He couldn't have disappeared? Surely?

He looked at his wife.

"There's no one here."

"But that's not possible." Some colour had returned to her face now and she climbed to her feet to go back to the car. She looked at the radiator and the bumper. There were no signs they had hit anyone. "But we must have done," she muttered to herself uncertainly. "We must have done, surely?"

"It's as if we both suffered a hallucination," Morgan ventured, and he tried to re-picture in his mind's eye just what the figure looked like. Tall - dark - presumably male. Yet what did he wear? A suit? Overalls? Jeans? *What?* But all he could see was something dark. "Can you remember what he was wearing?" Morgan asked.

His wife pursed her brows in thought.

"Wore?" The thought confounded her, and she showed it. "I don't know," she said slowly. "I didn't have time to take it in. It happened too fast." And try though she did, she could not remember anymore about the figure than Morgan.

"A fine couple of witnesses we'd make," he told her ruefully, relief that they hadn't hit anyone mixed with a feeling that something was wrong. It wasn't just that they should have hit whoever it was who strode in front of them, as the fact they *must* have hit them.

The sound of a vehicle coming down the road made them look up as a large van headed towards them in a cloud of dust.

"It's Paxley," Morgan said as the van drew up beside the wreck of the Orion, and the familiar figure of the sculptor could be seen pulling open the van door and climbing out. He looked at them in blank astonishment.

"For Christ's sake, man, what happened?"

They told him briefly the bare facts of the crash.

"And the bugger who caused it has gone?" Tom climbed up the side of the hedgerow and scanned the fields beyond it to see if he could spot something they'd missed. He shook his head bewilderedly.

"It's as if we hallucinated it all," Winnie said.

"A bloody dangerous hallucination," Tom said to her. "Here, I'd better give you a lift back to the house. Then I'll arrange for your car to be towed away for repairs. There's a garage in the village, though whether old Fred'll be able to do anything besides move it for you I don't know. Still, you'll at least be able to have a brandy or two at the house while I find out, eh?"

Unable to see any alternative to what he suggested, they agreed.

"It's a bit of a tight squeeze in here for three," Tom apologized as they climbed into the front seat of the van. Sketchpads and bags of charcoal had to be pushed to one side as they inched their way along the seat. Once in, Tom reversed down the road till he came to a farm gate set back in the hedge, then turned the van round and drove back to Elm Tree House. Only then did the full significance of their return begin to sink in. Morgan reached out for and clasped Winnie's hand. Her fingers tightened about his in response and it was as if they both shared the same feeling of disquiet. They glanced at each other while Tom rambled on beside them. Ahead of them the dark trees about Elm Tree House loomed into sight.

CHAPTER 13

Oliver did his best to make them feel welcome when they returned, his bitterness at their sudden departure forgotten in face of concern for their welfare. He immediately ushered them into the lounge, where he insisted on them taking a seat while he fixed a drink. Alicia said a warm cup of sweet tea would do them more good, that and a couple of aspirin.

"They'll ease the soreness of your bumps," she said as she bustled from the room to prepare it.

Oliver watched her go with a smile.

"Me," he said glibly when she'd gone, "I'd rather put my trust in a good *strong* drink."

He handed them a couple of generous brandies.

"Get them down. If they don't make you feel better, they'll at least make it easier to drink the tea Alicia will be making for you."

Tom Paxley dropped their suitcases in at the doorway.

"I'll be off now," he said. "I'll nip into the village and arrange for your car to be picked up."

"Thanks, Tom," Morgan said.

"Think nothing of it. It's the least I could do." He grinned at them suddenly, then left.

Oliver clapped his hands together.

"I'd better see about getting your bags to your room for you. If that's all right with you?"

He looked at them expectantly.

"We really should be making alternative arrangements for getting on our way," Morgan said.

"One night." Oliver raised his hands against their protests. "I insist. Neither of you are fit enough to embark on a journey after what you've just been through. Now are you? You might not feel it yet, but you'll be suffering from shock. It will hit you both eventually some time today. Mark my words. One night, that's all. Surely you can put up with one more night in my house? Morgan? Winnie? It will be better if you stay. If you insist on going, I can't stop you, but I'd hold myself responsible if anything happened to you as a result. I'd blame myself for not pressing you hard enough to stay."

"Perhaps it would be better to stay one night," Winnie said, looking at Morgan uncertainly. She felt nauseous after the crash, and her hands were trembling so much she couldn't even light a cigarette for herself properly.

"All right," Morgan said. He didn't feel too well himself. "One night, Oliver. But one night only." He smiled weakly. "And thanks for the offer, after what was said earlier. I'm sorry."

"Think nothing of it." Oliver spoke with a warmth that took them back to the way things were before Louise's death - this was the Oliver they knew. He picked up the bottle of brandy. "Would you like some more?" he asked.

Morgan laughed, tiredly.

"You'll have us both roaring drunk if you go on. I think I'll wait for the tea Alicia promised."

"Philistine," Oliver mocked as he poured a large glassful for himself.

To Winnie it was as if the whole of their journey from Elm Tree House, right up till the crash, had been a dream, a dream that was fading fast. She yawned tiredly, and she wondered if this was because of shock. All the strength seemed to have drained from her arms and legs, and she seemed to want nothing more than close her eyes and sleep. Her eyelids had become so heavy, in fact, that it was an effort to keep them open. She sank into a comforting darkness that wrapped itself about her and drew her down into its depths.

Only when she knew it was already too late to keep awake did she wonder why she felt as tired as she did. Then she slept - a deep, dreamless, endless sleep that seemed to last an eternity.

CHAPTER 14

The first thing Winnie became aware of when she awoke was an irresistible feeling of weakness, as if all the muscles in her arms and legs had wasted away and there was nothing there. A light, almost painfully bright, hit her eyes when she opened them, and it was a while before her overtaxed pupils were able to make anything out. By the time she had moved her head on the pillow beneath her so she could look about herself, she was able to see the window at the far end of the white-walled room. A plain, cream-coloured blind covered the top half of it, cutting out most of the glare from the sun, though what came through was enough to dazzle her. There was a strong smell of disinfectant that reminded her of a hospital. Confirming this, she noticed a number of charts on the wall by the closed door and a row of dark brown medicine bottles on a shelf beside it.

Feebly, she tried to force herself up on her elbows to see more of the room, but the effort was too much for her yet and she collapsed after a moment with a groan.

Unable to move again, she tried to call for attention, but even that was too much effort for her. Her throat felt dry as if she hadn't drunk for days. And when she managed to inch one of her hands to her head, she felt a bandage fastened tight about her temples.

When her fingers touched the bandage, she remembered the accident - the figure that stepped out from the hedgerow - the terrifying squeal of the tyres as they skidded on the road - and the sickening lurch of the car as it tipped on its side, and the door beside Morgan crunched and screamed against the surface of the road. She remembered climbing out with her husband's help, and the arrival of Paxley in his van. And she remembered, too, the fact that neither she nor Morgan had been hurt in the crash, apart from a few mild knocks and bruises.

Her fingers felt the bandage as she tried to remember more, as she became conscious how much her head ached beneath it. Had she hurt herself more than she seemed to recall? She stared at the unmistakable features of the hospital room she was in.

The sound of feet warned her that someone was approaching the door an instant before it opened. A nurse in a stiff blue uniform walked in, followed by a tall, balding, middle-aged man in a white coat, clearly a doctor. He smiled at her when he saw she was awake, and she noticed that one of his teeth was capped with gold. The nurse felt her pulse with a nod of her head.

"Still feeble, Doctor," the nurse said in a clear, impersonal voice as she tucked Winnie's hand beneath the blankets. She reached for the thermometer and placed it under Winnie's tongue with well-practised precision.

The doctor, his pockmarked face fixed in a smile, approached the side of the bed. Winnie wanted to ask what was wrong with her and how long she'd been here, but she had to wait for the thermometer to be removed from her mouth first. She stared at the nurse impatiently as she counted the seconds.

"Her temperature is down," the nurse said quietly when she finally read the thermometer.

The doctor nodded in reply.

"You are recovering well," he said to Winnie as he glanced at a chart hooked to the bottom of the bed. His voice was deep and had a curiously foreign accent. "That was a bad knock you had on your head. I wouldn't try to talk just yet," he said as she soundlessly opened her mouth in an effort to speak. "We had to give you a strong anaesthetic to ease the pain in your head and allow you to sleep. It will have left your throat feeling dry. That's quite normal and you need not worry about it. You will be weak for a day or two, so the best thing to do is relax. The more rest you have now, the quicker your body will recover. You are a lucky woman. It was a terrible crash you were in. It's a wonder you were not hurt far worse than you were."

Despite his words she tried to speak again. She had to find out about Morgan. If the crash was worse than she remembered, then Morgan might have been hurt as well, even though she could clearly recall that he wasn't. But that might have been a dream.

"Doctor," she managed to croak finally, "my husband... is he...?"

The doctor smiled reassuringly.

"He is in another room. I am afraid he was hurt worse than you. He fractured both arms and several of his ribs were broken. But he is doing fine, just as you are, I assure you. You will be able to see each other in a few days when you have sufficiently recovered. Till then, please rest as much as you can. The nurse will bring you something to drink in a minute." He patted her shoulder, then turned to the nurse to make a few comments in a voice too low for Winnie to hear what he said, then left.

The nurse tucked her sheets more tightly in, told her she was doing fine, then started to mix something in a plastic cup at the far end of the room. She returned to her with it and lifted Winnie's head from the pillow. Carefully, she tilted the cup to her lips and poured its contents into her mouth. It was almost oppressively sweet, like thin syrup. Thirstily, though, Winnie drank it till the cup was empty and the nurse lowered her head to the pillow again. Whether the drink contained something to put her to sleep, she was not sure, but a deep drowsiness soon came over her as she lay on the bed, and she quickly sank into a fathomless, motionless sleep even before the nurse had left the room.

Time passed, with brief spells of consciousness, when the nurse tended to her bodily needs, and long stretches of sleep. The weakness in her arms and legs did not lessen, and as one period of wakefulness succeeded another with a dreamlike uniformity, she cared even less. She even stopped worrying about Morgan, conscious only of the ever-present thirst in her throat and the lingering sleepiness that merged everything into a pale blur.

How long she was like this she did not know, since she was never really sure how long she slept, nor whether she woke up once or twice each day. She was barely even aware of the difference between night and day, since the blind at the single, square-shaped window was pulled down and closed after the first time she awoke and the room was lit only by a solitary neon light fixed to the ceiling.

Now and then she saw the doctor, but he rarely spoke to her, and when he did it was merely to reassure her she was doing fine and that everything would be all right provided she got plenty of rest.

Rest.

More rest.

More and more, and still more.

On and on.

It was as if her bed-ridden body, weakened to a degree she had never felt before, could not get enough rest, as if nothing could shake the lethargy that had taken hold of her.

Sleep.

More sleep.

On and on.

Her limbs seemed to meld with the mattress, to merge and sink into the clean white sheets, till they no longer seemed to exist anymore. Sleep. Rest. More sleep. More rest. More and more, till it seemed as if she had always been here in this tiny room, and only the faintest memories remained to her now of what it was like before she came here.

An eternity seemed to pass like this, an eternity of boredom.

Eventually, though, despite everything, there came a change.

At first she barely realized it, but her mind was less sleepy one day when she awoke, more alert and more active than any time since she came here, as if whatever it was that was making her feel tired had somehow begun to lose its grip. Her eyes still felt unbelievably heavy, and it was an effort even to keep them open for more than an instant, but she knew she would not drop back to sleep just yet.

For a while she lay still, too unused to movement over the past few days - or weeks - to do anything yet. She lay there and stared at the blind shut tight at the window. It was dappled with shadows from the trees outside as sunlight glowed across it. The smell of disinfectant hung thick in the air, though she was all but used to it now and hardly noticed it anymore.

As she lay there she thought.

At first she found it difficult to concentrate on anything for long, as if her mind was as numb as her arms and legs. When this struck her she turned what small concentration she could muster on making movements with her feet. First one toe, then a second was made to move. It was more difficult than she could have thought possible. Each joint in her toes ached painfully. But she did not relent. As the pain made her mind become more alert, she began to realize that she mustn't relent in her efforts. What it was that drove her - or why - she did not know, though a vague, intuitive fear lurked somewhere at the back of her mind - some insight she could not understand, but which would not let her relax into her apathetic drowsiness again.

Once she had managed to bring some sort of life back to her feet she began to concentrate on her fingers. And again she felt the aches and pains course through them as she forced them to move. Her face felt hot at the effort she was making. It was as if whatever it was that had relaxed her before had filled her joints with fine granules like sand, that grated against the sinews and bones inside them, rubbing them raw. She persisted - harder and harder she forced herself, ignoring the pain.

For an hour or more she worked on her arms and legs, turning from one to the other when the pain became too bad, till she was able to move about the bed sheets. Then the familiar sound of footsteps outside the door warned her an instant before it opened, and the nurse strode in. Before the woman had time to look at her, Winnie lay back as if she was still asleep. For a moment there was silence, then the nurse stepped towards her. Gently, she prised one eyelid open and studied her eye. Releasing her, she turned to the door. She was gone only a moment before she returned with the doctor.

"She appears to be wakening," the nurse said as they entered.

The doctor gave Winnie a smile. "How are you feeling today, Mrs Davies?" he said as he felt at her wrist. He leaned over and laid the palm of his hand against her forehead, then straightened up.

Winnie half opened her eyes as if drowsy and made the motions of saying that she felt all right.

"Very good," the doctor said. "I'm glad to see you are making progress. I told you, you would, provided you had plenty of rest." He looked at the nurse. "Prepare Mrs Davies a drink," he told her.

When he'd gone, the nurse went to the shelf and started to fill a plastic cup with more of the sweet, syrupy liquid she'd given her before. Too weak to resist, Winnie let her pour the potion into her mouth and swallowed it.

"You'll feel better now," the nurse said unemotionally. She patted the sheets till they were smooth and tucked them in again at the sides, then left. The door shut behind her with a quiet click.

No sooner had she gone than Winnie forced herself up into a sitting position. The syrup tasted almost sickeningly sweet in her mouth, and she was certain it was this that was making her sleep. Whether the nurse had made a mistake earlier and given her a weaker than normal dosage of whatever drugs it contained, or whether her body was gradually starting to build its own resistance to it, she did not know. What she did know was that she had had enough of lying in bed. She thrust two fingers deep into her mouth and forced them to the very back of her tongue till she felt as if she was going to choke. She gagged on them for a moment, then it started. The sweet stickiness of the liquid was nauseous enough. On top of what she was doing to herself the result was inevitable. And a moment later she was retching into her bed. Her stomach heaved once, twice, three times, and her throat felt as if it was being burnt. But whatever she had been given was almost completely purged from her system. More awake now than she had been for ages, Winnie slumped onto her pillow for a moment, exhausted, panting in lungfuls of air. Then she swung her legs over the side of the bed. Cold, cream-coloured linoleum covered the floor. She sat on it for a moment while she thought about what to do next. She was dressed only in a cotton nightdress, fastened at the back. But there was nowhere for her clothes to be in this room. Apart from the bed there were no other furnishings inside it.

For a moment she felt too depressed to do anything else, as she wondered how strange it was that clothes alone could give a person a feeling of confidence. If she had been able to slip on a pair of jeans, a top and a pair of canvas shoes, she would have felt able to cope with just about anything. Bare-footed and wearing only a frail nightdress, she felt vulnerable and weak.

Angry at herself, she clenched her fists and told herself to concentrate. First she must find out where Morgan was. He would know what to do. With this thought in mind she climbed to her feet, supporting herself on the bed as she walked towards the door. Balancing herself carefully, she reached for the handle. It turned easily in her grip and she felt the door move in towards her as she pulled. For a moment she listened before doing anything more. Hearing nothing outside, she decided to risk leaving the room. With a determined movement she held onto the door and swung herself outside. What she saw, as she stumbled forwards, made her gasp, and for a moment she felt too stunned to take it in. The corridor was long and narrow, with a varnished parquet floor. The walls were oak panels and dark, with windows at either end - windows that had tiny, diamond-shaped panes of glass.

It was, unmistakably, the redecorated upper floor of Elm Tree House.

Shuddering, bewildered, convinced until that moment she was in a hospital, the illusion was so complete she had to lean against

84

the wall for a moment. Then a feeling of anger at the deception surged through her, and she pushed herself to the next room down the corridor. She tried the door handle and pushed. Again she saw a room like the one she'd been in with plain white walls. And a bed. She forced herself in and slowly tottered towards the bed to see who was in it.

"Morgan!" Her voice came in a ragged croak as her fingers gripped hold of her husband's arm to shake him awake. "Morgan! Morgan! Wake up! For Christ's sake, wake up!"

But he was too deep asleep to be roused easily. She took hold of his hand and tried to squeeze some life into it, but it was nerveless and dead, and when she let go of it, it flopped onto the bed, motionless, as if it was nothing more than a life-like lump of clay.

Despair almost made her fold up there and then on the floor and give in. Bewilderment at what had happened to them was mixed with a feeling of betrayal. Why had they been drugged and kept here? Why had they been cynically tricked into thinking this was a hospital? She thought about Oliver, and wondered why he had done this to them. *Why?* He was their friend. He had been a close friend of theirs for more than twenty years. They had been close for so long. How could he have done something like this to them? Tears flooded her eyes as she thought about it. Then she pushed herself back from the bed and fell towards the open doorway. Outside on the corridor she forced herself towards the stairs with angry determination. Whatever reasons Oliver had for doing this to them, he was not going to get away with it!

Sunlight shone through the window at the end, where the staircase led to the gallery below. She gritted her teeth with effort as she started to make her way down the stairs, clinging onto the banister rail with the whole of her strength for support. If she could reach the ground floor she was certain she'd be able to get away. She concentrated on it. If she concentrated enough she could ignore her fears and doubts and confusion. The muscles of her face stood out like cords as she worked her way down the stairs, thankful that the house was silent, as if no one else was here, and there was a chance she would be able to drag herself out without being seen.

She knew this was her only chance.

Hers, and Morgan's too.

CHAPTER 15

Three times Nevil Wilkes tried to concentrate on his morning paper, and each time he found himself staring at the pages with a lack of comprehension, lost in a whirl of confusion.

"You've hardly eaten your breakfast, dear," his wife said to him finally. "You've hardly eaten anything for the past week."

He looked at her and apologized.

"I'm sorry," he said. "I was day-dreaming again, that's all."

Marian Wilkes poured him a cup of coffee, strong and black as he liked it.

"This should help to wake you up," she told him, with a smile of reassurance as she tried to hide the worry she felt for his health, certain something must be wrong with him that he was hiding from her. "Perhaps you should make an appointment to see Doctor Craddock. It's ages now since you last went to him for a check-up, and you always used to say it was better to have these things done regularly, just in case."

"Perhaps I will," he said. He drank some coffee, then sighed, dissatisfied with himself. Ever since he was threatened at the door of the library by Tom Paxley he had felt old and useless, his fears about what was going on at that house confirmed and intensified by that act of violence. In the days that followed he had hoped the Davies would come to the library to see him again, but he had seen no sign of them, either at the library or anywhere else in the village. Nor had anyone else he'd asked about them. Perhaps they had had enough and gone home. The thin thread of hope they represented after the shock of Tom Paxley's threats, had faded and gone, and he had sunk into a feeling of despair.

He looked at his watch and saw it was time to set off for the library. With a lack of enthusiasm Nevil put on his jacket and felt to make sure his keys were still in his pocket, then gave his wife a kiss.

"I'll be back at lunch," he told her.

It was a greyish sort of day. What promise there had been of bright sunshine earlier in the morning had been overshadowed by heavy clouds that had blown in from the west, and he supposed there would be rain before long. He picked up an umbrella from the stand by the door and went out. For a moment he stared at the garden, squared his shoulders, then strode down the street. A short while later he was marching through the village to the library, his head too full of thoughts for the usual small talk he normally enjoyed on the way.

At the library he felt the first spots of rain. Hurrying the final yards, he reached with one hand for his keys. As he inserted them in the door, he heard someone call his name. Startled, he spun round, his heart thumping in his chest as if he expected to be attacked again.

At the end of the building, where a row of privets blended with a wall, he saw a woman, dressed loosely in something white. For a moment he stared at her in shocked silence, unable to recognize her at first. Winnie Davies's face was so drawn and she looked so ill he wondered for an instant if he couldn't have made a mistake.

"Mrs Davies?"

She sobbed, broke free of the bushes and collapsed against him, shuddering weakly.

He pushed the library door open.

"Come in," he told her. He held her shoulders, so thin beneath the weak material of the night-dress that barely covered her, and kicked the door shut behind them. "I'll take you to the storeroom," he said, as he led her across the lobby to a closed door. Inside the storeroom he sat her on a wooden stand chair. He put his jacket round her shoulders. She looked frozen. Mud and leaves were plastered to her legs, and her arms were scratched, as if she'd had to claw her way through a forest. "Whatever's happened to you?" he said as she sat, shivering.

She looked up at him, and he saw her eyes were red. Dark shadows ringed their sockets, while her cheeks looked sunken, as if she'd hardly eaten for weeks.

"What on earth has been done to you?" he asked, a feeling of outrage boiling inside him.

She shook her head.

"I'm all right now," she said, her voice no more than a croak.

"Wait till I've got you some water," he told her, and he hurried to get a cupful from the rest-room. When she'd drunk half of it she lowered it from her lips and held it in her hands on her lap.

"Thank you," she said, and she smiled at him. "You saved my life."

"What's happened to you?" he asked again. "Where have you been?"

As she told him, he nodded. "Morgan and I have been at the house ever we saw you. I don't know how long ago that was."

"Ten days," he said.

She nodded again. She sipped more water, then handed the cup back to him.

"Ten days..." She seemed to draw upon almost exhausted reserves of strength before speaking again. "We left Elm Tree House the day after we saw you. But something happened - I'm not sure now exactly what - but we crashed our car only minutes after setting out."

"Crashed?" Nevil raised his eyebrows in surprise. "I've heard about no crash."

"I'm not surprised. Tom Paxley came by in his van only moments later - by coincidence, we thought at the time - and offered a lift back to the house. He said he'd arrange for our car to be towed to a garage in the village."

"He must have had it towed somewhere, but wherever that was no one reported a crash. In a place this size I'd have known it if they had."

Winnie stared at her hands for a moment, and Nevil noticed her fingers were clenched with tension. Then she said: "Oliver Atcheson offered us a drink to help get over the shock of what happened. I'd hardly finished mine when I began to feel tired. So tired... When I came to, I found myself in what I thought was a hospital. A nurse entered, followed by a doctor. They said the crash was worse than I remembered, that Morgan and I had been injured in it, even though I could clearly remember neither of us had been hurt worse than a few bumps and bruises. I thought I must have imagined that. I never thought for an instant I was being fooled. The nurse gave me a drink - I don't know what it was, except it was disgustingly sweet - but I could hardly keep awake for more than a few moments afterwards. And that's how I've spent the time ever since. Drugged, I suppose."

"And half starved by the look of it," Nevil said, his voice hard with anger. "You must have lost a couple of stones at least."

Nodding her head, Winnie went on to finish her tale, telling how she managed to escape and her frantic journey from there to the village in the early hours of the morning. She had been bewildered and scared, unable to think what she could do until she thought of him, then she hid by the library till she saw him turn up a few minutes ago.

"I suppose we should get in touch with the police," she said.

Nevil agreed with her.

"I'll phone from here, though Colin Merriman, our local constable, isn't terribly imaginative. Not a top priority qualification for a place like Endon, though." He shrugged. "Wait here for me and I'll ring him now. He shouldn't take long to get here."

His doubts about Merriman's lack of imagination were amply confirmed on his arrival ten minutes later, his uniform still streaming from the downpour outside. He shook off his helmet and placed it on the desk in the entranceway, before following Nevil to the storeroom. Nevil's assistant, Janet Sadler, had arrived by now, and he asked her to look after things when the library opened while he took care of Mrs Davies.

"Now then," P.C. Merriman opened, consulting his notebook with concentration, his jowelled face scowling with thought, "you say you and your husband have been kept at your friend's house under false pretences for the past ten days, that you thought you were in a hospital. You say they drugged you so you slept most of the time. Is that correct?"

Winnie nodded, her throat too sore to speak anymore than necessary.

P.C. Merriman scratched the back of his head, his hair cut so short it stood up on the back of his neck like bristles. He regarded Winnie for a moment, making no attempt at disguising the doubts he felt about what she had told him. He looked round at Nevil Wilkes.

"And what do you have to say about this, Mr Wilkes?" he asked.

"I think we ought to go to that place and find out what's going on."

The policeman raised his eyebrows quizzically.

"You think there's something going on there?" He stirred uncomfortably, as if he would sooner forget all about it.

"I have no doubts about what Mrs Davies has told us," Nevil said as forcefully as he could. "Her husband will be there. We must get him away and find out why they were being held, and why they have been deceived into thinking they were in a hospital for the past ten days. Don't you?"

P.C. Merriman moved his shoulders inconclusively, then raised himself from his chair.

"Very well," he said at last. "We'll take a look. Perhaps Mrs Davies would accompany us to show exactly where it was she alleges she was kept."

"Will we need a search warrant or something like that?" Nevil asked.

"I doubt it. We're only making enquiries. If they've nothing to hide they won't refuse permission to look round. If they have, then I'll get onto the station at Fenley for help. We'll see about getting a search warrant then. But we'll take things nice and slow to start with. No point in jumping the gun, is there?"

They climbed into the police car parked outside and Merriman drove them straight to Elm Tree House. Oliver Atcheson greeted them when they arrived.

When Merriman asked about the Davies being detained here, Oliver laughed.

"Surely you must be joking?" he said, incredulous. "Winnie, you aren't serious, are you?"

P.C. Merriman stiffened.

"I hope no one is joking," he said heavily; he cast Winnie and the librarian a serious look.

Winnie stared back at the policeman defiantly.

"Ask him to show us the rooms on the top floor," she said. "Then we'll see who's joking."

"Certainly," Oliver said. He led them to the stairs. "I've nothing to hide, as you'll find."

A feeling of apprehension stole over Nevil as they followed Oliver up the staircase to the gallery, then along to the stairs that led to the upper floor. Oliver was too confident to be trying to brazen it out. Nevil placed one hand on Winnie's shoulders as they reached the top floor, as if to reassure her, no matter what they found - or failed to find - he still believed her. To Winnie the corridor was exactly as she saw it hours ago.

"Now," Merriman said, "which room is it you said your husband's in?"

Winnie pointed at a closed door several yards down the passageway.

Oliver strode on ahead of them and pushed it open. He smiled as they stepped in.

There was a bed inside, but by no stretch of the imagination could it be mistaken for a hospital. A blue headboard covered in velvet stood at one end, while matching sheets covered it. By the window, beneath lace curtains, was a rosewood dressing table covered in jars of make-up. Lambskin rugs covered the polished floorboards, while the rest of the furnishings consisted of a small table with a record player resting on it and a stack of L.P.s, a rocking chair and a wardrobe. Colourful posters had been stuck to the walls to give the room a cheerful appearance, as unlike the one that Winnie remembered as she could imagine.

"You're sure - quite sure - this is the room?" the policeman asked.

Winnie nodded her head as Nevil pressed his hand reassuringly against her shoulder.

"I'll show you the other rooms on this floor," Oliver said co-operatively.

He led them along the corridor. The next room, which Winnie knew was the one she had been kept in herself, was as unlike the one she remembered as the previous one had been. A man's room now, the sturdy writing desk at the window and piles of clothes scattered about the floor by the unmade bed had an unmistakable lived-in look.

"They must have done this after they found I'd escaped," Winnie said when the policeman looked at her, his small eyes tight with annoyance.

"I'm quite sure they did, ma'am," he said, heavily.

Oliver smiled.

"Feel free to look anywhere you like," he said. "I've nothing - and no one - to hide," he added. "I'm afraid Mrs Davies has been under a lot of strain recently. Her husband, who's been a friend for years now, walked out on her recently. The usual thing, I'm afraid. A middle-aged man with a middle-aged wife getting involved with a younger woman. You know what I mean? I'm sorry to have to say that Winnie - Mrs Davies - couldn't face up to it. She still won't, as you can see." He shrugged helplessly. "I wish there was something I could do, but..."

"I quite understand," P.C. Merriman said.

Winnie shook her head vigorously. "He's lying, constable. It's not like that at all. Morgan hasn't left me. He's here."

The policeman looked at Oliver. "Perhaps we'll just take a quick look at the rest of the house on this floor. Just to satisfy Mrs Davies."

"Certainly - certainly. Indeed, I'd insist on it. I'll do anything to help her see things as they are. Though she needs help, proper, professional help."

They made their way along the corridor. Each room they looked in was furnished in similar styles. Nowhere was there any trace of the type of beds that Winnie had described, nor of her husband. When they had finished, Oliver insisted on showing them through the rest of the house. The policeman, convinced there was nothing in what Winnie had claimed about the place, grew impatient to finish. As if perversely enjoying himself, Oliver insisted on showing them more.

"I can't allow you to have any doubts," he said to them. "It would not be fair on me - nor on Mrs Davies."

It was nearly an hour before they had finished going through the rooms on the other floors. They ended at the generator room.

"Where does this lead to?" Merriman asked, indicating the door into the cellar.

"We can look down there if you like," Oliver said, "though it will take some time." He picked up a torch from a shelf inside the door and led Merriman down the worn steps into the gloom below. The policeman gazed at the vast reaches of the cellar. Oliver shone the torch between the grimy, web-draped pillars.

"I still don't know how extensive this place is," Oliver said, "though, as you can imagine, I've never felt any great need to explore it." He shivered theatrically at the cold inside it.

"I think I've seen enough," Merriman said. By the time they had returned to the hallway the policeman turned to Mrs Davies and said: "We've searched this place thoroughly, thanks to the co-operation of Mr Atcheson, and found no trace of your husband or anything to prove that you or Mr Davies has ever been held here against your will. I'm sorry, I don't think there's anymore I can do for you. I suggest you see your doctor as soon as possible. Perhaps you've been suffering from stress."

"Constable, what Mrs Davies told you is true," Nevil insisted.

"You saw Mrs Davies imprisoned here before she escaped? You saw the rooms that Mrs Davies described to us?"

Nevil shook his head impatiently. "I know her well enough to know she's telling the truth."

"Mr Wilkes, by your own admission, you only met Mrs Davies once before today." Constable Merriman closed his notebook and put it back in his tunic pocket. "Unless you come up with something more than what you've shown me so far, there's no more I can do." He turned to Oliver and said: "Thank you for your co-operation, sir. I'm sorry we had to disturb you like this."

"Think nothing of it, constable," Oliver told him. "I understand. I just hope Winnie takes your advice and sees her doctor."

CHAPTER 16

They took Winnie away from Elm Tree House in the back of the police car, Nevil beside her. At the last second before they climbed in her self-control deserted her and she tried to attack Oliver. She would not - *could not* - accept that Morgan was not in the house.

"They're hiding him somewhere," she screamed at the policeman. "Why can't you believe me?"

P.C. Merriman did his best to soothe her, while Oliver hovered in the background, assuring him he understood her feelings.

"She's been under a great deal of strain recently. It isn't her fault."

The policeman thanked him as they restrained her.

"Calm down, Mrs Davies," he told her. "You're doing yourself no good acting like this. No good at all."

Nevil Wilkes took hold of her shoulders.

"I'll take her to my wife," he said. "She can stay with us till she's better." He stared at Oliver Atcheson defiantly. "Her health's been undermined. She needs feeding. *And* some rest."

"So long as you're sure you can cope," Merriman said doubtfully.

"I'm sure." Nevil squeezed Winnie's shoulders reassuringly. Sobs shuddered through her body. "I'm absolutely sure." He looked again at Oliver. "She'll be safe with us."

Merriman drove them straight to Nevil's house. When he drew up outside Merriman turned to the librarian and said: "If you have any problems," (He nodded at the ashen-faced woman) "don't hesitate to contact me."

"I won't," Nevil said. He took hold of Winnie's hand and led her to his house. Marian Wilkes appeared at the door. "Marian," Nevil said to her, "we've a guest who'll be staying for a few days with us. Winnie Davies. She's been through a trying experience and needs our help." Together they helped her indoors.

"Remember," Merriman called from his car. "Any problems at all, call me." Nevil waved back as the policeman drove off, then he shut the door behind him and looked at his wife with a sudden feeling of warmth.

*

Nevil rang the library and told Janet he would not be in again today.

"I might be off for the next few days, in fact," he said. "I'll let you know."

Then he went into the kitchen, where Marian was preparing some hot soup. She had loaned Winnie a dressing gown, and she'd taken a seat at the table. Quiet sobs racked her shoulders, though her tears had stopped now.

Marian looked across at him as he entered. While she ladled soup into a bowl, then cut some slices of bread, he related what had happened.

"I know it may be hard to accept," he told her, "but you have two people who know it's true."

After he had finished, Marian said: "Why didn't you tell me about the threats that horrible man made against you? And why didn't you report what happened to the police when it happened?"

"I didn't want to worry you. And two, I had no witnesses and it would have been my word against Paxley's. It would have been a waste of time and might have been dangerous too."

"And isn't what we're doing dangerous, if this is true?"

He admitted it was. "But there didn't seem any choice. Perhaps, there isn't any choice," he said as Winnie glanced up from her soup, a look of gratitude on her face.

"If it wasn't for you," she said, "I don't know what I would have done. I can't cope with this by myself. Not yet."

Nevil turned to face the two women and said the first thing to be done was to get themselves organized.

"I've said there is danger," he went on, with an encouraging smile to his wife, "and there is. Let's not fool ourselves." He paused for a moment to let them digest this before going on. "Marian, our guest will need new clothes. She's taller than you, so I doubt any of yours will do. Perhaps you could ask for her sizes, then pop into the village and get her what she'll need for the next few days? I'd suggest something robust, and perhaps some jeans. You can sort that out between you. And while you're there we'll need some money from the bank. We can't stay here, not with Atcheson knowing where Winnie is - and knowing what we'll have been told by her. We have to get away for a while to sort ourselves out and decide what we should do. We

95

can't stay here and wait for them to act first. Go to our bank and draw out a thousand pounds."

"That's nearly all our savings," Marian reminded him.

"Don't worry about that," Winnie interrupted. "Once we're away from here I can get some cash from my bank and pay you back."

"We'll sort that out later," Nevil said. "Let's deal with first things first. While you're in the village I'll pack the car with what we'll need, so as soon as you're back Winnie can get dressed and we can leave."

"Where to?" Marian asked, bewildered by what her husband was telling her, but too convinced to argue against him. She knew him too well to distrust his judgement.

"We'll decide where we're going when we set off. That's not important. What is important is that we should get away from here as quickly as we can and go somewhere neither Atcheson nor any of his friends at Elm Tree House will know. Do you understand?"

Marian nodded. "All right, Nevil. You know best, obviously. I'll get my handbag and be off." She delayed only to ask Winnie for her sizes and the type of clothes she'd need, then left. The rain had returned and the road looked grey as she set out, her head bowed beneath her umbrella as water bounced from the paving stones about her feet.

"Thank you," Winnie said when she and Nevil were alone. "I hope I haven't dragged you and your wife into something I shouldn't have done."

"I was involved already, like it or not," Nevil said as he took a seat at the table and sipped some tea. "That's why Paxley made his threats against me. They know I know too much already. Perhaps it was only a matter of time before things between us came to a head."

"What do you suspect?" Winnie asked.

He shook his head. "I'll tell you when Marian is with us and we're on our way out of here." He stood up. "In the meantime I'll start packing a few things. If I were you I'd take the opportunity to nip upstairs and have a bath before Marian gets back with your clothes. It will help you feel more like your normal self."

By the time Marian returned with her purchases and the money she'd withdrawn from the bank, Winnie had finished her bath and her face looked well-scrubbed and healthier than before, though there was no mistaking the pinched look of enforced starvation or the dark rings about her eyes. It would take days of rest and nourishing meals to right the effects of what had been done to her.

Nevil clumped downstairs as Marian handed Winnie her clothes, suitcases in his hands. He dumped them in the hallway while Winnie dashed upstairs with his wife to dress. By the time they had finished he'd stashed the suitcases in the back of the car and was ready to set off.

"Just one thing more," he said when they joined him. He went into the study, where he unlocked a heavy mahogany cabinet near the window. Inside, broken into two sections, was a double-barrelled shot gun. Its butt was of polished walnut, and there was elaborate silver chasing on its barrel. Next to it were several packets of cartridges.

"This used to belong to my grandfather," he said as he stuffed it into a duffel bag. "I haven't used it in years."

"He did a lot of shooting once," Marian explained, "mainly crows."

"I hope I won't need it, but I'd be a fool to leave it behind," he said.

Winnie shook her head sadly. "If they're prepared to do what they did to me - and what they're doing to Morgan - we'll need it," she said. "I know we will."

Nevil patted her arm. "We'll see."

They dived out of the house into the rain and climbed into Nevil's car, a small hatchback Datsun Cherry he'd parked at the gate while the two women were getting ready. Winnie climbed into the back while Marian took the front passenger seat next to Nevil.

"Take care," Winnie warned as they set off. "Remember what happened to Morgan and me."

"Till we're away from here I'll keep my speed to a minimum," he said. He smiled grimly, alert as he had never been before in his life as he turned onto the main road to head out of Endon in the opposite direction to Elm Tree House. Rain slashed across the windscreen like angry whips, and he slowed even more. No one and nothing were going to stop them from getting away from this place. His knuckles were white as he gripped the steering wheel and carefully guided the car down the road through the drenched fields that rose on either side to the grey, dismal, cloud-covered sky.

Not till they had left the countryside well behind and were parked up for lunch a couple of hours later in the fourth town they'd passed, did Nevil ask Marian to fish out their *A.A. Guide to Hotels* from beneath the dashboard.

"Look up some hotels in Birmingham. That's another forty miles from here. We should be safe enough there."

When she'd picked out a couple, Nevil climbed out of the car and went across to a line of telephone boxes in the shopping precinct nearby. He returned minutes later with a grin of satisfaction.

"All done," he said when he'd climbed in out of the rain. "I've booked two interconnecting rooms for us in the Georgian Hotel for tonight. We'll decide later if we're going to stay any longer once we've had a chance to discuss things. Okay?"

*

The Georgian Hotel was a modern, plate-glass, reinforced concrete tower twelve storeys high, built by a complicated roundabout not far from the exit off the motorway. They drove into the hotel car park, which was under the hotel down a concrete ramp, then made their way to the Reception Desk. A few minutes later they were guided up a stainless-steel lift to the sixth floor where their rooms were situated.

"The restaurant opens for dinner in another hour," the porter said with a stiff face as he pocketed his tip and left.

Nevil and his wife had been given a large room with a window in one wall that looked out through a set of adjustable blinds across a panoramic view of the motorway less than a couple of hundred yards away. Grey, rain-swept hills rose in the distance beyond the ribbon of tarmac road to a sky that was unseasonably dark.

By the time they had unpacked it was time for dinner. They knocked on Winnie's door, then went down to the restaurant where they ordered themselves something to eat.

"Let's pick up our spirits with something," Nevil said as he tucked into a plateful of beef cooked in red wine. "I don't know

98

of anything guaranteed more to do that than something good to eat. Fill a man's stomach and you double his courage."

When they had finished, Nevil suggested they should go into the bar for a few drinks while they talked. He ordered a martini for his wife, a gin and tonic for Winnie and a bottle of lager for himself.

"After this we'll stick to tea or coffee," he said when he returned to the table they had settled around in a quiet corner of the bar. Potted ferns and hanging baskets of plastic flowers seemed designed to induce an atmosphere of sedate tranquillity in the room. "We want to keep clear heads," he added. "The clearer the better." He drank some of his lager reflectively, then said: "Marian's been splendid." He gave her an encouraging smile. "She's obviously bewildered," he told Winnie, "as are we all to some degree or another by what's been going on."

"I've told your wife what happened to me," Winnie said.

"It's dreadful," Marian said, shaking her head in consternation. "What that man is up to I can't even guess. He must be insane."

"If there was only Atcheson involved I might agree with you," Nevil said, "but there are others. There were four other people staying there when Winnie and her husband arrived at the house. Since then at least two more have arrived - the doctor and the nurse who were supposed to be looking after them. There may be more."

"Oliver did say more people were due to arrive in the next few weeks," Winnie said. "He never indicated how many, though."

Nevil frowned. "From what you know of the house, how many do you think it's capable of holding at the moment?"

"I don't know." Winnie shrugged. "Perhaps a dozen," she said.

"From what I saw this morning I would agree with you. A dozen would be right. Perhaps one or two more. Which would make a nice figure for a coven," he said with a wry, almost whimsical smile that caught both women with surprise. "What do you know about Tom Paxley?" he said suddenly.

Winnie shook her head. "Not a lot," she admitted. "I know he's a sculptor and some of his work has received some sort of critical acclaim. Besides that, I really don't know much about him at all."

Nevil carefully unfolded several sheets of A4 paper from the inside pocket of his jacket.

"I got hold of these a week ago from the library archives at

Fenley. A friend of mine looked them up for me, then photocopied them after Paxley's threats. I knew there had been something about him in the press a few years ago, but I couldn't remember the details. This is what my colleague managed to unearth."

He laid the photocopies on the table between them. Large block headlines on one of them read:

SCULPTOR DENIES BLACK MAGIC CHARGES

Smaller headlines below read:

PAXLEY FLEES TO SCOTTISH HIDEAWAY

Adrian Cotton, son of the writer Peter Simpson Cotton, was found dead in his flat in the early hours of Sunday morning. Initial signs indicate that Mr Cotton killed himself. Police say there are no suspicious circumstances surrounding the death of the 39-year-old, one time member of the 'Satanic Order of the Hidden Way', who was given a suspended six-month sentence earlier this year for his part in the desecration of a church. His live-in lover, poet, 25-year-old Hazel Metcalfe, was taken away by friends in distress afterwards and refused to discuss her relationship with Mr Cotton.

"How old are these articles?" Winnie asked.

"The Tom Paxley was only three years ago. The one about Hazel Metcalfe was early last year." He drank some more of his lager, then said: "I've asked my colleague in Fenley to see if he can find any more press cuttings for me. I'll ring him tomorrow to see how he's doing, though I think what I've already shown is clear enough."

"Who's this?" Winnie asked. She held up one of the other sheets they hadn't been through yet. There was a photograph of a man climbing into a car. Though not very clear, the man's face had some obvious features. Bald, with a narrow, jutting forehead, Winnie recognized him at once as the doctor who treated her in Elm Tree House. She read out the article attached to it after she told them who he was.

TOP SATANIST FLEES COUNTRY

Ramon Tarradellas, alleged to be a leading member of the notorious 'Order of the Hidden Way' fled Britain under mysterious circumstances after claims he took part in the desecration of St. Mary's church, Copley Sudderton. Police sources state he left Britain only hours before a raid was carried out on his Brixton home by a special unit set up to deal with the rising tide of Black Magic cults in the area. A quantity of items was taken away, though the police refused to discuss what had been found at this stage. Police Inspector John Melling, in charge of the operation, said: "A number of items were removed by members of the task force employed in searching Mr Tarradellas's property. A full statement about these will be issued later."

"Oliver spent the winter recuperating in Spain after his nervous breakdown," Winnie said when she'd finished reading the article to them. "He might have met Tarradellas while he was there."

"Unless he already knew people like Paxley. You said Atcheson told you he'd planned this so-called artists' colony for years."

"Unless his original idea was different to the perversion he has now," Winnie suggested defensively.

"Perhaps. However, the facts as we have them show your friend has a number of people staying with him who have known connections with Satanism. In view of what's happened to you, I think we can assume they're still involved with cults of some kind."

Winnie frowned as she realized the awfulness of what they were talking about.

"But why should they have drugged Morgan and me? What possible purpose could that serve?"

"I don't know," Nevil admitted. "I'd hate to speculate. But there must be some reason. It's the 25th of June today. The 29th is Midsummer Eve, one of the great occult festivals of the year. Maybe they wanted you at Elm Tree House on that date for a reason." He halted, unwilling to say anymore as a look of distress spread across her face. Winnie took a long sip of her gin and tonic as Marian lay a hand gently on her arm. Nevil's wife looked across at him, her face pale.

"We're in too deep to get out of it now, aren't we, Nevil?" she said.

He nodded slowly. "I'm afraid so."

101

The bar was beginning to fill with other hotel guests as Winnie thought about what Nevil had revealed to them, finishing her drink. She smiled at him.

"I don't know about sticking to tea and coffee after this. I could do with another of these." Despite her smile there was a bleak look in her eyes that revealed far more about the way she felt than the facade of resilience she had adopted since they set out earlier in the day from Nevil's house.

"Perhaps we could all do with another," he conceded. He went to the bar and made the same order as before. When he returned with their drinks, Winnie said: "How much do you know about this kind of thing?"

"Satanism? Black Magic? Devil worship?" He grimaced. "Not a lot, I'm afraid. I'm a librarian in an out of the way village, that's all. Most of the stuff I deal with is popular fiction. The nearest I've come to that kind of thing is the occasional Dennis Wheatley, and I haven't seen one of them for years, I might add."

"But we'll need to know more to cope with this. Can the police help? Is there no way we can get them to do something about it?"

"By now I should think Elm Tree House will be even more innocent than when we went with P.C. Merriman this morning. The only thing we could tell the police is that some of the people staying there have known connections with Black Magic in the past. As far as I'm aware, apart from Tarradellas, no charges have ever been levelled against any of them, only sensationalized allegations in the press. I'm sure Tarradellas would be nowhere in sight if the police did swoop on the place. He'd either be well disguised or hidden away elsewhere. We'd come no nearer to finding Winnie's husband than now. All we'd achieve would be to discredit any future allegations we might make to the police about what is going on and make it even more difficult to get co-operation out of them. For the time being I think we'll have to look on it as our task and our task alone. Premature use of the police would only be counter productive. It may even be disastrous," he added sombrely.

"Is there no one we can turn to?" Winnie asked, exasperated by the sheer enormity of the task facing them. "There are only the three of us. What can we do by ourselves?"

"Couldn't we turn to the Church? Surely they'd be interested in the activities of a Black Magic cult?" Marian suggested hopefully.

"Maybe, but you know as well as I do that Satanism is not one of its overriding worries these days."

"Isn't it? I don't know about that. You keep your nose buried too much in your books," Marian admonished. "There's more concern about it than you think. The Church doesn't treat it lightly. If you bothered going to church more than once every blue moon you might have heard our curate warning people about the dangers of dabbling in the occult."

"He was probably talking Ouija boards and stuff like that," Nevil said.

"Even if you're right, how much more worried do you think he would be about people who organize Black Magic Masses and desecrate churches?"

Nevil considered what she'd said, then looked at Winnie. She nodded her head. "We have nothing to lose," Winnie said. "We do need all the help we can get."

"Okay," Nevil said. "I'll phone the curate and see if he can help. Even if he can't do anything himself, maybe he'll be able to put us on to someone who can. I'll get his number from Directory Enquiries now."

The two women felt a surge of morale as he stood up to go to the telephone outside the bar, as if this small act was something positive at last.

When Nevil had his number, he rang the curate straight away. Quigley's seventeen-year-old son, Raymond, answered the phone.

"Is your father in?" Nevil asked. "It's Nevil Wilkes."

"Dad's out visitin'. Don't know when he'll be back. He never said."

Nevil could easily visualize the sullen expression on Raymond's sulky face.

"Can you give him a message?"

"I s'ppose so. What is it?"

"Tell him I rang - tell him it's very important that I speak with him and I'll ring back tonight at nine. If he's not back then I'll ring later. Okay?"

"Okay." The phone was put down at the other end even before Nevil could take the receiver from his ear, and there was a painful burr of clicks that made him swear. He put down the receiver and returned to the bar. "He's not in," he told them as he sat down. "I've left a message with his son that I'll ring back later."

When he tried, though, at nine he found the Reverend Quigley was still out visiting. His son's voice was almost insolently sullen as if he'd been dragged away from something important - probably *Sonic the Hedgehog*, Nevil thought. He told the boy he'd ring back at ten. That time, though, the telephone was engaged. It was still engaged half an hour later, and at eleven when he tried again he knew that Raymond must have left the phone off the hook so he wouldn't be disturbed from whatever it was he was doing.

Angry now, Nevil told the others they would have to leave it till morning.

"There's nothing else we can do tonight, except try and get some rest. Tomorrow could be a very busy day."

CHAPTER 17

When they went to their rooms for the night, Winnie found herself too keyed up to sleep. She'd slept so much over the past week under the influence of the drugs they'd been using on her she supposed her body had acquired a need for them now in order to rest. Without them she felt nervous and tense, with an almost irresistible urge to bite her nails. Even the gin and tonic she'd drunk in the hotel bar had done nothing to relax her. They'd certainly done nothing to deaden the feelings of concern she felt for what might have happened to Morgan - or what might be happening to him now. Where had they taken him? What were they doing to him? And why? Why?

She took a shower to clear her head, then climbed into bed. It was large and soft, and the sheets felt unbelievably fresh to her aching body. For a while she watched the television at the foot of the bed, but the programme irritated her in her present mood, and she switched it off. Without it there was only the gentle hum of the air conditioning to disturb her as she lay back in the warm twilight. Its curtains only partly closed, the window glowed from the ambient light of the sodium lamps along the road six floors below.

Despite the ache of anxiety in the pit of her stomach for her husband's safety, exhaustion eventually eased her into the semblance of sleep. How long she lay like that she did not know. Some time later, though, despite her exhaustion, she started to stir. Something had moved inside the room and her sleep was broken. Her mind slipped almost instantly into an acute wakefulness as she lay, alert, her body rigid with fear.

There was an awful, smothering smell of decay, as if something rotten had been dumped in her room while she slept. It was so overpoweringly nauseous it was impossible to ignore however much she wished she could. Opening her eyes, she noticed a subtle change in the light, a dull, sickly kind of glow radiating from the window. Cautiously, she raised herself onto her elbows and stared at the curtains. They seemed to be billowing towards her, though the window was shut. In fact, as she had found out earlier, it couldn't be opened on this floor, possibly for safety reasons. Then it was that she saw the hand - it was long and thin. Reaching towards her, it seemed to beckon her. Winnie's heart missed a beat as she sat bolt upright in bed, a scream caught at the back of her throat. A tall, manlike shape stood in the gloom of the window. It seemed to have been merged with the glass, half in, half out of the room. A large hood covered its head as it stared towards her. The smell became thicker, more pungent, and she gradually began to make out more of the dim blur beneath the hood, till she could see the outlines of its cheeks and nose, and the empty, depthless, pit-like sockets of its eyes. The hand that reached out for her was white, fleshless, with foot-long, tapering, dagger-like nails.

Even this was not so bad as the fungoid decay that had rendered what little she could see of its face into a leprous softness that sagged before her eyes into a filthy, leering, lipless smile.

She screamed.

Again and again, as she stared at the thing, her lungs emptied themselves, as the thing reached for her, as it struggled to force the rest of its emaciated body through the glass. At some point during her screams she became aware of someone knocking at the door. But she could not move to open it. The sheer unmitigated evil of the thing had left her paralysed with fear. All she could do was to scream - again and again - endlessly - as if this alone would fight the thing off and keep it from her.

The door burst open and Nevil Wilkes, ashen-faced and dressed only in his pyjamas, fell into the room. He looked at the shape towering before him at the window. In that instant he felt a desperate urge to be sick. Choking back the acidic bolt of bile that rose in his throat, his eyes darted about the room for a weapon of some sort. In a frantic effort to stop the thing from reaching Winnie he threw himself towards the bedside table. His fingers grasped hold of its drawers, frantically pulling them open. Winnie could hear his breath come in harsh gasps. Then he tugged back his hand. A red-bound book was clenched in it. In one movement he hurled himself back from the drawers, turned and threw the book as hard as he could at the abomination in the window.

"*In the name of Christ -!*" he began to cry out. The rest was lost in a howling shriek of agony as the stench grew even worse than before. Where the thing had been a moment before a black, sticky, tar-like mass dripped from the window. What looked like bones were mingled with the noxious fluids as if churned up inside a filthy stew of decay.

An instant later Winnie heard Marian's voice at the doorway, and the light was switched on. Nevil staggered to the bed. Where the blackness had been a moment before there was now no more than a stench of decay. A book, its spine broken and some of its pages torn loose, lay on the floor. Too shaken to realize what she was doing - or why - Winnie climbed out of bed and picked it up. She looked at Nevil when she realised what it was and showed it to him.

It was a Gideon Bible.

CHAPTER 18

Though P.C. Merriman liked a peaceful life, and had found his ideal niche with his posting in Endon, where the worst offences were double parking on the main street through the village at weekends by visiting tourists or the occasional drunk on Saturday night, something about his visit to Elm Tree House irked him. It was as if he knew he could have done more. In fact, it was worse than this. It was as if he knew he *should* have done more. And that hurt his sense of self-respect, blunted though that had become over the years, under worked by his superiors in Fenley and overfed by his wife in Endon. Just as she was doing now, he thought as she added two more baked potatoes to his already heaped plate. He rolled up his shirtsleeves and looked across at his two sons, Colin and Brian. They'd be big lads too one day - the elder, just gone eleven, was already starting to thicken out, especially at the neck. "Takes after his father," his wife said the other day. Merriman felt at his collar and loosened his uniform tie. He'd need the next size up anytime soon if he didn't start to lose some weight. His mind wandered from this back to the problem of Mrs Davies. Should he have got in touch with his superiors at Fenley? At the time, tired after too many cans of beer in front of the television last night, and with a dull headache coming on, he hadn't wanted to be bothered. And that bothered him now. That bothered him a lot.

"Can you put this in the oven to keep warm for me, love," he said to his wife - a woman as large in her ample way as him. She looked at his plate suspiciously.

"Is there something wrong with it?"

"No, love, 'course not. It's just there's something I've got to check on first." He walked into the hallway and looked up Nevil Wilkes's telephone number. He let the telephone ring for several minutes, then replaced the receiver. Still raining outside, it was too early yet for the pubs to be open – even if Nevil Wilkes was the kind of man to go out at this time for a drink anyway. And he'd not be out walking in weather like this. P.C. Merriman frowned with concentration.

On an impulse he reached for his tunic on the coat stand by the vestibule door.

"I'm just going out for a minute," he called to his wife, thrust on his helmet and thudded down the path of their threadbare garden to his car.

A few minutes later he pulled up outside the Wilkes' house. Even from where he sat the place looked deserted, and he knew, even before he wheezingly pulled himself out of the car and plodded to the door, it was empty. Nevertheless, he rang the bell a few times to make sure and peered through its windowpanes. Why he wanted to see Wilkes and the Davies woman again, he wasn't sure. He hadn't thought it through that far. But the disappointment he felt at being thwarted only added to his dissatisfaction with himself when he climbed back into his car and drove off.

Later that night trouble at the Squire's Arms called him out again after he'd finished his tea and settled in front of the fire. By the time he reached the pub things had quietened down and a few gruff words of caution were all that were needed from him. Pat, the landlord, pulled him a pint of bitter before he left.

"What's gotten into Teb tonight?" Merriman asked as he reached for his beer, drinking it down in long, slow gulps that barely showed in his throat.

"Don't know," Pat said. "Ain't seen the daft bugger like this for years. Someone just said somethin' to 'im about that 'ouse?" (he nodded knowingly in the vague direction of Elm Tree House) "and 'e started up."

P.C. Merriman tucked his helmet out of sight on a stool and placed his glass, now drained, on the bar.

"I'll have another one, Pat." He turned around and glanced at the other customers in the pub. Teb was sat in his usual spot by the window, his head hung low over the untouched pint of beer in front of him. He looked pathetic, his broad shoulders sunk into bony arches behind his head.

"He still gets upset about that place, does he?"

"Upset?" Pat laughed lopsidedly as he finished pulling Merriman's pint. "Daren't even so much as mention that bloomin' place once 'e's 'ad three or four beers inside 'im."

"What's someone been sayin' about it tonight to upset him?"

The landlord handed him his pint and leered.

"Well, I would 'a' thought you'd know better 'n most, seein' as 'ow you've been up there today."

"I see the village grapevine's as active as ever." Though he was not surprised. Little went on in the village that didn't become common knowledge before long. "So?" he prompted.

"So, we were talkin' like, as you do, 'bout what was goin' on o'er there these days since that newcomer bought the place. What with all those others there as well. An' that woman you 'ad with you this mornin'." He laughed at the back of his throat, then coughed gutturally. "Not of'en as we get 'alf-naked women wand'rin' round 'bout the place, now, do we? More's the pity, like. Teb, though, 'e can't see no 'umour in it, can 'e? Not 'im, the po-faced bugger. Starts tremblin', don't 'e, as if the Devil 'imself were creepin' up on 'im. An' Bob, who's got a bit of a sense o' 'umour, as you know, starts eggin' 'im on, like. Well, that were it. What with that an' everythin' else, 'e blew up, didn't 'e?"

P.C. Merriman slowly drank his beer, contemplating the talkative landlord with distaste.

"Proper little bundle o' fun you lot can be at times, can't you? Like nothing but a nest o' vipers."

Pat's Adam's apple bobbed up and down as if it was stuck on top of an explosive hiccup that couldn't work its way out.

"The old bugger over there's been a sick man for years. An' one of your best customers too, by all accounts. Don't you think it's about time you and the rest o' the wits in here left him alone?"

The policeman snorted his disgust, picked up his drink and took it with him as he wove his way through the pub to the back and seated himself opposite Teb.

"Mind if I join you for a few minutes?" he asked.

Teb looked up from his beer and shrugged. His eyes had a haunted look to them, as if they'd been searching through dark labyrinths of memories into the distant past. If they had, Merriman knew what night he had been looking at.

"You been thinking about it again?" Merriman asked. Though Nevil Wilkes was right in his estimation of Merriman's imagination, the policeman was not without some perception. "Was it bad?" he asked, probing gently.

Though at any other time or asked the same question by someone else, this might have sent Teb into a fit, the old poacher merely nodded his head.

"Bad," Teb repeated quietly, part of the stretched side of his face twitching slightly, as if a vein was pulsing inside it. "It were bad. It were worse 'an bad."

"Yet there are people living there now, aren't there?" Merriman said, watching him carefully.

Teb nodded his head.

"I've seen some of 'em in the village," he acknowledged.

"What do you make of them?"

"Make of 'em?" Teb seemed to struggle with the thought. "Make of 'em?" His voice became doubtful and strange. "I don't make anythin' of 'em. I don't want to make anythin' of 'em. I don't want to 'ave anythin' to do with 'em. Any of 'em at all." He looked Merriman in the eyes, and the policeman felt uncharacteristically disturbed. "They're evil," Teb said. "Like *it* was evil. They're evil. The lot of 'em. Sick with it, they are. Sick." He nodded his chin at his beer.

Merriman drank his own beer quietly for a moment as he wondered how much of that Davies woman's story might have been true. At the time his distrust of over-emotional, distraught women had prejudiced him against her. Yet, the all-too-suave, cool collectedness of Oliver Atcheson disturbed him too. Something about him didn't ring true. He'd been like an actor playing a part. And too co-operative. He knew he should have seen that at the time. That was suspicious, if nothing else, he thought. Yet the rooms they looked in had been nothing like the ones that Davies woman had hysterically insisted were there. Though Nevil Wilkes had been convinced by her story - *and* had met her before, her and her husband. And, perhaps, after all, it would have been perfectly natural she should have been as distraught as she was - and as hysterical as she eventually became - if she'd been through what she claimed had happened to her.

Merriman finished his beer and bid Teb good night.

When he left the pub, the policeman climbed into his car and drove towards Elm Tree House. Dark clouds had brought dusk earlier than normal tonight, and the woods were almost black when he pulled up at the gates. He opened one of them wide enough for his car to get through, then carried on to the house. A number of cars were already parked in front of it, and lights showed through the heavy curtains at some of the ground floor windows.

Slamming the car door shut behind him, P.C. Merriman strode towards the house and gave the knocker on its heavy door a

111

hefty bang. He gazed about the drive as he waited for the door to be answered and, unimaginative or not, began to understand something about what Teb might have felt all those years ago when the place was still deserted.

A moment later the door opened, and Merriman recognized the bulky figure of Tom Paxley standing there.

"Mr Atcheson's busy at the moment," Paxley said when Merriman asked if he was in. The sculptor led him into the hallway. "Did you want to speak to him about something in particular?"

Merriman shook his head as he sniffed the air suspiciously.

"I was just passing by," he said. "I don't want to disturb him unnecessarily." He looked around the well-lit hallway. "What's that odd smell?" he asked finally.

"Smell?" Tom smiled. "Some incense someone must have lit in the lounge. It *is* a bit strong, isn't it?"

For the first time in his career, Merriman wished he knew more than he did about drugs. He'd smelled incense before - old Mrs Leyland, whose husband worked for an export firm out East till he retired years ago, was always burning the stuff in little brass holders. He'd visited her house often enough since her husband's death when she was worried, as she always was, about burglars, and this was nothing like the stuff she burned. It was sweeter, sicklier, with an undercurrent of something that was not at all pleasant, like meat gone rancid.

"How is Mrs Davies?" Tom asked, his eyes narrowed.

"I've no idea, Mr Paxley. I haven't seen her since this morning."

"I hope she's all right. She was in such a frightful mess."

Merriman hesitated, uncertain. Apart from Tom Paxley none of the others staying here had appeared, though subdued voices could be heard somewhere.

Merriman looked again at the sculptor, who was patiently waiting for him to make the next move. Beginning to feel uncomfortable in his uncertainty as to what he should do, Merriman hesitated a moment, then said: "I'll be on my way." Merriman hesitated again, frowned at himself with annoyance, then continued on his way to the door, whatever it was he was going to say forgotten.

"Good night," Tom called as the policeman climbed into his car. Merriman looked back, disgruntled at himself, and said: "Good night." As he drove off, he stared at the trees, certain there was something about this place he didn't like. And although he knew it would probably be a waste of time, he decided he'd start to keep a keener eye on it. There was something suspicious about it - something too suspicious to ignore.

As he turned his car onto the road, his heavy face was troubled, though he could not grasp quite why.

CHAPTER 19

After everyone had managed to calm down again, it was decided Winnie would share the same room as the Wilkes, while Nevil slept on a couch. There were a few bad moments with the night porter, a swarthy man with bad breath, upset at complaints from other guests at the hotel about the noise. Nevil did his best to pacify things with a hasty and somehow unconvincing explanation about Winnie having been recently ill. A clumsy attempt to appease the porter with a ten-pound note only resulted in the man storming off, ominously muttering something about having to report it to the hotel manager in the morning.

"It doesn't matter," Nevil said to the two women after the porter had gone. "We'll not stay here another night anyway. It's obvious Atcheson and his friends know where we are."

"And have the means to get at us." Winnie shuddered as she remembered the thing at the window.

"Thank God there was a Bible in those drawers," Nevil said.

"Did you know there'd be one?" Marian asked, as she sat on the bed.

He shook his head. "I was too terrified to think coherently enough for that. I just wanted something, *anything* I could lay my hands on to hurl at it. It was blind luck I chanced on a Bible."

"Luck?" Winnie paused for a moment. "Was it blind luck you shouted what you did?"

Nevil wondered about that too. "Finding the Bible, yes, that was luck - pure luck. Those words... I don't know. As soon as I touched the book the rest all seemed to happen automatically, as if something was guiding me."

"We need help," Marian said. "We're out of our depth in all this. We got through what happened tonight by the skin of our teeth. We can't go on like that. If *they* have the power to do what they did, they'll try something again. Something worse. Something we might not be able to stop next time."

It was a sleepless night for all of them, and it wasn't long after dawn before they dressed and went down to the hotel restaurant shortly after it opened for an early breakfast. Pre-empting a pointless interview with the manager, they checked out afterwards and went to Nevil's car. The day was brighter than yesterday, with a sky only slightly scudded with clouds, and the early morning air felt cool and fresh and clean.

"Where are we going next?" Winnie asked as they sat for a moment in the car. "If they found me so easily last night, surely they'll be able to find me anywhere no matter where we go?"

Nevil thought about this, then said: "I think it's time we contacted this curate of yours, Marian. If ever we needed spiritual help, it's now." He put the car into gear and drove up the concrete ramp to the road, then headed on into the heart of the city. He parked a short while later at the Bull Ring and they walked down New Street, the early morning crowds of office workers and sales assistants giving them a feeling of safety after the perils of the night. Spotting a vacant telephone box, Nevil signalled for the two women to follow him while he fished out the curate's telephone number from his pocket.

"He should have noticed the phone's off the hook by now," Nevil muttered as he prodded at the buttons. After a moment's silence, there was an answering *trill* at the other end of the line. A woman answered it. "Mrs Quigley?" Nevil asked. "Hullo, it's Nevil Wilkes - I'm fine, thanks, fine - I wanted to contact your husband - Is Francis in?" He cupped the speaker in his hand and turned to the women, crammed in the box beside him. "She's gone to get him," he explained.

"Nevil?" The voice was well modulated, distinctively urbane. "Is that you?"

"Thank God I've got through to you at last," Nevil said. "I tried to get hold of you last night but you were out."

"That's right, I was," Quigley said without explanation. "What's upsetting you? I can tell something is from the tone of your voice? Is it Marian?"

Nevil pressed one hand against his forehead for a moment as if that would aid his concentration. "It's very complicated - too complicated to go into over the phone. We're in serious trouble and we need your help."

"We? You and Marian?" Francis Quigley's cultured voice showed concern for the first time.

"And a friend of ours, Winifred Davies. She's with us now."

"And what kind of trouble? How on earth can I help?"

"You'll have to bear with me, Francis, because it's important. It may sound improbable - or impossible even - but, God help us, it's true. I hope you'll excuse the language, but if you'd been through what we went through last night you wouldn't be too self-controlled either." Nevil was only just beginning to realize how much the sheer horror of it had affected him. He gripped hard onto the phone and went on: "You spoke recently about the dangers of people dabbling in the occult?"

"I did - three Sundays ago, in fact." Quigley's voice became cautious. "You've not gotten yourself involved in that kind of thing, have you, Nevil?"

"Not in the way you're thinking, Francis. This is worse, far worse. Look, we'll have to meet. Can you get away for a few hours this morning? We could meet at Fenley. Outside the library, perhaps."

"What time? I've nothing I can't postpone, especially if this is as important as it sounds."

"Make it eleven. We can be there by then. We're in Birmingham at the moment."

"What on earth are you doing there? Good grief! You're not on the run, are you?"

"In a way, I suppose we are," Nevil said. The pips sounded in the phone. "We'll see you at eleven. Don't let us down, Francis. This is even more important than you think."

*

As they headed towards Fenley, Nevil drove with fanatical care, conscious of what happened to the Davieses. Although he did not think they could be got at so easily en route, he was not prepared to take any chances. As a result, it was already eleven o'clock by the time they arrived at Fenley. Its bustling streets, tight-packed with shoppers, slowed them down even more, and it was eleven twenty by the time the stone colonnade of the library building came into sight. Nevil turned onto the car park where they saw Quigley, a black overcoat over one arm, stood at the top of the library steps. He turned his deeply freckled face towards them, shielding his eyes against the sun as they climbed up the steps. His balding forehead, fringed with wisps of reddish-brown hair, was peeling from the recent hot weather. He held out his hand to Nevil, who shook it warmly.

"I'd just about given you up," he said when Nevil had

116

introduced him to Winnie. "It's fortunate you told me this was important. And that I believed you."

"You'll only appreciate how important it is when we've finished telling you the full story," Nevil said. "I suggest we go into the library restaurant where we can tell you everything."

*

Inside the restaurant, with its views of Fenley Cathedral across the square, they seated themselves round a table while Nevil ordered coffee and sandwiches at the counter. When he returned with a tray, he sat down and started to relate to Quigley what had happened. Winnie and Marian broke in now and then while he spoke to back up or elaborate certain events, and to reassure the curate that what he was being told was the truth. Quigley listened in silence, his square-shaped hands cupped round his coffee almost as if he was in silent prayer. He nodded his head now and then, and his eyes passed thoughtfully from one person to the other. When they'd finished, he drew his breath in quietly, then breathed out, opened his hands and stared studiously at his nails for a moment before speaking.

"You're all quite certain about this?" he asked. The look on their faces, the signs of stress and fear so clearly impressed on them by recent events, were confirmation though.

"As certain as we're sat here now," Nevil said.

The curate shook his head with an attempt at reasoning it out. "I'm not sure what I can do," he said finally. "This is bizarre. If it were almost anyone else - and, God knows I've known you and Marian for the past ten years or more - if anyone else were to tell me all this, I wouldn't have heeded more than a part of it. Even so, I'm out of my depth. What can I do? What can I suggest?" He rubbed his hands together in thought. "Perhaps the best thing I can do is contact someone with a specialized knowledge of this kind of thing - of cults like the one you've been talking about - this Order of the Hidden Way. They're beyond the experience of most people - of most clergymen as well, for that matter. When I spoke up about the dangers of dabbling in the occult, that was one aspect, of course. I attended a lecture a short time ago about the threat posed by Black Magic groups like that. Though I never expected to be confronted by one. Perhaps the best person to contact would be the man who gave the lecture - Professor Krakowsky ⸗ Joseph Krakowsky. By all accounts he's been investigating them for years. He was a lecturer for a time at Edinburgh University. I remember he told us something about how he came into contact with cults like these while he was there, how they engineered the death of one of his students who'd inadvertently become involved with them and wanted to get out. For a number of years I've also had more than a passing interest in the subject myself, ever since I was curate at a church in Devon that was hideously desecrated by a local coven. If you've ever seen what they do to a church, especially the holy relics stored inside it, you'd understand why I had an interest in them. Only when someone's had personal experience, as you have had to an even greater degree, can you begin to appreciate the utter, detestable evil of them."

"This Krakowsky," Nevil asked, "do you know how to contact him?"

"The lecture was organized by a church committee. My Bishop is a member of it. I'll contact him first to get the professor's telephone number. Then I'll try to fix up a meeting."

"As soon as possible," Nevil urged. "We haven't much time. If Atcheson and his friends could reach out last night and almost get Winnie, they'll try something again. Next time might be even worse."

The curate nodded his agreement. "I'll not waste a second, I assure you. I appreciate the seriousness of the situation." He touched Winnie's arm reassuringly.

*

It was less than an hour before the Bishop's secretary had found them Professor Krakowsky's telephone number and the Reverend Quigley had spoken to him. The professor was recuperating in his London home after the exhaustions of his lecture tour. But as soon as he heard the full details from Nevil of what had been going on in Endon, he wasted no time in offering his help.

"I shall be in Birmingham within the next few hours," he told Nevil in his strong Polish accent, which over forty years of residence in Britain had done little to blunt. "I'll meet you at New

118

Street Station. I know it well. There's a fountain in the shopping precinct overhead. I'll meet you there. Check with British Rail when you arrive what time the first train from London is due. I'll be away from here within the hour. Can you make it by then?"

"Certainly," Nevil told him, the strong reassurance of the old man's voice giving him a feeling of determination. "There'll be myself, my wife, Marian, and Mrs Davies." He looked at the curate, who nodded his head. "And the Reverend Quigley."

"Excellent," Krakowsky said. "In the meantime, I'll leave it for you to book rooms for us all at a convenient hotel. We'll use that as our base tonight and discuss what action should be taken. Okay?"

"Okay. I'll get that done straight away." Nevil looked at the others when the phone had gone dead. "We've a stiff drive ahead of us. We're off to Birmingham again. We've to meet the professor in three hours."

"Give me a minute to ring my wife to let her know I won't be back tonight," Quigley said, "and I'll follow you. My car's only parked a few streets away."

"Then we'll rush," Nevil told him. "We haven't much time to get to Birmingham." He felt the exhilaration of impending action stir through his veins. It was as if, at last, the blackness that had seemed to seal them in had been halted. Or would be soon.

*

When they reached Birmingham, they parked their cars at New Street Station. Nevil enquired when the first train from London was due and, on learning they had half hour to wait, Winnie said she would use the time to telephone her bank manager to arrange to get some money, while Nevil and the others went to book hotel rooms for the night. They agreed to meet again as soon as possible at the fountain in the shopping precinct above the station.

Fortunately, Roger Mitton, Winnie's bank manager, was a personal friend, as well as being a member of the same Masonic Lodge as her husband. As soon as he heard that she was in urgent need of cash and didn't have a cheque book or cheque guarantee card with her (these had all disappeared while she was being held at Elm Tree house) he told her he would send a cheque book to their branch on New Street, together with a fax of her signature. "I'll contact the manager by phone and let him know you're all right to cash cheques over the counter there. And make sure you have no problems. If I send the cheque book by first class post today they should have it by tomorrow morning."

By the time Winnie reached the fountain the others were already there. Nevil told her they'd booked a suite of rooms on the top floor of the Kingsway Hotel, just off New Street, with adjoining bedrooms for them all.

"This professor we're waiting for," Winnie said, "what do you know about him? Is he reliable?"

Francis Quigley answered her. "From what I remember of the details given about him before his lecture he was a member of the Polish Government in Exile during the War. He fought during the occupation of Poland in 1939 and was captured by the Russians. Although he was tortured by them - and badly, I believe, at the hands of the K.G.B. - he managed to escape. After the War he settled in Edinburgh, where he lectured on Philosophy. Since then he's been involved in a number of investigations into Black Magic groups throughout Britain. I understand he was involved in bringing about the destruction of one group only a year ago, during the course of which he suffered some horrifying injuries. When I met him he gave me the impression of being a tough, pragmatic type of man, a ruthless man - a man who could be a formidable enemy - and a stalwart ally. Just the kind of man we need, in fact."

As he finished speaking, they saw an old man heading towards them, walking sticks clenched in both hands. A young girl, perhaps twenty years old, walked beside him, carrying a couple of suitcases. The man was just over five feet tall, with broad, muscular shoulders and a hard, aggressive face, its hardness and aggression emphasized by a short white beard and a pair of pale grey eyes that glittered intelligently from beneath his bushy eyebrows. He wore an old tweed jacket with leather patches at the elbows, the stem of a pipe jutting conspicuously out of one overstuffed pocket. The girl was dressed in jeans, with a denim jacket. She was pretty, with long, dark hair, though Winnie could not help noticing a look of sadness in her eyes and lines about her otherwise youthful mouth that seemed to indicate that she had had more than her fair share of emotional suffering in her short life.

"Professor Krakowsky," Quigley greeted him, rushing forward. "I'm pleased you could come here."

The old man stopped and leaned forward on his walking sticks for support.

"After what you told me on the phone, Reverend, I had no choice." He eyed the others keenly as Nevil stepped forward to introduce everybody.

"And this," Krakowsky said, indicating the girl, "is Vivian Connors. Miss Connors is my personal assistant. She has had some experience of occult matters." There was a momentary hint of tiredness in his hard, grey eyes, which was immediately swept back, as if by the strength of his will. His bearded chin jutted forward authoritatively. "Have you arranged accommodation for everyone?" he asked Nevil.

"I'll take you there now. It's only across the street from here. The Kingsway Hotel. We have a suite of rooms on the top floor."

"Excellent, excellent. Then lead the way. Perhaps you could give Miss Connors a lift with these cases? They're heavy."

Marian Wilkes exchanged glances with Winnie as if they sensed the change in atmosphere amongst their small group at the old man's arrival, as if at last they had found the strong leadership they had so far lacked. Despite his walking sticks and crippled legs, there was a strength about Krakowsky that impressed them profoundly, that he was a man who could not be easily beaten.

By anything.

CHAPTER 20

P.C. Merriman wiped a hand across his broad, unintelligent face and stared at the beads of sweat that had gathered on his palm. The telephone receiver was still warm from his hand, and his eyes turned to it, wonderingly. His call to the drug squad at Fenley had left him with a sour taste of disillusion - with the police, his superiors... and, worse, himself.

Detective Inspector McCree, head of C.I.C. at Fenley, who specialized in drugs, had been piercingly sarcastic over his suspicions about Elm Tree House, especially the smell that worried him last night.

"Sweet and sickly, with a hint of bad meat? Are you having me on? You'd only just gone through the place that morning and you think - under those circumstances - they'd be burning some kind of exotic drug? They'd have to be more than a bit stupid to pull a stunt like that, don't you think? Besides," (and McCree's voice had turned icily dismissive) "I've never heard of drugs that smell like that. Take my word, what you smelt was incense, with a touch of bad meat in the background - real, genuine bad meat probably - the kind you get maggots in, you know. Forget about drugs. We've heard nothing here about them in that area. And we'd have heard something by now if there were. We'll get in touch with you if we do hear anything. Till then - forget it. Okay?"

Forget it. *Okay?* Okay my arse! Merriman clenched his large, ham-like fist. There was something going on at the house whether Detective *God Almighty* McCree believed him or not.

With unusual speed Merriman stood up and strode back and forth in his stark office. Somehow he would find out what was going on. Even if he didn't get another night's sleep in a month!"

CHAPTER 21

While P.C. Merriman simmered in his office in Endon, Nevil Wilkes led Professor Krakowsky and his assistant, Vivian Connors, into the suite of rooms he'd booked in the Kingsway Hotel. The main room was a long, well-lit lounge, with draped windows down one wall. A modern beige sofa and several armchairs, a large television, a glass-topped coffee table and a number of gilt-framed pictures comprised its furnishings. Krakowsky immediately seated himself on one of the armchairs and let his walking sticks clatter to the floor with a look of relief on his face. After a moment's rest he looked up at the others and, with an irritable gesture of his head, told them to be seated so the discussion could start.

"We have a lot of information to sort through before tonight. And even more decisions to be made. *And* plans to be settled on," he rasped, fumbling in his jacket for his pipe. By the time he'd filled it and got the thing lit, they were ready. He looked at them speculatively, as if assessing their potential calibre. His brows knitted together tight. In his own mind, despite his own advancing years, he would have preferred a few younger men. The curate was the youngest here, and he was in his forties, while Nevil Wilkes, for all his determination, could not have been much more than ten years younger than the professor's own seventy years. Krakowsky looked at Vivian Connors, and gave her a thin, reassuring smile, that vanished when he raised his head to address them all.

"Last night," he said, his strong Polish accent adding authority to his voice, "Mrs Davies was subjected to a vicious occult attack, undoubtedly launched against her by her former friend Oliver Atcheson, and by one or more of the people staying at Elm Tree House."

"Probably all of them," Nevil interrupted heatedly. He held out the photocopied newspaper cuttings he had about Tom Paxley, Hazel Metcalfe and Ramon Tarradellas. "They've all been involved in Black Magic or Satanism in the past. And still are, I'm sure."

"You are certainly correct," Krakowsky said. He scanned the cuttings. "This Tarradellas I have already heard about," he said. He stared at the picture thoughtfully, then flicked it to one side.

"He is probably the leader of the group, rather than Atcheson. In reality Atcheson is very much the neophyte amongst that group of seasoned Satanists, the rawest of beginners - if not their dupe... their relatively wealthy dupe, I might add."

"I wouldn't say Oliver was exactly wealthy," Winnie said, "but he isn't without money."

"He had enough money to buy this curious place - this Elm Tree House - and have it renovated to live in."

"Why should he have chosen that place?" Nevil asked. "Because of its picturesque past? Because of what's happened there, and its long connections with Devil worship?"

"Some places," Krakowsky said, with emphasis, "have a special quality about them which attracts occult phenomena, almost like a kind of psychic loadstone. Why this should be, I cannot profess to know. Whether it is what has happened there in the past that has created this special quality, or whether this special quality existed there from the very beginning and caused what happened, no one has ever satisfactorily answered. What does seem to be beyond argument is that Elm Tree House, and in particular the area surrounding it - "

"The woods," Winnie interjected, with a shudder of remembrance.

Krakowsky nodded. "Such as the woods," he said, "yes. About these it seems undeniable they have this quality. From the ancient and bloody worship of Moloch in Roman times - and who knows what before then – down through the ages to the depraved monks of the ruined abbey and the diabolism of Sir Robert Tollbridge."

"Tollbridge?" Nevil sounded surprised. He looked at the curate, who smiled knowingly and nodded his head in acknowledgement.

"I did not know anyone outside the Church - and few inside it - knew about Sir Robert Tollbridge's diabolical practices," Quigley said.

"I know it is a closely guarded secret of the Tollbridge family, which still holds extensive interests in that area. And that the Church has co-operated in keeping this secret as close as it has."

"And this diabolism," Nevil asked, "what form did it take?"

Krakowsky shrugged. "The usual forms of Devil worship and raising of demonic spirits, by all accounts. It was a short-lived career. Whether by accident or design, Tollbridge was challenged to a duel by a distant cousin, who was also an associate of the Marquis, their uncle. Details about what happened that chill March morning in 1661, three years after Elm Tree House was built, are vague, though the outcome was conclusive enough. Sir Robert was killed with a pistol ball to the brain. Though I have heard that other wounds were seen on the body before it was buried."

The curate agreed. "It's said he was executed by a party of men raised by the Marquis to end his activities at Elm Tree House."

"Which leads to speculations," Krakowsky continued, "whether the fear that made Sir Robert's murder a necessity was because of what he was doing... or *where* he was doing it." He waited for this to be digested by his listeners, then said: "I believe the people with Atcheson now - Tom Paxley and his wife, Hazel Metcalfe, Howard Brinsley, Ramon Tarradellas and however many others have arrived - brought him into their coven for the sole purpose of acquiring Elm Tree House. Just what their purpose is I do not know. Nor, indeed, do I know whether they are there because they chose to be in that place or because they themselves were chosen."

"By this psychic loadstone?" Nevil asked.

"Perhaps."

"Which would mean, surely," Marian said, " some other intelligence was guiding them. If so, professor, what?"

"I wish I knew the answer to that question," Krakowsky said. "Perhaps the curate knows more."

But the clergyman merely shook his head.

"What I do know," Krakowsky said, "is that something big is being prepared. That much we know from what has happened to Mrs Davies and her husband. I have no doubt that both of them were being prepared for something of symbolic importance. The lack of nourishment, apart from the thin, syrupy liquid, was a way of purifying the body, of purging it. The somnambulistic state in which they were drugged, apart from helping to keep them prisoners inside the house, was also serving to purify their minds - to melt their individual consciousness. I suspect, in fact, that what Mrs Davies was being given was some distillation of the Golden Poppy of Tibet, specially prepared into a dehumanising drink that can eventually turn a man - or a woman - into nothing more than a zombie."

"Morgan!" Winnie exclaimed suddenly. "They still have him. They'll still be giving him that vile drink. They'll still be destroying his mind, turning him more and more into a... a..."

Nevil clasped her shoulders and eased her back onto her seat.

"It is up to us to get him away before that happens," Krakowsky assured her.

"This Tarradellas," Quigley asked, "what do you know about him?"

Krakowsky shifted in his chair, then frowned. "I wish there was more than just the darkness of his reputation to go off. He is a clever man, always one foot, as you say in this country, ahead of the law. To my knowledge he has been involved in diabolic covens throughout Europe. Warrants have been issued for his arrest in France, Greece, Sweden and Germany on various charges, including murder."

"Murder!" Winnie buried her face in her hands, and Krakowsky looked at her in concern.

"I am afraid this must be said, Mrs Davies," Krakowsky told her. He glanced at Nevil and his wife. "Perhaps it would be better if Mrs Davies rested in one of the bedrooms while we discussed this. It's obviously distressing her, especially after what she has been through."

But Winnie shook her head. She applied a handkerchief to her eyes.

"I'll be all right, professor. Thank you for your concern, but I shan't break down again. I promise." She smiled bravely, her cheeks still shiny with tears.

Krakowsky regarded her carefully, then nodded. "Very well." He moved his gnarled but muscular hands about the arms of his chair, then said: "Tarradellas is an evil man. A dangerous man. A suspected adept of the highest order of Satanism, he is most likely the leader of this particular coven, this Order of the Hidden Way. However, we must discover what they are up to and find a way to get Morgan Davies away from them. These are our first objectives. These, and ensuring that Mrs Davies is safe from any further attacks tonight."

Winnie shivered as his words brought back her suppressed memories of what happened last night - of her helplessness, and her utter horror of the thing that reached from the window to her. And she knew she could not face something like that again.

It would drive her out of her mind, however many reassuring words the professor or anyone else uttered to her. She looked at Krakowsky. She wondered how much he could help, that tough-looking, but nevertheless crippled old man, with his craggy, wearied, world-weary face and bright grey eyes.

"Before tonight some of us must pay a visit to Elm Tree House," Krakowsky said. He smiled grimly at the startled expressions this immediately drew from his audience.

"Beard the Devil in his den?" the curate asked with a troubled frown. He tried to smile but found the prospect too daunting for bravado. All he could think of was what his wife would say if she could see him now, discussing how to combat a coven of Satanists.

Krakowsky clenched his fists and slammed them hard against the arms of his chair.

"If we do not beard this Devil in his den, as you so accurately put it, your Reverence, then we might just as well disband here and now, because we can achieve nothing otherwise. Nor can whatever protection I place around Mrs Davies for tonight against these people, effectively safeguard her night after night. If we do not fight back, she is doomed. And so is her husband. Do we surrender to that?" He glared at them demandingly, and for the first time Nevil saw the real hardness of the professor, the almost fanatical, uncompromising hostility he felt for the forces arrayed against them.

"Which of us should go?" Nevil asked.

Krakowsky cast him a brief look of thanks, then said: "You, the Reverend Quigley, my assistant, Vivian Connors, and myself. Mrs Wilkes should stay here with Mrs Davies and help keep her nerve if anything happens while we are away."

Nevil glanced at his wife, alarmed.

But Krakowsky waved his concern aside. "I'll ensure they are effectively protected against whatever is sent against them. Do not worry about that."

Marian tugged at her husband's arm. She stared at the professor steadily and said: "I'm sure the professor knows what he is doing. He'll make sure we're safe while you are away. In fact, I'd rather stay here with Winnie than go to that horrible place with the rest of you. I don't envy you that. We'll be much safer here. The worst thing for us will be worrying about you. Is that right, professor?"

Krakowsky chewed on the stem of his pipe before answering her. "I'm not a man to lighten the hardships we'll be facing - nor the dangers. And I'd be a fool to play down any of the dangers you'll be facing too - and they exist, even here, I'm afraid, in this nice, comfortable suite of rooms. But if you and Mrs Davies keep your heads, you'll be safe - far safer than we'll be, I assure you of that. Though we'll take precautions too," he hastened to go on, as he noticed the doubts that swept across the curate's face.

"What form of protection are you going to give us, professor?" Winnie asked.

"A pentacle," he said. He met the raised eyebrows of the curate steadily, then added: "The only effective protection against this kind of attack is a pentacle drawn on the floor, within which you must remain throughout the hours of darkness. Neither of you must venture outside it for any reason whatsoever, whatever threats or promises are made to you. Do you understand that? Mrs Davies? Mrs Wilkes?"

They exchanged glances, then slowly nodded their heads.

"That will be enough?" Nevil asked, uncertain.

"You ask me that, yet a Bible was enough for you to scatter the horror that threatened Mrs Davies last night? Am I correct?" Krakowsky shook his head. "Would you rather we gave them a gun? I assure you - and I'm certain the Reverend Quigley will agree with me here - a pentacle will be immeasurably more effective against the kind of perils Mrs Davies and Mrs Wilkes will have to face while we are away tonight than any number of guns. It is the *only* effective protection they can be given, in fact. Of that I am certain."

"And for us," Quigley asked, "what form of protection are you going to give us?"

Krakowsky regarded them coldly for a moment, then said: "For us there can be no elaborate protection. We must rely on our wits, our speed and our resolution. I can offer little more."

Nevil Wilkes glanced at his wife, then picked up his duffel bag from the floor. "Perhaps this will help a little," he said. He pulled out the two halves of the shot gun he'd stashed inside it the day before. With expert hands he fixed the two halves together and clicked back the hammers. "I have plenty of cartridges," he added, with a firm glance at Francis Quigley. But the curate merely nodded his head, saying: "That's more like it, Nevil." He turned to the professor. "At least that will put the fear of God in them," he added with a sardonic smile.

Krakowsky agreed. "Which is why I have this," the old man said. He asked Vivian Connors to bring one of their suitcases to him. When she'd laid it at his feet he bent forward and unlocked it. Inside, he rummaged through the tightly packed heaps of old books and papers he'd brought along for reference, till he found a large, wooden box. Carefully extracting it from the suitcase, he placed it on his lap. There was a brass lock at the front of it, which he unfastened with a small key from his pocket, then opened the lid. Inside, held firmly in place by the worn velvet lining, was a well-oiled Colt 45 automatic. "Fully loaded," Krakowsky informed them, taking it out and carefully weighing it in his hand, as he had done on hundreds of occasions before. "But remember this," he told them sternly. "We are dealing with the occult. Guns and bullets will prove effective against Atcheson and his colleagues - even against Ramon Tarradellas - but they will have little or no effect against whatever creatures of the dark they raise against us. The book you threw at the manifestation that menaced Mrs Davies last night was far more lethal than any number of guns would have been," he told Nevil. "You may as well fire arrows at a bolt of lightning as bullets at a thing like that. Be warned." Krakowsky looked at his watch. "Time passes," he said. "As soon as possible we should set off for Elm Tree House. Ladies," he went on, turning to Winnie and Marian, "it is time for the pentacle." With a grim smile fixed on his face, he forced himself up from the chair as Vivian stooped for his walking sticks and handed them to him.

From the suitcase he had already opened, Vivian went to take out some chalk, a length of string and a large carton of salt. Krakowsky directed the men to clear the furniture back into a corner of the room, then roll back the carpet to bare the floor beneath.

"Excellent, excellent," Krakowsky murmured as Vivian tried the chalk out on it. Then, using the string, he supervised the measurement of as large a pentacle as the available space would allow. Vivian marked out the outermost lines of the five-pointed star, before going over the chalk marks with a line of salt. "Whatever you do during the course of this evening," Krakowsky warned them, "do not disturb the salt. This is the barrier against which whatever is sent against you will be held back. Stay within it and you are safe. Cross it or break it and I cannot answer for the consequences. You understand?"

Both Winnie and Marian nodded their heads in silence, more disturbed than either would admit now that preparations were being made for their protection. To Winnie it looked too frail, too feeble a barrier to protect them from the kind of horror that had come for her last night. Would such a simple thing as this hold it back if it came for her again? She clasped Marian's arm for comfort as she wondered if she had the strength of will to have faith in the pentacle's effectiveness.

"Professor?" she asked, when the pentacle had been completed. "How certain are you that this will make us safe?"

Krakowsky pressed her arm. "As safe as anyone can be, that is how safe you will be. Do not worry. The worst thing would be for you to give way to fear. Have faith in the pentacle and you will be safe. But remember: no matter what happens, do not allow yourself to be tricked or panicked or lured outside it. If you do..." He shook his head and tightened his grip on her arm. "Just have faith, that is all."

That is all! To Winnie that seemed such an awful lot. The professor had not seen what she saw last night, alone except for the horror in her room. He hadn't felt the mind-numbing terror that filled her, so that the only thought left in her mind had been to scream and scream and scream, till the world seemed to rip itself apart all around her in her tearing hysteria.

He hadn't seen the horror of its face!

*

Finally, they were ready. Nevil stashed the shotgun away again in his duffel bag and slung it over his shoulder. It was decided they would set out in two cars: Nevil and the professor in the librarian's Datsun, and Vivian and Francis Quigley in the curate's battered Ford Zephyr. It was shortly before seven when the convoy set out from the hotel car park, and the sky, despite the time of year, was already beginning to turn grey, presaging an earlier than usual nightfall. It was an ominous sight as they drove Northwards out of Birmingham into a skyline filled with black, low-hanging clouds, and not one of them was left unaffected by it.

130

CHAPTER 22

In the hours that passed after the others had gone, the women watched TV. The professor had sternly instructed them not to leave the pentacle again, and they were adhering to his orders. Their memories of what happened in Winnie's room last night were far too vivid for either of them to underestimate the danger they were in.

By half eleven, though, they had both become weary of the television, and Marian nipped outside the pentacle to switch it off. As soon as she had done it she hastened back to the pentacle, her heart racing in her chest. She stared at Winnie for a moment, then burst into giggling laughter. Winnie watched her, white-faced, then she started to laugh as well. Hysteria lurked near the edge of their laughter, as they were both too well aware. Yet they laughed till tears began to stream from their eyes, and they clung to each other like two young girls in a dormitory frolic.

"A few weeks ago, and we would have laughed our sides out, seeing us here, out of our wits with fear," Marian said, when some of their laughter had died away.

Winnie nodded, though she would have given anything to exchange that for the fear that gripped so tight to her heart, giving it a squeeze now and then out of viciousness as if to remind her that it was still there, waiting to show itself again. She wiped her face with the back of her hand and stared round the room.

"Marian," she whispered softly - too softly for Marian to hear. "Marian," she repeated, louder this time, some of her fear showing itself in her voice. "Is it my eyes, or is the light growing dim?"

"Growing dim?" Marian gazed round the room. She narrowed her eyes as if to pierce the greyness that seemed to be flowing into it, like a mist whose presence could only be detected by a lessening brilliance of the light.

Within several minutes neither of them had any doubt that the room was growing darker. Shadows lengthened. The harsh glare of the light bulbs became pale and sickly. While the air became chill. Icily chill. Winnie clamped her arms about her and shuddered as she breathed.

"Marian, it's starting - it's starting again - like last night," she

131

whispered. The women clung together again, silent now as they stared into the grey shadows drawing in about them.

"We're safe within the pentacle," Marian said in a shaky voice that lacked conviction. Her plump face mirrored this as she held onto Winnie. "We're safe," she repeated.

The shadows thickened in the air as the light grew dimmer, as if gaseous grey tendrils of darkness were reaching out, coiling about each other into an interwoven network of gathering greyness that blurred what light there was as it seeped across the floor. As the gloom drew up to the thin lines of the pentacle, so there developed a distinction now between the colour of the floor within the star and that outside. Instinctively the women drew even nearer the centre, their arms wrapped tight about each other as their bodies shivered at the intensifying coldness of the air and the fear they felt building inside them. Winnie's face, its urbane sophistication long since drained away from it, was drawn with terror. Thin lines, cut deep into her flesh like long-worn wrinkles, marked the edges of her mouth as she strained against the scream, she felt coiled inside her throat. Her hair hung dishevelled about her shoulders, tangled with sweat. Her finger nails tightened into Marian's shoulders, drawn to a hair-trigger tenseness.

"Marian," she whispered, "you'll not let it come - not again - not here..."

Marian brushed a hand through Winnie's hair as she pressed her head to her shoulders, her own fears smothered for the moment as she concentrated on her friend's distress.

"We're safe here, Winnie; trust in what the professor told us. He knows what he's doing. We're safe. Quite safe. Stay here with me and whatever happens out there can't hurt us. Can't hurt us at all."

They rocked back and forth in each other's arms as the cold grew dank, like the damp chill deep inside a disused sewer. A smell of decay drew about them, rancid and foul. The thickening darkness rose on every angle of the pentacle, pressed tight against it, as if it was trying to crush it inwards. Higher and higher the gloom began to weave itself, and to their eyes, as they watched, it was as if a dense layer of spiders' webs was being built all around them. Soon most of the room was hidden behind it, and its density, as it piled up higher and higher, increased

132

with it, as if it was adding inches to its thickness as it rose, foot by foot from the floor.

For maybe an hour it coalesced, rigidly mirroring the geometric lines of the pentacle, so that it seemed, after a time, as if the network of webs was part of the pentacle's protective walls, paradoxically adding to their appearance of security, and Marian could feel Winnie's tension gradually subside. She relaxed her own grip as their fears started to fade.

"Do you feel better?" she asked, and Winnie nodded, not trusting herself to speak, her throat too dry. Marian peered at the webs of darkness - they looked solid, as if she could reach out and feel them, like matted lengths of hair, thick and grey.

Gradually, she eased herself from Winnie's arms and stood. The cold was still as severe as before, and her fingers and toes were becoming numb from it. The air misted before her mouth as she breathed.

"Some air conditioning this place has!" she muttered to herself in an attempt at humour. With a sudden stab of determination, she took two steps towards the pentacle walls and stared at the webs - or whatever they really were, she thought, repelled by their coarseness. If they were real webs, they were old ones, heavy with dust. Nearer to, they were more like hair, tangled, unwashed, knotted hair woven into mats. Reinforcing this image, she noticed thousands upon thousands of small insects crawling through them. She squeezed her eyes with the knuckles of her hands and looked again. There they were: minute insects, round, white, hump-backed bodies and wriggling rows of almost invisible legs. Mites - or lice. Like head lice. Hair - she felt almost tempted for some insane reason to test the reality of the stuff surrounding them, despite the thousands of mites swarming across it. Her fingers twitched, and she had to make a conscious effort to restrain her hand from touching it - the professor's words came back to her, and she knew if she touched the strands her fingers would have passed beyond the protection of the pentacle. She held back and took a deliberate step away from it. Winnie stood close by beside her.

"What is it?" Winnie asked. Her voice trembled even now, though Marian felt calmer, reassured by the inability of the grey fibres to pass beyond the thin protective lines of salt.

"Something they've sent against us," Marian answered. "What

it's supposed to do to us, I don't know. It looks harmless enough, despite those disgusting creatures crawling through it, but looks don't mean anything, I don't suppose."

The cold grew worse - *impossibly* worse. And Marian wished they had thought to bring extra clothes with them inside the pentacle, but the earlier warmth of the hotel's air conditioning had lulled them.

"Something else must be happening," Winnie said. Her eyes seemed to open unnaturally wide, till their whites could be seen all around them. "This cold - something else is here - something worse." Her memories of the thing at the window last night, beckoning her with the leprous remnants of its fingers, rolled back across her mind, and she shuddered. Her knees felt weak and she had an overwhelming urge to urinate.

Something stirred behind the webs in front of them. First one, then two gaps were ripped through them. Fingers - *dead* fingers - curled into them, bunching them into balls that were tugged back and violently scattered to the side. More hands - more *dead* hands - joined in the work. Larger gaps were torn in the webs, as if this barrier, separating them from whatever horror had crept into the room, was being destroyed so whatever was there could reach and attack them.

"It's getting through!" Winnie screamed. She pulled herself from Marian. "*It's getting through!*"

Marian glanced from Winnie to the webs. Rotten fingers, their nails like chewed-up claws, tore down the webs. Only half-seen, leprous, swollen faces peered at them. She felt her stomach muscles tighten, and she knew one glimpse more and she would throw up.

"They're coming through!" Winnie cried. Through her nausea, Marian realized that Winnie was in a state of hysteria. She tugged her eyes away from the creatures tearing at the webs.

"We're safe," she said to Winnie, but the woman wouldn't listen.

"They're coming through, I tell you. They're coming through!" She grovelled before them, mewling through trembling, bloodless lips.

"They're not! We're safe."

Winnie screamed. She jumped to her feet in panic.

"We've got to get out of here. They'll trap us. *Kill us!*" She

134

punched Marian's hands away from her and ran across the pentacle to where the webs still stood as a solid, implacable barrier between them and the rest of the room. "We've got to get out of this place!" Winnie shrieked.

She reached for the untouched webs.

"For God's sake, *stop!*" Marian screamed out to her.

But her hands were already at the webs. For a moment Winnie ripped into them, then her screams rose even higher into an ear-splitting shriek of terror. Hands, like the decaying claws of a score of lepers, fastened themselves to her arms. Thick fingernails scratched, then caught in her skin. There was blood from the wounds they gouged into her. Blood that dripped onto the floor. Winnie shook her head violently from side to side as she desperately tried to tug her arms back inside the pentacle, but more hands gripped her, tugging her to them with a hard, relentless strength that dragged her feet, scrabbling uselessly, across the floor.

"Marian! Help! *Help me, please!*"

Marian leapt to her. She hooked her fingers in the belt around her jeans and pulled. Bent double, she tried to use all her weight to slow her, to stop her, to pull her back into safety again, but it was no use. Her own feet slithered on the floor, unable to gain a purchase as she saw the webs being torn apart in front of them, and more dead faces stared at them. Hands, held back by the pentacle, hung poised in the air, splintered fingernails, like blackened shards of splintered wood, ready to reach out and grab them once they were past the pentacle.

Her stomach felt as if it was going to burst as she tugged and tugged at Winnie's belt, all her strength concentrated in the grim effort. It hurt. It hurt bad. And her teeth were ground into a grimace as she strained to hold on, to pull her friend back, to keep her feet from being dragged across the floor. Winnie's shrieks rose even higher as she writhed and twisted her lithe body in an effort to wrench herself free of the hands. But it was no use. Marian saw this - felt this - as her hands reached the edge of the pentacle. She hung on even now, unwilling to give up, to let her friend be dragged from her grasp. Then the pain hit her arms as nails scraped and gouged thick grooves into her flesh. She saw her blood flow to her elbows as the fingers scratched her arms. She strained, opened her mouth in a last-minute protest of despair as she felt her grasp start to weaken, releasing the belt. She kicked herself backwards. The fingers made a grab for her arms, and her hands were torn as she rolled into a sobbing, huddled ball in the centre of the pentacle. She clutched her hands to her and felt the hot wetness of her blood as it soaked through her jumper. A howling, shrieking Bedlam of hysteria swirled around the room beyond the pentacle, but she screwed her eyes shut against what was there. She doubled up till her knees were pushed against her chin and her eyes were pressed into the damp, dark heat of her hands.

"Oh, Lord have mercy," she mumbled to herself, as if this and only this could save her sanity from whatever was going on around her. "Oh, Lord have mercy, have mercy. Oh, Lord have mercy."

It was the beginning of the longest night of her life.

CHAPTER 23

When the two cars drew up outside the gates to Elm Tree House the first thing they noticed was the unlit police car parked alongside. Although night had drawn in and the sky was black, no stars showing through the thick depths of clouds overhead to lighten it, the small white car was unmistakeable.

"I wonder what Colin Merriman's doing here," Nevil said, recognizing the car.

"Maybe he's suspicious about this place as well," Krakowsky suggested as he undid his seat belt and reached for his walking sticks.

Francis Quigley and Vivian Connors had already climbed out of the curate's Zephyr by the time Nevil and the professor were out. They stood shivering by the roadside, staring through the tall gates along the drive beneath the trees.

"I understand now what you meant about the atmosphere of this place," Krakowsky said after staring at the gloom beneath the elms for a few moments. "This place has an aura, no doubt about that. No wonder Tarradellas was drawn to it. You may as well have waved a rotting carcass at a jackal."

"What do we do about that?" Nevil asked, indicating the police car.

"We follow him," Krakowsky said with disarming bluntness. He pointed one of his walking sticks at a footprint in the wet soil by the gates. "From the size of that I imagine it was made by a policeman. Yes?"

Nevil compared his own shoe and smiled in appreciation. It was a good inch and a half longer than his size 9.

"That will be Merriman's all right," he said.

"Well, if he has no objections to doing a bit of trespassing, why should we scruple?" Krakowsky asked, with a humourless chuckle. "I would leave that shot gun of yours in the car for now," he added to Nevil.

"And your gun?" Nevil asked.

Krakowsky patted his inside breast pocket.

"I doubt if the police would think of searching a harmless old cripple like me. At seventy-one I'll risk it. I've risked far more for less reason. Besides, it's not so obvious as that great elephant gun of yours, is it?" he added with a grin.

They made their way along the edge of the drive, keeping in the shadows. There were few lamp posts along the road, and the one that faced the gates at the end was soon lost from sight as they walked along the great, broad curve of the drive towards Elm Tree House.

The building stood as a large patch of darkness ahead of them. Several lights showed through thick curtains at some of the windows on the ground floor, though they did little to lessen the leaden atmosphere of the place.

"What do we do now? Break in and confront them? Or what?" the curate asked as they paused several yards from the front door by the row of parked cars. His voice shook with suppressed tension. His flesh crawled under the layers of clothing he wore, and he was glad that he was not alone - not here, not now, not knowing what he did about this place.

Krakowsky ignored his question for the moment. Instead he limped towards one of the lit windows and listened at its panes. The indistinctive sound of voices could be heard through them.

"We'll go to the back of the house and see if they have locked all the doors. If we can get in undetected, we'll see what we can do."

They stole by the empty west wing. The derelict gloom of the tumbledown walls and dirty windows, and the rank smell of neglect, of rotting wood and mouldering plaster, gave a squalid air to the place. They had barely reached the end of it and turned to head for the back of the house when something moved on the ground ahead of them. Tense already, they stopped in silence. Krakowsky let one of his walking sticks fall to the ground with a clatter as he reached for the gun in his pocket.

"What is it?" The curate's voice was a harsh.

Nevil clenched his fists, even though he knew how useless blows would be against anything like the thing he saw last night.

When what they were staring at came no nearer, Krakowsky limped forwards, the heavy automatic held unwaveringly ahead of him. A faint sound of panting came from the thing.

"Come here quickly," Krakowsky whispered. "Look to him, Nevil, if you can. If I'm not mistaken, it's your policeman."

Nevil rolled P.C. Merriman over, while Vivian held the man's head in her hands. Merriman's breath came easier now, but it was obvious to all of them that he was in a great deal of pain.

Vivian freed one of her hands from beneath his head and wiped his brow. She looked up sharply when she touched him and met Nevil's eyes in the gloom.

"His face is covered in blood," she whispered. Her slender fingers carefully felt about his face. "It's as if he's been slashed again and again with something sharp."

"By claws?" Krakowsky murmured in a low voice as he stooped to see what had been done. He put away his gun and reached instead in his pocket for a torch. In its light they saw deep grooves had been scored across the policeman's face. Some were so deep that they reached the bone, severing or tearing the stretched muscles and fat underneath. One of his eyes had been ripped free of its socket. Nevil bit back the convulsions that automatically started in his stomach. This was no time to be sick, he told himself.

"It were white."

Merriman's remaining eye opened to stare upwards, though he did not appear to see them as he started to babble.

"White?" Krakowsky rasped, leaning nearer. "What was white?"

"It were white... all white... like bones... wagl nagl... no, no, no!... I can 'ear it... wagl nagl... f'tharg... starin' eyes... all white an' dead an' dry... go away! No!" He flung his arms in front of his face, throwing Vivian against the wall of the house.

"Steady, now, steady," Nevil urged him. He took hold of the policeman's arm and firmly but gently pressed it back to his chest. He felt the sticky blood that covered his tunic. *"Could you shine your torch down here for a moment, professor?"* he asked in a sickened whisper.

In its light they saw that the policeman's tunic had been as badly ripped as his face.

"This man needs getting to a hospital right away," Nevil said. "God knows how deep some of these gashes are. He'll bleed to death."

Quigley agreed. "Whatever we came here for must wait till he's been seen to. If we delay, he'll die."

The professor raised his torch to the policeman's face and studied it in silence, his brows knit in thought. He looked at the others and shook his head. "He already has the look of death," he said. "I've seen too many violent deaths - during the War and

139

since - not to recognize when there is no hope. He's lucky to have lasted as long as he has." He pressed a hand to Merriman's shoulder, and there was a return to some kind of consciousness again by the policeman. "This thing," Krakowsky said, "that attacked you, where was it?"

"I saw it from the road... suspicious... drugs... think I'm useless... out here... alone... but I saw it... followed... never thought it'd be waitin'... must've been...waitin' for me... *No! Get away!*... tried to stop it... the *pain*, God, the *pain!*..."

Merriman drew in a deep breath that seemed to take every effort in his body. A shudder passed through him and he coughed. The cough died in his throat, and Merriman with it.

"He's gone," Krakowsky said a moment later. They let the body sink to the ground. "Murdered."

"By what?" Quigley asked, shaken by the enormity of what was happening, of what he had allowed himself to get drawn into. "By what, professor? *What* murdered him?"

Krakowsky subconsciously felt for the gun inside his jacket, though he knew more than the rest of them the uselessness of it against whatever killed the policeman. He stood up, leaning on his walking sticks.

"We have a job to finish. Is that not right?"

"It is." Vivian Connors spoke calmly, and Nevil wondered what could have happened to her in the past that had hardened her as it had. He felt far from hardened himself. In fact, he was far from certain just how much more of this he could take. Despite his fear, despite the metallic sickness in his mouth, that made him want to leave this place and try to forget what he'd seen and what he knew was going on and everything that had happened, he nodded and said: "I'm ready. Let's get on with it." He hardly recognized the lifeless tones of his voice as he stood and followed the professor past the rest of the derelict wing, till they reached the rear of the house.

The trees had encroached much nearer the house at the back, and the darkness here was even denser. Not far ahead they saw the dim shape of a doorway.

"That will be the kitchen," Nevil whispered.

There was a crackle of twigs being trodden underfoot in the woods. Instantly stopping, they looked back, tensed and listening. The cold seemed even worse, as if they were stood within the shadow of a colossal iceberg. It was a cold that seemed to rush upon them, though there was no wind, just a warmth-sapping chill that penetrated deep into the bone.

"Quickly now!" Krakowsky said. "To the door. Don't waste time looking back. *Whatever killed Merriman is there!*"

In a panic-stricken huddle they rushed ahead, heedless of what noise they made. Behind them the undergrowth parted, and Nevil glimpsed something staring at them. Then he turned away from it and brought up the rear as Krakowsky reached for the handle of the door and thrust against it. Even had the door been locked it was likely the sheer momentum of his body crashing into it would have smashed it open. As it was, the door opened straight away, and they almost fell over each other in their haste to get into the unlit room.

Krakowsky was the first to regain his composure. Panting heavily he pushed the door shut behind them.

"We are safe enough here. It cannot pass through that doorway. As you have no doubt already heard, this house was deliberately built with misshapen door and window frames. A fact Sir Robert Tollbridge used to ensure a safe haven for himself from the monstrous things he conjured up in this place."

"Like a vast pentacle?" Vivian suggested.

"Exactly," Krakowsky said as he eased himself onto a chair with a subdued sigh of relief.

"Where do you think Tollbridge conjured up his demons?" Nevil asked.

Krakowsky massaged his right leg. "I would imagine the most obvious place would be the cellar," he said. "That's where the original temple to Moloch lies. What more perfect place for the kinds of devilish rites Sir Robert performed than in the cellar beneath this house on land long used for sacrifices in the past?"

"Is that where you think they'll be, Atcheson and the rest?" the curate asked.

"Without a doubt. They'll be concentrating what forces they can raise against Mrs Davies."

"And the voices we heard from outside?"

"If I'm right, we'll soon see about that," Krakowsky grunted, as he pushed himself onto his feet again. "This way." He clenched hold of his walking sticks and led them out of the kitchen into the hallway. For a second, he glanced from side to side, as if to

141

sort something out in his mind, then clumped towards the lounge. A faint light showed beneath the door into it, and he paused for a moment to ready his gun, then indicated for Nevil to open the door for him. A blast of noise greeted them as the door was thrust back and they rushed in, but the room was empty. Krakowsky grunted at the back of his throat, as if what he saw confirmed his suspicions. All of the noise they had heard from outside came from a radio. "Camouflage," Krakowsky muttered. "Camouflage to make anyone calling here mistakenly think there were people in this room." He glared at his companions. "There's only one place they'll be." His cold eyes turned towards the hallway. "The cellar."

Although they did not know where the door to the cellar was, they systematically started to search the rooms at the back of the house. Less than five minutes later Vivian Connors found the door in the generator room. She rushed to fetch the others as soon as she'd opened it and heard the noises inside. Gathering about the open doorway, they listened for a moment to the murmurs - to the dull, repetitious chants - *and* the evil, discordant twitterings that set their teeth on edge. The curate drew a crucifix and muttered a prayer, but Krakowsky cautioned him to silence.

"Let's not disturb whatever is down there till we are ready," he warned sternly. "*Then* pray. *Then pray for all you are worth!*" He tightened his grip on the automatic and took a cautious step down the steep flight of well-worn blocks into the darkness below.

The sounds grew louder as they neared the bottom of the steps, and none of them doubted that what they were hearing was some kind of satanic rite.

Ahead of them, flickering between the huge pillars across the dim depths of the cellar floor, they saw a mass of light. Krakowsky stared at the candles that had been lit in a broad circle far ahead of them. A number of shapes could be glimpsed now and then passing between them.

"Stay silent. Our lives depend on it," Krakowsky said. "Do nothing till I act." He stared each of them in the eye in turn, as if to impress the importance of his instructions. Then he turned and headed between the pillars, hidden by the darkness that filled the cellar with a claustrophobic density beyond the distant candlelight.

142

A foul odour quickly struck them as they crept nearer the Satanists - an odour of decay, of a reptilian rottenness and of a vile, chemical sort of stench that none of them could identify. Sweat poured from their faces despite the unearthly cold that filled the place - a cold that almost seemed to hold them back like a physical barrier as they silently, slowly made their way between the pillars. Nevil hung close to the professor, wishing he had even a fraction of the man's determination. But the occasional cackles that echoed through the air from the distorted, silhouetted shapes ahead of them unnerved him - unnerved him far more than the rising chants of the Satanists.

When they were no more than ten yards away from the edge of the candlelight Krakowsky motioned for them to gather round behind him. Figures stood beyond the candles, dressed in robes that reached to their feet. As they swayed, they chanted. Nevil recognized the florid, square-shaped face of Tom Paxley amongst them, as well as the long brown hair of Hazel Metcalfe. There were about a dozen, quietly moaning their intricate chant. A further figure, bald-headed and pock-marked - obviously Ramon Tarradellas from the descriptions he had seen of him - stood nearer the centre of the ring at a low, stone-built altar. On the paving stones in front of it a dark triangle had been drawn, and a candle flickered from each corner. At the base of the triangle, facing Tarradellas, they could make out the letters:

I H S

A cross was drawn on either side of them.

The ceremony seemed to have been going on for some time, since the candles had melted down and great clumps of hot wax had run down their sides to gather around them on the floor.

Tarradellas called in a loud, clear voice:

"By the great Key of Solomon I command you to act. Aglon Tetragram Vaycheon Stimulathon Erohares Retragsammathon Clyoran Icion Esition Existion Eryon Onera Erasyn Moyn Meffias Soter Emmanuel Sabaoth Adomai..."

Krakowsky raised the gun in his right hand and took aim at Tarradellas. He leaned against one of the pillars for support.

"When I fire, I want you to start the Lord's Prayer, Reverend." He gripped the gun with both hands, carefully, slowly pulling on the trigger. The cold grew unbelievably even more intense than before, and the air seemed to well towards them. Jerking

143

his head from the figure he was aiming at, Krakowsky started to say something when a black shape crashed into him and he was sent sprawling across the floor. He squirmed as the others stared on, paralysed by shock. He fired at the tangle of shadowy darkness that covered him. Two powerful gunshots thundered in the cellar like cannon fire, amplified by the echoes that rolled deafeningly back and forth across it. The short but brilliant flames from the gun were like bursts of lightning as Krakowsky fired at the thing that was attacking him. An instant later Quigley took a grip of himself.

"In the name of the Lord I command you to stop!" he cried out, raising his crucifix high above his head. He leapt at the thing, bringing the crucifix down in his fist against the shape. There was a scream that burst like an explosion in his face and there was a stench of rottenness far worse than anything they had smelt so far. The thing on top of Krakowsky melted inwards, its body boiling black and sticky and foul. A thick, glutinous, mucus-like matter dripped from the old man as he struggled to his feet, his face scored with deep scratches that bled into his beard. He wiped his hands down the sides of his jacket as the Satanists, gathered in front of them, menacing in the sudden silence. A faint twittering echoed from somewhere in the distance, and Tarradellas stepped towards them. A smile lurked at the corners of his mouth - a mouth that was almost as lipless as a human mouth could be.

Krakowsky defiantly raised the Colt once more towards him.

"Don't be a fool," Tarradellas said. His voice was soft, with just a hint of a foreign accent. "I have more than one protector in this place to stop you. And your Nazarene friend may not be so lucky next time to save you from the folly of your actions." He held out his hand for the gun. "Your only hope was to strike while my attention was concentrated elsewhere. You know that as well as I do. Don't be a fool."

Despite the prickling of the hair at the nape of his neck, Nevil felt like mentally urging the professor to fire whatever shots he had left at the man. At that range, less than ten feet from him, he couldn't possibly miss. And Tarradellas would almost certainly be killed. Yet, insanely, Krakowsky did not fire. Nevil opened his mouth as if to protest at his delay, when Krakowsky suddenly reversed the gun in his hand and held it, hand-grip first, towards the Satanist.

"*Why?*" Nevil cried. "For God's sake, why?"

"Because you have failed," Tarradellas answered him. He threw the gun onto the floor. It skittered across the flagstones into the darkness.

"If I could have shot him before he realized we were here," Krakowsky said, his voice harsh with anger at himself, "we could have destroyed them."

"But now it is you who will be destroyed," Tarradellas said. Sweat dripped from his pockmarked cheeks. "You have saved us a great deal of effort in coming to us like this. A great deal of *wasted* effort."

Tom Paxley beamed behind him. "I warned you, Wilkes. You should have heeded me when I told you to keep your mouth shut. Now you'll have to find out what the consequences for talking too much are."

Nevil turned, looking back across the empty space between the pillars, back towards the cellar stairs, hidden in the darkness, knowing they were too far away for escape.

CHAPTER 24

How long she lay huddled in the pentacle, shuddering with horror, Marian did not know. Eventually, though, as the warmth of the sunlight that shone through the window soaked into her, she felt the tensed constriction of her muscles relax. She unfolded her arms from about her knees and looked up. Her bleary, blood-shot eyes seemed incapable of focusing properly, and it was minutes before she was certain the room was empty and that everything seemed normal. *Normal!* Tears welled in her eyes as she remembered what happened. Unable to take it in, she climbed to her feet and dragged herself across the floor to the bathroom, where she soaked her head beneath the shower. A glance at her watch showed it was seven thirty-five - late enough for the others to have returned by now from Elm Tree House. A feeling of presentiment crept over her and she had to sit for some minutes till she could collect her wits again.

Of the grey webs - or hair - that had piled in the room during the night, there was now no trace. Nor was there any trace of Winnie Davies, or of any of the things that had entered and dragged her away. That she had been able to survive their attack convinced her of the effectiveness of the pentacle, and she was careful to repair any damage she'd made when she walked across it on her way to the bathroom in case she might need its protection again. Then she unlocked the door to the corridor outside, hung the *Do not disturb* notice on the handle, then went down for breakfast. The practical side of her nature uppermost again, Marian told herself she would need all her strength to face whatever hardships lay ahead today, and for that she needed food. She ate without appetite, though, worrying about her husband and the others, but she ate stolidly and did not allow herself to stop till every plate set before her had been cleared. She then went down to the reception desk to ask if any messages had been left during the night. That there were none did not surprise her. She telephoned her home in Endon on the off chance that Nevil had taken everyone there as a refuge during the night, but there was no answer. She replaced the receiver with a feeling of weariness, unable to think of anywhere else they might have gone, unless they were still on their way back. She nodded her head with an attempt at optimism, unwilling to consider the other alternative: that they might have failed and been captured.

Or worse.

As she stepped out of the call box, she saw two men step into the lobby and head for the reception desk. She recognized Tom Paxley as one of them, and stepped back at once into the kiosk, hiding most of her face behind the receiver as she watched them speak to the receptionist. They appeared to be arguing with her, and Marian was sure they were trying to get information out of the girl about the rooms they'd booked here. Knowing it would only be a matter of time before they got the information they wanted, Marian slipped out of the call box while their backs were turned and hurried as quickly as she could out of the lobby, pushing the swing doors open before her and rushing down the steps onto the street. Without hesitation, she turned left and merged with the passing crowds. Not till several blocks separated her from the hotel did she slow down. Then she headed back towards New Street Station, where she enquired about hire cars. Less than an hour later she had arranged for the hire of a Ford Escort and was heading down the motorway towards Fenley, a lump in her throat as her hands gripped tight on the steering wheel. Her round face was pale beneath her deep suntan, and there were shadows about her eyes that would have reminded her of Winnie Davies the day before if she had looked in the mirror to see them, but there was a firmness of purpose to her small mouth and a look of determination in her smooth, unwrinkled brows that showed a strong difference between the two women. Smaller than Winnie, and stockier in build, there was a steadfastness about her that told of deep reserves of strength - not only of physical strength, of which she had plenty in her own way, but in strength of character. It would take much to rattle her - much more than what she had been through so far.

Her foot kept the accelerator pressed as she drove swiftly down the motorway for Fenley, counting the turn-offs with a barely restrained impatience. At Fenley she drove on, taking the direct route for Endon. This took her past Elm Tree House, and she slowed as she neared it. There was no sign of any of the cars that had been parked along the road, nor anything to show that anyone had been here during the night. The place looked all but deserted as she slowed almost to a standstill at the gates. Then she pressed down on the accelerator again and drove past.

At the village she called to see the Reverend Quigley's wife, but the last time she had heard from her husband was a telephone call the previous afternoon to say he would not be home that night. A tall, harassed-looking woman with a wayward, teenage son, Marian said nothing to her about what had been going on, leaving her as soon as she could to drive back home. As she parked outside her house, Mrs Jolliby, a neighbour, waved to her. "Have you heard about P.C. Merriman?" Mrs Jolliby called in a loud voice even before Marian had been able to climb out of her car.

"I'm afraid I haven't. What's wrong?"

Mrs Jolliby leaned her over-bright face nearer and whispered in a theatrical voice: "The poor man's been murdered. They found his body out on the hills. A nasty mess, I've heard tell. A very nasty mess." Her eyes twinkled with enthusiasm, and Marian could tell that she would go on re-iterating the few scraps of information she had about whatever had happened to the policeman for as long as she would listen, but she didn't have time.

"I'm sorry. You'll have to tell me later. I'm very busy."

A look of disappointment unrolled itself across Mrs Jolliby's face, but Marian ignored it. "I'm sorry," she repeated. She searched for and found her door key and let herself in, shutting the door behind her in Mrs Jolliby's face with a feeling of relief.

CHAPTER 25

It was late morning now, not far off lunch, and the heavy curtains at the windows in Elm Tree House had been drawn back to let in some light. It shone with a watery pallor across the room, matching the washed-out faces of Professor Krakowsky and his companions as they sat on the long, comfortable sofa. Ramon Tarradellas and Oliver Atcheson reclined in armchairs facing them. They'd discarded their ceremonial robes of the night and were dressed in slacks and open-necked shirts. A thick gold bracelet hung from one of the Spaniard's wrists as he cupped his hands beneath his dark chin and regarded them in a thoughtful silence for several minutes. Four of the other male Satanists stood guard behind the sofa, though there seemed little need for them. There was a subtle air of authority about Tarradellas, and Nevil sensed that this relied more on a firm belief in his own ability to handle anything they might try to do than on the help of his associates. Those black eyes of his bored into them with a power that Nevil could feel, though Krakowsky returned his gaze with a steady, vehement look of hatred on his face, its harsh lines even more severe than before, with dried blood caked about his cheeks and beard.

"That was a foolhardy escapade you dragged these unfortunate innocents into last night, professor," Tarradellas said, finally breaking the silence that had filled the room since they were led here from the cellar. "So eminent an expert on the occult as yourself would have been expected to have acted with more caution. And far more wisdom. Or were you too concerned about the welfare of Mrs Davies? Was that the weakness that brought you here with your pitiful band of followers? And led you, finally, to this?"

"What do you intend doing with us now?" the curate asked. A note of defiance showed through the tremors in his voice. There was a deep cut on his forehead from a blow he received when he tried to resist being brought into the lounge a few hours earlier, as if at that last instant he thought he could break free and escape. His face was even paler than the others', and Nevil, seated beside him, was unsure whether the blow hadn't been worse than it appeared to have been at the time.

Tarradellas turned his gaze from Krakowsky to the curate.

There was a hint of malevolent amusement in his eyes.

"The Nazarene shows his fangs, does he?" There was hatred in that voice, Nevil realized, and he felt suddenly afraid for the curate - more afraid than he felt for himself.

Oliver Atcheson remained silent, sunk in thought, despite the token prominence accorded him in sharing in the interrogation of their prisoners. One of the other Satanists, though, clamped his hands on the curate's shoulders and tugged him back against the sofa with a vicious jolt.

"You'll find out soon enough what we've got planned for you, filth," the man snarled.

Tarradellas shook his head slightly. "No need for that, James." He spoke quietly, but with unmistakable authority. The Satanist released the curate's shoulders and straightened up.

Nevil glanced at Quigley's face, saw him gulp, then wipe his forehead, clearly shaken. Nevil glared at Tarradellas.

"Well?" he asked, surprised at his own mounting anger. "What do you intend doing with us?"

Tarradellas looked at the librarian, studying him with amused curiosity. Nevil felt his blood start to boil, and his fingers ached to get hold of the gun that Krakowsky had handed over to the Satanist hours before.

"Since fortune has been so benevolent as to let you fall in our hands, it is obvious you are intended to help us in our aims." The Spaniard spoke slowly, carefully, his stilted English somehow pregnant with a sinister undercurrent of meaning that Nevil knew was intentional. The dull craters on the Spaniard's pockmarked cheeks seemed to deepen as the light glanced sideways across them from the windows, like the ravages of an awful decay.

"You're shit!" Vivian's voice snapped through the silence that followed the Spaniard's words. Nevil saw the man's eyes shift angrily towards her, and he half moved forwards as if he was about to hit her. Nevil felt his muscles tense in response. Then Tarradellas eased himself back into his chair with a dry, artificial chuckle. His gold-capped tooth glinted as his mouth moved into a smile of appreciation.

"I hope you can keep that keen wit when you see what is planned for you, young lady."

Krakowsky moved his broad shoulders and looked more keenly at Tarradellas. "If you are planning to raise more than you already have, you do realize you're creating a release of power too great for any man - even any group of men - to control, whatever promises you may have been given so far?"

"I know my own powers, professor," Tarradellas said.

"You *think* you know your own powers, seignior. The forces you are hoping to use have a way of misleading those they tempt, especially how much control they have. Greater men than you have tried to use these forces, only to find, in the end, it is *they* who are being used."

Tarradellas acknowledged the old man's argument with a nod of his head. "I know you will try to undermine my confidence too. You will not succeed." He spoke to the Satanists behind them: "Prepare some of the sleeping draft. It's time to end this interview." He looked at the professor: "The twenty ninth is Midsummer Eve. We were going to offer two sacrifices - six would be better though. As it happens, you came in time for us to prepare you over the next few days to be suitable offerings."

"Six?" Nevil asked. "But Mrs Davies got away from you."

"For a while. For all your pathetic efforts to save her she could not escape us for long."

Nevil felt his stomach muscles cramp with despair. If they'd got Winnie, what about Marian, what had happened to her? He knew his wife would not have let Winnie be taken without a fight.

Tarradellas cast him a smile of contempt. "With six such as you all the power we need will be ours. Then nothing can stop us. Nothing at all."

Krakowsky studied him intently. He noted the addict-like look in the Spaniard's eyes. He'd seen that corrupted look before. For all the Spaniard's appearance of self-control, it was an act. He was no more the master of himself than a back-street junkie. All this was just the thinnest of all acts - so thin, in fact, it would take little to destroy it, to reveal the unthinking fanaticism beneath the facade. Krakowsky grunted to himself as one of the Satanists left the room.

"Both Morgan Davies and his wife are in this house?" Krakowsky asked.

"Under sedation," Tarradellas said. "As will you in less than ten minutes from now, till the twenty ninth," he added. "Though by then none of you will be capable of doing very much, I'm afraid."

"The drug?"

"It weakens the will as much - if not more - than it weakens the body. You no doubt noticed its effect on Mrs Davies, even though she was only on a light dose at that stage. Neither the mind nor the body can survive the kind of dose we will be giving you during the final stages for long. It debilitates the life force too much."

"I see." Krakowsky appeared to consider what he'd said. "It looks as though I underestimated you, seignior."

"It would appear you did." Tarradellas smiled, amused at the compliment.

"Would it be permitted for us to share a last drink before we are drugged? I don't suppose it would affect it, would it?"

"Nothing will affect it, professor. Of that I can most certainly assure you." He nodded to one of the Satanists behind them. "Pour what they wish to drink. We can at least give them the passing courtesy of one last drink. After all, they will soon be helping us immeasurably, whether they like it or not."

"Make mine a brandy," Krakowsky rumbled. "A large one." He stared hard at Nevil as the Satanist poured him a glass from one of the decanters. "And you, Mr Wilkes?"

"A brandy for me too," Nevil said, confused by the professor's behaviour. He wondered how wise they had been in turning to him for help, though it was too late for doubts now.

The curate, wrapped in his own gloomy thoughts, turned down the offer of a drink, but Vivian defiantly ordered vodka.

"A large one," she added. "Don't skimp." She gave the professor a grin of appreciation and a flash of her eyes.

Glass in hand, the professor struggled to his feet.

"A toast, gentlemen," he said solemnly. Bemused by the old man's behaviour, Tarradellas indicated for a drink to be poured for him, then stood as well.

Krakowsky faced him with an old-fashioned formality, tilted his glass in salute, then hurled its contents in the Spaniard's face. Tarradellas cried out as the alcohol hit his eyes like a glass of acid. In that instant, while everyone stared in surprise, Nevil spun round and threw his own drink into the face of the nearest Satanist to him. Simultaneously, Krakowsky reached for his walking sticks and cracked one of them hard against the side of the other Satanist's head, sending him reeling across the room with a shattered nose, gushing blood. Vivian dashed her own drink at the last remaining Satanist, but he threw his hands before his face in time. She called him a fucking bastard, snatched a carafe from the table and hurled it at him. He grabbed her arm and tightened his grip till she cried out in pain, then struck her hard across the mouth. Nevil reached for his collar, gripped it from behind and pulled. Overbalanced, the man fell backwards, and Nevil caught him a glancing blow on the side of his head with his knee. There was a thud, and Nevil felt a spurt of agony dart up his leg, sickening him. But it had hurt the Satanist more. He curled up, groaning, as blood leaked from his ear.

Krakowsky swung his walking stick, hit Tarradellas on the back of the neck as he was about to get up and sent him sprawling on the floor.

"Let's get out of here!"

Vivian picked up a wooden chair as Krakowsky shouted and hurled it at one of the windows. It crashed through, breaking more than half the leaded panes. She reached round to help Krakowsky toward it, as Nevil picked up another chair, swung it at Oliver Atcheson, then leapt to follow them through the window. In the confusion, Quigley staggered to his feet, saw that Tarradellas had wiped the drink from his inflamed eyes and was steadying himself with an effort of will to bring order again. The curate bunched his fists and threw himself at the Satanist. Too late for him to escape with the others, he knew he had to do what he could to hold back any attempt at recapturing them, whatever the cost. Hands gripped him to drag him back, but in the cold fury that possessed him Quigley was conscious only of the need to fix his hands about the Spaniard's throat, and the pain and blows inflicted on him were as nothing as he grappled with Tarradellas.

Outside, the others ran as fast as they could down the tarmac drive. The professor grimaced with agony. Both his legs were still recovering from severe injuries less than twelve months before and hurt abominably when he put any strain on them.

"If I hold you up, keep going," he grunted between gasps, but Nevil and the girl told him not to be a fool.

"We need you," Vivian said as they took hold of his arms and helped him down the drive.

Behind them they heard someone shout. There was the thud of feet racing after them. When they reached the gates, Nevil tugged one of them open and they squeezed through the gap. Two men were only ten yards away up the drive. Nevil stooped by the roadside for a stone and hurled it at them.

A car horn sounded as brakes squealed down the road.

"*Nevil!*"

A blue Ford Escort pulled up in front of them. Nevil looked round at the cry as Marian's head bobbed out of the car.

"Get in! All of you!"

The two men pursuing them hesitated when they saw the car. In the pause Krakowsky was bundled into the back of the car by Vivian, who climbed in after him. Bewildered at seeing his wife, Nevil slumped in beside her. Marian slammed her door shut, put the car in gear and drove off with a squeal as men ran out into the road in front of them, waving their arms aggressively.

"Run them down if you have to," Krakowsky said.

The men darted sideways into the hedgerow as Marian swerved at them, sounding her horn.

"Keep going!" Krakowsky said between gasps of breath, his face strained with pain from his overtaxed legs. "Back to Birmingham," he added. "We have plans to make." He slumped back, exhausted, in the rear of the car. Vivian undid his tie.

"Rest, professor. You've done enough. More than enough."

Marian glanced at her husband, a look of relief on her face.

"I'd just arrived home," she told him, "when I decided to drive to Elm Tree House. I was going to confront Atcheson. I knew something must have gone wrong last night. I was certain."

Nevil shook his head, unable for the time being to tell her just how badly things had gone wrong.

"They've got Winnie again," he managed to say as they drove away from the village.

Marian shot him a look of astonishment. "Thank God for that!" she exclaimed. "I thought she'd be dead - horribly dead." She told him what happened last night. "I was sure she'd been killed by those things. They were vicious." She showed him what their claws had done to her arm. Though the blood had dried, the wounds were swollen and hideously discoloured.

"If they'd got you out of the pentacle," Krakowsky said, "they would have been *murderously* vicious. They must have been given specific orders to get Mrs Davies back to Elm Tree House alive."

Marian drove fast and it was not long before they joined the flow of traffic on the motorway for Birmingham.

"Back to the Kingsway?" she asked as she counted the turn-offs. She told them about having seen Tom Paxley in the hotel reception earlier that morning.

"The Kingsway," Krakowsky confirmed. "No matter where we go it won't take them long to find out where we are. It would be better not to lull ourselves with a false sense of security. And we can get all the protection we need from the pentacle."

"Shouldn't we go to the police," Marian asked, "now we know they have the Davieses - and the curate?"

"*Because* they have the Davieses and Quigley we dare not contact the police. Tarradellas knows this. If the police moved against them, none of their captives would live longer than it took the Satanists to cut their throats - unless Tarradellas has prepared something worse for them."

"His demonic allies?" Nevil asked.

"You saw the thing that attacked me last night," Krakowsky said. "There'll be others of that ilk."

"We can't just leave them there," Marian insisted.

"Till the twenty ninth they're safe enough," Vivian said as she pressed the professor back into his seat to relax.

"Which gives us two more days," Nevil said.

"Two days in which to keep out of their clutches and elude whatever creatures they send against us. Two days in which to try and get the Davieses and the curate free and stop whatever plans those bastards have."

"At whatever cost Tarradellas must be stopped," Krakowsky said. "At whatever cost." There was a hard edge to his voice. "At whatever cost," he repeated more quietly as he sank back and closed his eyes.

CHAPTER 26

Before they reached Birmingham the professor insisted on turning off the motorway to find a hospital. Marian's arms were beginning to hurt and some of the deeper scratches looked infected. They made a few enquiries on the roadside and were soon directed to a hospital on the outskirts of Wolverhampton. When they'd parked up by the casualty department, Krakowsky took Marian inside, where he arranged for the two of them to have tetanus injections and their wounds cleaned up. Afterwards they continued on their way, and within the next hour arrived at the Kingsway Hotel. Once inside the hotel Krakowsky suggested they freshen themselves up before going down to eat in the restaurant.

It was a subdued group that seated themselves a short while later, with none of them showing much appetite.

"We have hard work ahead of us. It would be foolish to weaken our reserves of strength by allowing what has happened to put us off eating," Krakowsky admonished. He ordered a bottle of wine to raise their spirits, though the thought of the Davieses and the Reverend Quigley still in the hands of Tarradellas disquieted all of them, and it was with some relief when they finally reached their dessert and Krakowsky raised his napkin to his lips and said he'd eaten as much as an old man could manage. He leaned back in his chair.

"This afternoon I intend taking the first available train to London," he told them. "I should be at Euston Station by four. It is only a short journey from there to the British Museum. There are a number of books I wish to consult which may help us. With any luck I should be able to get back tonight. If not, I'll stay overnight at my place in London and come back tomorrow. In any event, I'll ring you to let you know. You'll be safe if you stay inside the pentacle tonight. I'll be all right in London in my own house. I have adequate protection there."

"Is it absolutely essential?" Nevil asked, daunted at the prospect of facing what Marian experienced the night before without the professor.

"It is," Krakowsky told him.

"I'll come with you," Vivian said. "You'll need some help."

"I'll need no help poring through a pile of old books, my dear," he said. "You'll be more use here with Mr and Mrs Wilkes." He shook his head when she tried to insist. "I'm an old enough fox to be able to look after myself for a while. Whatever walking I have to do will only be from the train to a taxi, that's all, and surely I'm not so infirm I can't manage that?"

"What is it you're looking for?" Nevil asked.

Krakowsky drained his glass of wine and placed it back on the table.

"When I came to help you, it was with the mistaken impression we were dealing with nothing worse than a group of Satanists. Most covens are made up of pleasure seekers with a sick need for grotesque perversions, usually assorted with a bizarre mixture of sex and blasphemy. For the most part these people are a greater danger to themselves than anyone else. My concern was that their misguided activities at Elm Tree House might inadvertently stir up dangerous forces. Even when I became aware of the presence of Ramon Tarradellas I suspected no more, despite the apparition you saw. For all the violence and death he has been associated with throughout his notorious career, it has always been human violence - sadistic violence, all too often - but human enough in its own sick way. I never for one instant suspected he had delved as deeply as he obviously has into the forbidden regions of the occult. Last night taught me otherwise. He must be an adept of the first order. His command of the things he has raised show this. As does the hypnotic power of his eyes."

"Was that why you handed him the gun last night?" Nevil asked.

"Certainly. Once his attention was focused on me, I was incapable of pulling the trigger. I tried - believe me, Mr Wilkes - I tried, but I could no more do it than I could push my fist through a brick wall. When I handed him the gun, I was only admitting what I already knew - that for the moment he had won. After that it was a question of waiting for an opportunity to disable him or divert his attention long enough to get away."

"To lull him into a false sense of security and strike when his guard was down?"

"And a damn close thing it was too, I don't mind admitting. If we'd been given the drug they were planning to administer to us we would have been lost."

"Professor," Marian interjected, "what is it they hope to achieve at this house? What are they planning for the twenty ninth?"

"The twenty ninth is an important date. The dark forces they are tampering with will be at one of their four great peaks of strength during the year that night. Precisely what demoniacal force it is they are striving to raise, I do not know. Something, though, has used that house as a focal point for contact with our world for millennia, and I presume some flaw in the fabric of the universe exists at that point - some weakness that makes it easier for these creatures to leak into our world. Tarradellas hopes to master this force. He is confident in his ability to do so. It is not unusual for men of his character to be beguiled by the forces of darkness, though. Their inflated egos are easily led to over-riding caution and commonsense, so that they are fooled into thinking themselves in greater control of what is happening than they are. For all the wisdom available from the past, for all the grim warnings from Solomon down, that should put the wary at bay, men like Tarradellas - and others in his group - are naive children, scornful of caution, and blind in their self-confidence. Their self-confidence is both their strength but, ultimately, their weakness. It gives them the will to face things that would crush lesser men into gibbering idiocy. But it tempts them to attempt things beyond their means to control. This is what I fear at Elm Tree House. The build-up of occult forces there is already strong. Too strong for any single man - or group of men - to govern successfully for long. To release even more power there would be disastrous. Yet this is exactly what they are intent on doing on the twenty ninth, God help us. And the Davieses are part of the means by which they intend to do it."

"As a sacrifice?" Marian asked.

Krakowsky nodded his head. "As a sacrifice to the arcane gods or demons or whatever you choose to call those abominable things that have been drawn to that place."

"And if we can get the Davieses away from there, will that spoil their plans?"

"I don't know. The sacrifice is part of an elaborate plan by Tarradellas to increase his own control over whatever it is he intends to release. By that stage, though, the forces might be strong enough to be drawn here without blood being spilt. In fact, my friends, I am convinced it is solely in order to impose his control that Tarradellas needs the Davieses."

"Would that be enough?"

"He thinks it is. But he has probably, also, been misled. Those forces will never be mastered by men for long and are likely to have worked on Tarradellas's mind without him being aware of it, to convince him it will be enough in order to lure him on. Only when their rites have been completed will the truth be known. By then it could be too late."

Nevil shook his head, bewildered.

"What can those fools hope to achieve?"

"What fools have always hoped to achieve - wealth, power, beauty, youth - the list is endless. Some strive for pleasure - for limitless pleasure, and the ability to enjoy it to the full. Others have political ambitions or just want wealth. These forces are skilful at finding and offering succulent bait. Some may seek revenge for past wrongs, real or imagined, while others seek the means to cause pain and suffering." Krakowsky glanced at his watch. "I am afraid I must hurry if I'm to catch that train. Vivian, will you help me to the station?" With that he threw his napkin down and pushed himself to his feet. "Till tonight, my friends," he said to them, "till tonight."

*

When Professor Krakowsky eased himself onto his first-class seat on the London train thirty minutes later, waiting for it to pull out of New Street Station, he was far from relaxed. He would have expected any normal satanic coven to have broken up and scattered by now after what he and his newfound friends had achieved. Fear of the authorities should have been enough to put the wind up them and sent them into hiding - even sent them fleeing overseas - as, indeed, Tarradellas had done before in the past, passing from one European country to another as a fugitive. That they were prepared to go ahead with their sacrifice of the Davieses, who were hardly the anonymous derelicts such groups often took as their usual victims, indicated an uncharacteristic disregard for the consequences. This, more than anything, dissuaded Krakowsky from contacting the police. Oliver Atcheson was probably no more than a pawn in their plans. His was the house they were using. And he would be the inevitable scapegoat if things went wrong. But Tarradellas obviously did not think anything, even now, could go wrong for them. With

159

the forces he already controlled he undoubtedly felt certain any loose ends left when he had finished - like the Wilkeses, Vivian Connors and even himself - could be dealt with. Krakowsky remembered the savage fury of the thing that attacked him in the cellar. With ferocious and deadly allies - and an increase of the strength with which he expected to command them - Tarradellas would be able to pluck any of his enemies to their destruction at will.

Krakowsky pressed his fingers down hard against his temples, as if to suppress a threatening headache.

The train began to move. He breathed in slowly, forcing himself to relax as he looked out of the window at the interlacing networks of railway lines as they drew out of the station into the grey sunlight. The train surged forward with a steady acceleration that took them speedily down the line. He closed his eyes as the motion of the train gently rocked him from side to side.

Despite his worries and the pain in his legs, he was soon asleep.

CHAPTER 27

It was 9.45 when the telephone trilled in their hotel suite. Vivian reached to turn the television down while Nevil answered it.

"Hullo?... Professor?... Will you not be able to get back tonight?"

Krakowsky's voice came clearly through the phone.

"There was a hold up on the line - a signal failure, I think. Or so we were told," Krakowsky said. "It was too late by the time I got here to go to the Museum. I'll have to go in the morning."

"But you'll be back tomorrow night?"

"I hope so, I sincerely hope so, my friend, though I don't know yet how big a task I've set myself in finding this information - if, indeed, I can find it at all."

"Is there anything we can do to help?"

Krakowsky said: "No. You are safe enough where you are. Remember to stay inside the pentacle tonight, though I don't suppose I need to remind you of that."

As, indeed, he didn't, Nevil thought as he looked at his wife. Marian had been glancing out of the window for the past hour, watching the sun as it slowly sank towards the high rooftops to the West. Already its shape was blurred and ragged, discoloured to a dirty red as it merged with the smoke and grime in the sky. Another few minutes would see it fall behind the bird-covered concrete roof of an office block across the road. Then they would have to settle inside the security of the pentacle.

"Do you think Tarradellas will try anything tonight?" Nevil asked. "After all, he knows we'll be ready for anything he could send against us. He can't hope to do us any harm surely?"

"Physical harm, no. But he will still try to wear you down and make you less able to thwart his plans. He'll not let you rest. Not now. So beware. And take care. Take the utmost care, my friend - all of you."

When the professor had finished, Nevil replaced the receiver and put on his jacket.

"We'll pile a few blankets inside the pentacle as well," he said, remembering the cold that invariably accompanied the creatures sent against them. They switched off the television set as the sun touched the top of the office block. They draped some of the blankets over their shoulders and settled down, huddled in the

161

centre of the star. Nevil reached for and gripped his wife's hand. "We'll be all right," he told her. She returned his squeeze and snuggled against him.

The first few hours passed peacefully, and by two in the morning they had managed to fall asleep despite the tension they'd felt to start with. Then, as the street outside fell silent of traffic, the temperature within the room began to drop. It fell swiftly now. Within seconds they began to stir in their sleep as the unnatural cold penetrated the blankets and through their clothes. The first of them to wake, Nevil peered into the well-lit room, sensing the change. For a moment he felt disorientated, then Marian moved against his back and he reached to cradle an arm protectively across her shoulders. In the next few minutes the temperature continued to fall, and it was not long before Marian opened her eyes and stared at him.

"Has it started?" she asked in a whisper.

Nevil nodded as she tightened her arms about him. The electric light bulbs dimmed. Dark shadows stole across the walls. There was a breath of wind that fluttered the few newspapers they'd left on the floor outside the pentacle.

"Are you all right?" Marian asked. Vivian moved on the floor beside her.

The girl sat upright and stared about herself for a moment, rubbing her eyes. Something grey and rotten fell from the window with a wet plop on the rolled-up carpet beneath. They tensed in anticipation as a thick smell of stale excrement billowed towards them. Nevil flinched before it, then snapped his eyes back to the window. The glass - black and shiny against the night - was mottled with blotches of grey matter, like decaying slugs, that dripped to the floor as more of them appeared on the window, almost as if they were oozing through the thick glass.

"We're safe enough here," Marian said in a strained voice. Nevil squeezed her shoulders encouragingly, though he could feel the tension of his body as he stared in nauseated fascination at the window. More of the blotches appeared on it, growing from insignificant dots of dirty mucus to large lumps that dripped to the carpet in the space of a few seconds.

The accumulated blobs of matter continued to build up on the carpet into large heaps. They dripped forwards, and there was a dim impression of splayed, bulky, misshapen fingers in the dribbles of matter that spread before them, as if horribly glutinous, malformed hands were taking shape from the lumps to drag themselves on with blind, spasmodic movements. Nevil saw one of the finger-like shapes start to raise itself from the carpet with a quivering gesture, as if it was trying to point towards them.

"Let's pray," Marian whispered. She took hold of their hands and pressed them together. "If nothing else it will concentrate our minds on something other than the things out there."

Vivian smiled appreciatively. "Spoken like the professor," she said as they turned their eyes away from the gathering darkness.

"The Lord is my shepherd, I shall not want," Marian started. Their voices, subdued at first, joined hers, drowning out the sounds of movement beyond the pentacle. "He girdeth me..." The night passed inexorably onwards. Hour after hour. Each time they completed their prayer they started again, relentlessly, till it seemed to mesmerize their minds like the words of a mantra, sealing them from the horrors that crept and dripped and slithered about the hotel room. By dawn the next morning, as sunlight splashed with a fiery brilliance across the mirror-like windows of the office block across the road, they had fallen into a doze, while whatever had been sent to pollute the room had gone, melted away in the sunlight as if it had never been.

CHAPTER 28

After the brutal murder of P.C. Merriman the village hall in Endon was temporarily handed over to the police as a local headquarters from which to co-ordinate their enquiries. In place of the usual notices about church fetes and whist drives and Mothers' Union meetings that normally covered the pale blue walls inside the long, rectangular room, large scale maps of the district had been fixed up, while rows of desks lined the scuffed linoleum floor with geometric precision. There was an atmosphere of intense activity and purpose in the place as uniformed police officers moved in boxes of files and various pieces of electronic equipment, while a small group of British Telecom engineers were busily wiring up telephones. Lengths of wire were strung about the floor and from the ceiling as they worked. A radio operator already sat at a console by the largest of the maps, her pen writing notes on a pad in front of her as messages were relayed in.

Chief Inspector Maurice Miller, the man in charge of the investigation, strode brusquely into the apparent confusion and nodded to one of the CID officers sorting through piles of paperwork on one of the desks.

Inspector Peter Dickinson, his round, normally cheerful face set in an expression of concern, put down the reports he had been trying to digest and stepped over.

Miller was a large man, with a ballooning paunch that had developed over recent years despite continual dieting and a rigorous, almost Puritanical abstention from all forms of alcohol. His long, fleshy, suntanned face regarded the inspector with a gloomy disdain.

"The autopsy report on Merriman's death shows he died as a result of a massive loss of blood caused by the wounds to his head and chest and abdomen," Miller said tonelessly. His lower lip drooped in a petulant pout that always reminded Dickinson of Alfred Hitchcock. Fifteen years younger than his boss, Peter was built like the amateur rugby player he'd been till a knee injury four years ago resulted in a permanent limp, which he tried his best to disguise.

"There are still no reports about the curate," Peter said. "Not a word. It's as if he's disappeared off the face of the world."

"And the Wilkeses?" Miller shook his head in exasperation. "What's going on in this place? The Reverend Quigley, the librarian and his wife, all gone missing, and our man found murdered." He reached for one of the wooden chairs and sank onto it, breathing a sigh of relief as he took the weight off his aching feet. It seemed as if he'd been stood on them for years. He'd hardly had time to rest for more than a few minutes since Merriman's body was found on the hills to the West of the village twenty-four hours ago.

"Do you think they're connected in some way?" Peter asked.

Miller shrugged helplessly. "You tell me," he said. "A sleepy village suddenly has its local bobby ripped apart by God knows what, while prominent locals disappear without trace - good, sound, normally reliable locals at that. Add the report about Mrs Wilkes returning home yesterday in a strange car she'd never been seen in before, staying no more than a few minutes before setting off again. In the meantime, she visits the curate's wife - says nothing of any importance to her, then leaves. And that's the last we hear of her. Or her husband."

"The drug squad mentioned that Merriman was on the phone to them the day before about suspicions he had about drugs being used locally," Peter added.

"And?"

"They fobbed him off. It appears he called on a newcomer to the area - Oliver Atcheson, a novelist. He bought a run-down place about a mile outside the village called Elm Tree House. It's got a bit of a bad reputation locally - supposed to be haunted and all that. Anyway, for reasons Merriman didn't make clear, he called to see Atcheson and thought he smelt some kind of drug being burnt in the house. Said it smelt sweet, sickly and rotten, like bad meat. The drugs squad discounted it, though they did say they intended following it up later just in case. They claim they fobbed Merriman off to stop him putting the wind-up whatever operation Atcheson and his friends might have going here. They didn't have much of an opinion of Merriman's discretion. Either that or they wanted the glory for themselves if there was something going on. You know what devious buggers they can be at times."

Miller scratched the side of his head thoughtfully. "Perhaps Atcheson would be worth a visit," he said. "See to it, will you?

165

I'm not having one of our men butchered and not move heaven and earth to find out who did it and why. I want every clue followed up, however thin. This Elm Tree House, what kind of a place is it? Large?"

"Very. Till Atcheson bought it earlier this year it was derelict, but he's spent thousands on having the place done up."

"Respectable type?"

"From what I can gather, decidedly so. Writes historical novels. The wife's got a few. Says they're good. *Very* good."

Miller stared at his clasped fingers. "Hardly the type to go around murdering policemen, I suppose. Still, everyone will have to be seen and questioned. He might have seen something. You never know. Go around this afternoon and see what he's got to say. Meanwhile arrange for every farm to be visited as well. I want a report on anything unusual seen hereabouts for the past month. Anything at all. Understand?"

Peter spent a few minutes talking to his colleagues, arranging for the Chief's instructions to be carried out, then stepped outside to his car.

The village was quiet as he drove through it - subdued, he supposed, by the sudden influx of police. It must have seemed like an invasion in a sleepy place like this. Nearby, outside the Hare and Hounds, he caught sight of a group of reporters and paparazzi from the national press, and an outside broadcasting unit from the local radio station, Radio Barchester, based at Fenley. The murder of P.C. Merriman was big news, though so far the press had not hit on the apparent disappearance of the Wilkeses and Reverend Quigley.

The road to Elm Tree House was quiet as he drove along it, and it was only a few minutes before he turned onto the drive and drew up outside the house. A man in a thick duffel coat stood by the entrance, hands in his pockets as he strolled up and down the tarmac drive.

"Mr Atcheson?" Peter asked when he'd climbed from his car.

The man had a dark, unshaven face and a large nose, with prominent tufts of hair in its nostrils. He looked startled on seeing the police car pull up in front of him, and Peter had the distinct impression he was in two minds as to whether to run or not. Peter had seen the same kind of shifty-eyed guilt on too many faces not to recognize it now.

For a moment the man hesitated.

"N-no," he stuttered when he finally managed to pull himself under some sort of control. "I ain't Atcheson. 'E's in there." He jerked a thumb at the house. "D'you want 'im?"

"I wouldn't have asked if I didn't," Peter snapped, hoping to undermine what self-control the man had been able to grasp together. "What's the matter? Never seen a police car before?" Nearer to, he recognized the borstal daubings on the man's knuckles: HATE on one and LOVE on the other.

Peter stepped past the man and rang the doorbell. While he waited he looked at him again.

"What do you do here?" Peter asked.

"I 'elp out."

"Gardening?"

The man's eyes caught at the idea with transparent eagerness. "That's right," he said. "I does the gard'ning."

Peter glanced at the trees that hemmed in the drive. "You've got your work cut out here," he said dryly. "Been doing it long?"

"Not long."

"How long?"

The man shrugged. "A week," he muttered reluctantly, after some thought.

"Took you long enough to remember," Peter said. "I'll have a word with you before I leave. Don't go away."

A thin, grey-haired woman answered the door.

Peter told her he was a police officer. "I'm investigating the murder of one of our men. Constable Merriman. He was stationed in the village. He was found dead earlier today."

A look of sympathy appeared on the woman's face as she showed him in.

"I'm Alicia Paxley," she said. "My husband and I live here with Mr Atcheson. I'll take you to Oliver straight away."

Peter glanced at the entrance hall, impressed by its size. As the woman led him across it he sniffed carefully to see if he could detect any trace of the smell Merriman had rung the drug squad about, but there was nothing now, only mustiness.

Oliver greeted him cordially at the door to the lounge.

"What can I do to help?" he asked.

Peter explained about the murder as they stepped inside. "We're also looking into a number of disappearances that might or might not be connected with it. We don't know yet." He mentioned the librarian and his wife and the Reverend Quigley.

"Surely a day isn't long enough for the police to start showing concern about someone's absence?" Oliver said. "Especially adults."

"Normally I'd agree with you," Peter said. He studied the room carefully while he spoke, though he could see nothing out of the ordinary. "But when there's been a murder as savage as this," he went on, "and a policeman in particular, things are different."

"Yes?"

"Yes." Peter studied him closely. Were his reactions a shade too careful? Too guarded? "I believe Constable Merriman called to see you a couple of nights ago?"

Oliver said that he had. "Though why, I don't know. I was busy at the time - typing the final draft of my latest novel - I'm a writer," he explained.

Peter said that he knew. "We've some of your books at home," he said. "My wife's one of your fans."

Oliver smiled. "As I was saying, I was busy when Constable Merriman called, and it was one of my guests, Tom Paxley, the sculptor - you may have heard of him?"

Peter shook his head.

"Well, he answered the door. Whatever Constable Merriman called for couldn't have been important because he didn't stay long. Tom asked if he should disturb me but the constable said no, it could wait, then left. And that's the last we saw of him."

"I see." Peter mused for a moment, unsure. Again he had a funny feeling about the novelist's reactions. "Do you mind if I take a look around myself?" he asked.

"I don't..." A look of confusion appeared on Oliver's face. "I'm not..."

Just then Peter heard the door open behind them. He became aware of someone staring towards him. A shiver of apprehension crept up his spine, and he looked round with a start. A bald-headed man in dark, expensive, casual clothes stood in the doorway, one hand touching the handle. There was a foreign caste to his pockmarked face that seemed vaguely unpleasant, though this was lost to Peter as he stared towards him into eyes that seemed suddenly to tug at his brain with a powerful intensity.

"I think I can help you," the man said as he took a step towards him.

*

"And you checked the place thoroughly?" Miller asked. He drummed his fingers on the desk in front of him. His other hand, deeply veined, clasped a plastic cup of coffee that steamed hotly.

"Clean as a whistle," Peter said. "Upstairs and down. I couldn't have had more co-operation if I'd asked for it."

"Hmmm." Miller glanced at some notes spread before him. "And this business about drugs, what do you reckon to that?"

"Nonsense. Merriman had no experience in that field. I'm sure he smelt nothing worse than a few joss sticks. That was the opinion of the drugs squad when he phoned, and I've seen nothing to alter that view. Quite the opposite, in fact. Oliver Atcheson gave me the impression of staid respectability."

"And the others? I believe there are a number of artists? Did you speak with any of them?"

"All of them," Peter said. He opened his notebook. "I have all their names listed here, and their addresses." He passed it to Miller, who scanned it rapidly. "Tom Paxley - Alicia Paxley - Hazel Metcalfe." He looked up for a moment. "Yes, I've heard of her. The youngest daughter's doing some of her poems at school." He looked impressed. "Howard Brinsley - Robin O'Donnell - James Patmore - Gwen Patmore - Georgette Fuller - Elizabeth Molyneux - and Graham Spereall." He passed Peter back his notebook. "That's the lot?"

Peter nodded. "Every one of them."

"And you've checked them against the computer?"

"Apart from a few traffic offences and a G.B.H. charge ten years ago against Paxley, nothing."

Miller thought for a moment, his eyes half closed in concentration. "I seem to remember reading somewhere that Paxley - a sculptor, isn't he? - was involved in some sort of witchcraft scandal."

"If he was," Peter said, "no criminal charges were brought against him."

"*Successfully* brought against him," Miller amended meaningfully. "If charges brought against him were dropped or

169

failed in court they wouldn't be on the computer, would they?"

"Of course not."

"Which doesn't mean he wasn't guilty, does it?"

"No," Peter said.

Miller scanned his own notes again. "I'm not too happy about that place. The thing doesn't gel."

"It seems okay to me, sir. Everything was in apple pie order when I looked it over."

"A hive of industry?"

"There were some paintings part finished, yes, and sculptures. And its atmosphere was right."

"Artistic?" Miller's attention was still on his notes. "I'd like you to look into Tom Paxley some more for me. Contact your friends in the press. See what they can dig up for us from their archives. And any of the others staying there. Something useful might crop up. You never know."

*

It was not till the early hours of the evening that Peter finally drove home. He'd rung his wife to let her know he was on his way, and tea was ready when he arrived. He ate it quietly as Jeanette plied him with questions about his investigation. The evening paper was full of it.

POLICEMAN BUTCHERED

screamed the headline of the *Fenley Guardian* above photographs of Merriman and his widowed wife and children. But Peter felt no appetite for discussing the case. In fact he felt no appetite for talk at all, as if his work during the day had drained him completely.

In the few hours before bed he sat watching TV without concentration, his mind elsewhere. Jeanette supposed he was more upset than he'd cared to admit by the murder. By half past ten she suggested an early night.

"You look done in," she told him.

Peter looked up, already half asleep as *News at Ten* drew to a noisy conclusion. He nodded his head.

"I think you're right. I'm whacked." He struggled to his feet and padded upstairs while she turned off the lights. Their seven-year-old son, Martin, was already asleep when Jeanette glanced at him in his bedroom, his curly hair hidden beneath his blankets as she tucked him in. A toy jeep was clutched in one fist, and she shook her head indulgently as she noticed the toys scattered about his blankets, as if a miniature battle had taken place across them.

When she went into their bedroom, Peter had already climbed into bed.

"Too tired?" she asked as she climbed in beside him. The sheets felt comfortably heavy on top of her.

Peter grunted. He rolled over, already almost asleep.

"Don't say I never asked," she said to the back of his head with a wry smile, then switched off the light.

A freezing chill a few hours later woke her up. Although the room was dark, she could sense something wrong. Instinctively she felt across the bed for the reassuring presence of Peter, but he was not there. Where he'd been lying was still warm, so she knew he couldn't have been out of bed for long. She wondered why he hadn't switched on the light. So as not to disturb her, she supposed, though the light in the stairs hadn't been switched on either.

Shivering, she reached for the lazy switch, then pulled on her dressing gown and rolled out of bed, feeling for her slippers on the floor. Fully awake now, she picked her way to the door and looked downstairs into the hallway. It was dark there too. Why would Peter have got up without putting on any of the lights? She brushed her hair out of her face and looked into Martin's room. The door clicked softly as she opened it. A dim glow shone through the half open curtains from a street lamp further down the avenue. She leaned over Martin's bed, though he seemed to be sleeping sound enough. Yet the room was cold, so bitterly cold. It raised gooseflesh down her arms as she reached to feel her son's forehead to see if he was warm enough or whether he needed a few more blankets on his bed. Then she saw the black mark that had spread from the side of the boy's mouth. It opened into a glistening circle on his pillow. Jeanette sucked in a breath of air, suddenly, terribly afraid. Her fingers felt at the mark by his mouth. It was warm. It was wet. Vomit burned at the back of her throat as she realized what it was.

171

"No, Martin, *no!*" Her fingers brushed the boy's cheek and she watched, immobilized with horror, as his head rolled over - and over again, till it fell with a solid thud on the floor. As she screamed, she felt a hand grip hold of her shoulder. It tightened till the pain made her stop. She wrenched herself free and turned, panicking. In the half-light she recognized her husband stood behind her.

"Oh, Peter!" she cried. She threw herself against him in despair.

Ignoring her tears, he fastened a hand about her throat, thrusting her away from him. Fear took over as she looked at his face and saw the hard, brutal, mindless hatred that twisted his features in the gloom.

"Peter!"

She saw the knife in his hand, recognizing it despite the stains still covering its blade, as a carving knife she kept in the kitchen. He raised it. Weak with terror, she tried to stop it with her fingers, but her neck was suddenly squeezed in his grip. She flung her hands up to prize his fingers from her. As she did so, she saw the knife move upwards. Once, twice he jabbed it hard into her. She heard the meaty *chunks* as it stabbed through her nightdress and entered her stomach. The pain hit after an instant's horrible delay, paralysing her with its intensity. It took away her breath. He wrenched the knife out with a twist of his powerful wrist and stabbed her again. She fell against the bed behind her. Blood splattered about her feet. Like a machine he hacked and hacked at her as she lay there helpless, till movement had been stilled in her twitching limbs. Then Peter took hold of her hair and gave it a tug as he set about sawing the side of her neck with maniacal strength, his teeth clenched tight in concentration.

A few minutes later Norman Goodspeed, picking his way along the avenue after a night out at the Top Hat Club in town, saw someone run out of the privet bushes ahead of him. For a moment he wondered if he'd had more rum and peps than he remembered. He felt at his tie with a peculiar feeling of disorientation, as if he'd awoken in the middle of a dream that refused to end but went on and on, unreeling before him. The man, hopping out across the road, looked bewilderingly like Inspector Dickinson, who lived a few doors away from him. But he didn't seem to be wearing anything more than his pyjama bottoms. In the lamplight the blood on the knife held clenched in one hand looked unreal. Then Norman saw the stains that covered the policeman's clothes.

And the look on his face.

Throwing himself sideways, Norman scrambled in panic through the pampas grass that someone had planted in their garden. He'd never become sober so fast before. Either that or he was still asleep, he thought, bewildered, as he parted the tall blades of grass ahead of him, before falling over a gnome that shattered beneath his feet with a loud crash, then hammered at the first door he reached.

"Help, for Christ's sake, *help!*" he screeched. He looked back and saw the inspector hop over a miniature bush. Norman shook his head, as if to clear the last dregs of confusion from his mind. For an instant he could have sworn he saw something long and thin holding onto Peter Dickinson's arms and legs, helping him on his way. That must have been the darkness playing tricks with his eyes, he told himself, as Dickinson paused at the end of the path and glared at him. Norman cringed against the door as a light came on behind him. For a terrifying instant he saw the twisted, maniacal look on the police inspector's face. Then Dickinson rushed towards him, the knife raised above his head. Norman screamed, falling back into the hallway behind him as the door swung open.

CHAPTER 29

Professor Krakowsky had barely arrived back at the Kingsway Hotel when the first of the morning's newspapers, announcing the murders in Fenley, were put on display.

POLICEMAN MURDERS
WIFE AND CHILD

Krakowsky reached for some change in his waistcoat pocket and bought a copy in the hotel lobby, then continued to the lift, reading the article as he walked.

"Well," Nevil asked when the old man finally reached their suite on the fourth floor, "what do you make of it?"

Krakowsky tossed the newspaper to one side. "A smoke-screen," he said dismissively. "I'd wager everything I have this police inspector they're so busily searching for recently visited Elm Tree House as part of their investigations into Merriman's murder."

"Do you mean *they* got to him?" Marian asked, appalled. "And *made* him kill his wife and son?"

"I suspect Tarradellas got at him. He has the power." Krakowsky slumped onto one of the armchairs, exhausted. "It is just to put the police off the scent and throw their investigation into confusion. They will be using all their resources to search for this unfortunate man, who will almost certainly already have been killed." The professor closed his eyes for a moment.

Vivian asked him how he was feeling. She looked concerned as he smiled back at her and said, "I've felt better, my dear. It's one of the inevitable problems of old age. I don't have the stamina I had in my youth. Now and then this unfortunate but unavoidable fact is brought home to me."

"Please take it easy for a while," Vivian told him. "I'll ring for something to eat. I expect you've had next to nothing all day." She looked at Nevil and his wife and said: "The professor is excellent at giving advice but not so good at following it."

Krakowsky smiled bleakly. "We haven't much time for rest," he said.

"You have time enough for a good, square meal. We all have," she added. "I'll order four meals to be sent up now, then we can talk while we eat."

"Tell them to send up a bottle of wine at the same time," Krakowsky told her. "It may be a bit early, but I need it."

By the time room service brought their order, Krakowsky had had time to catch his breath, and he tucked into his food with furious gusto. When he'd finished he looked almost renewed. He pulled out his brier, filled it with an earthy-looking tobacco and lit it, sinking back in his chair with a look of pleasure spread across his face. Odin at rest, Nevil thought as he drained his wineglass. Briefly, he told the professor what happened last night.

"Tarradellas's attention was concentrated on Inspector Dickinson. By the time that was over he would have been too exhausted to concentrate on breaking through the pentacle. In any event, there was never much chance of him succeeding here, not unless one of you panicked into leaving the safety of the pentacle, as Winifred Davies did, and I am sure he did not really have any hopes of that."

"Were you successful at the British Museum?" Nevil asked.

"Partly," the professor said. He sucked at his pipe for a moment in thought. "I learned that Tarradellas's position is both stronger and potentially more dangerous than I thought. And that any ideas we might have about simply going back there again, as we did last time, and taking him by surprise would be even more suicidal than before."

"You don't sound optimistic we can do anything to stop him," Marian said. "Does that mean there's nothing we can do, any of us, to save the Davieses? Or the curate?"

Krakowsky put down his pipe. He smiled encouragingly.

"I've never given up against the kind of evil these people represent." He reached for the newspaper he'd tossed to one side earlier. "At the end of this article there's a reference to the killing of P.C. Merriman. It says the police are looking into the disappearance of several people from Endon." He looked at the Wilkeses.

Nevil glanced at his wife in consternation, then back at the professor.

"How does that help us?"

"Because we have a means of casting confusion of our own into the ranks of the Order of the Hidden Way. Tonight, we stay within the pentacle. If we return to Endon now there's too much of a risk the police will be watching your house. But tomorrow night is Midsummer Eve."

"When Winnie and - " Marian started to say, before faltering.

Krakowsky glanced at her kindly.

"When we get them away from whatever fate Tarradellas has prepared for them," he said matter-of-factly. "Because tomorrow night we return to the village, prepared this time, and with luck and the help of Providence, the means to end this diabolical evil." He pulled out a sheaf of notes from his inside pocket. "Tarradellas's grip on the forces he has raised so far is strong. But they are treacherous allies, hating all men with an instinct as old as time. That one of them should have intervened and saved him when I tried to shoot him shows how strong his grip on them is. Even the strongest grip, though, can be weakened given the right opportunity. That, my friends, is what you will give me tomorrow night."

"How?" Nevil asked. The possibility they could fight back and end all this both excited and terrified him.

"Although we cannot turn to the police for help - they would not believe us - we could still make use of them, though - with the two of you," he told Nevil and Marian, "as bait."

"Bait?" Nevil stalled at the word. "I don't see what you mean."

Krakowsky reached for his pipe, tapped the dead ash out of it and started to refill its bowl with painstaking care.

"You will," he said.

When they had discussed his plans, Krakowsky checked the pentacle to make sure it would protect them during the night, repairing any damage to it.

"Tarradellas's attention will be focussed on the four of us tonight. He might try to use this opportunity to wreak as much harm as possible - mentally and physically," Krakowsky said. "Last night you did well, but tonight will be worse."

"Is there nothing you've learnt that would enable us to fight back in some way?" Nevil asked.

"I could attempt something, yes," Krakowsky admitted. "But it would be premature to show my hand. Let him think we are helpless against his attacks. He is a powerful adept - too powerful to face head on." Krakowsky reached for his travelling bag and took out a couple of guns. He handed one to Nevil. "I assume you did National Service," he said, "so you'll have some idea how to use it." It was a Browning automatic.

Nevil admitted that he had as he felt the all too familiar weapon. "A good bit of time has passed since then, but my memory's good."

"And for myself I managed to get hold of a semi-automatic pistol," Krakowsky said. "They are fully loaded, so take care till you need to use it."

"I thought bullets were useless against what they've been sending against us," Marian said.

"So they are," Krakowsky replied. "But don't forget, besides Tarradellas and Oliver Atcheson, there are nearly a dozen Satanists, including Tom Paxley. They are dangerous enough. Indeed, knowing how secure we have managed to make ourselves against their demonic attacks, there might be an attempt of a different sort against us." Krakowsky took out two smaller guns for Marian and Vivian. "I don't suppose either of you have ever used one of these before, but all you need remember is to aim at whatever you want to hit and pull on the trigger slowly. I got small calibre guns for you which do enough damage, believe me, if you hit whatever you're aiming at."

Marian looked at her gun, unsure if she could use it or not. It felt strange in her hand. Nevil patted her encouragingly as he slipped his gun inside his jacket, out of sight.

That night Krakowsky made sure the door into their suite was locked, then pushed one of the armchairs behind it. Again they took a pile of blankets into the pentacle as the sun sank towards the office block across the road. Krakowsky opened a King James Bible on the floor in front of him.

When dusk came, they immediately knew Tarradellas was not going to waste any time in launching his next attack against them. As soon as the sun had disappeared beyond the concrete roof opposite, the temperature began to fall, while the light bulbs dimmed to dull blurs on the ceiling. What light they cast seemed to make the room extend outwards like a vast, shadowy, comfortless cavern.

They looked in surprise as the television, which had been switched off, suddenly began to crackle. Waves of sparks coruscated across its screen like a build-up of static. Dots of light milled about it. It was as if the set, switched on again, had not been properly tuned into a channel. A hum reverberated through the floor as the dots of light increased in number and a picture, distorted, unfocused, started to take shape on the screen.

As it became clearer, they could see it was a large cellar, lit by candles.

"Remember: whatever we see is meant to break us down. Don't be taken in by it. Or react to it," Krakowsky said.

Slug-like lumps of grey matter spotted the window, just as they had the night before, as the picture on the TV zoomed in on a figure hanging from a wooden cross. It was the Reverend Quigley, stripped naked, spikes hammered through the palms of his hands and through his feet in an obscene effigy of the crucified Christ. He seemed to hear something, perhaps someone off-screen, because he suddenly looked up. Threads of blood covered his freckled face. His eyes looked sunken, pain-wracked from the wounds in his hands and feet. Bruises covered him and it was obvious he had been badly beaten. Quigley turned his head to one side as if someone was approaching him, causing him to squirm, despite the pain it caused to his hands and feet. A naked woman walked up to him. Her long hair hung down her back as she reached out to touch the curate's chest, stroking it gently. Quigley turned to her, saying something that made her laugh as her hand moved lower down the curate's chest towards his stomach, slowly, languidly...

"This is obscene," Nevil grunted. He touched Krakowsky's arm. "Is there nothing we can do to stop this?"

The woman's hands, their objective all too obvious, slid down the curate's body with a slow, sensuous motion, meeting and parting down his abdomen as he pulled back from her.

Krakowsky reached into his travelling bag and took out the machine pistol and a metal tube, which he screwed to the end of the barrel. He pressed a lever to one side of the gun for single shots, aimed at the screen - and fired. There was a dull thud from the gun and the screen imploded with a muffled crump. Something laughed - or screamed - or both - none of them was ever sure afterwards, before their attention was turned to the outside door behind the armchair. Nevil realized that, while they were staring at the television screen, distracted, someone had been working on the lock on the corridor outside.

"Your gun - get ready!" Krakowsky whispered urgently.

The door jammed for a moment as it was pushed open, held by the armchair. Something black, reaching up from the piles of mucus on the floor beneath the window, skittered behind the curtains. As they glanced at whatever had jumped, the door burst inwards, buffeted by a man's shoulder. He was burly and strong. In the instants in which they had time to see him as he rushed in, Nevil saw he had a rough, street fighter's face. There were scars on his cheeks - razor scars. Dressed in black in a wrinkled suit that bulged at the shoulders and about his arms, his fists were clenched as he clambered past the armchair and headed straight for the pentacle.

"If he touches it we're doomed," Krakowsky shouted. He aimed and fired. A black spot, like a burn, appeared as if by magic above the man's eyes in the middle of his forehead. His head was flung back by the impact of the bullet that burst through his skull, throwing him off his feet. It sent him sprawling on the armchair. His fingers twitched for a moment, then stilled.

Coming as if from nowhere, a wind whipped at the pentacle with a futile rage. It slammed the door shut, before rushing about the room, ripping at the curtains and sending papers and books hurtling before it, before dying as quickly as it came.

"Will they try again?" Marian asked, her voice unnaturally loud in the silence that followed.

Krakowsky shook his head.

"Not with men, not now they know we have guns. They haven't enough of men to waste on efforts like this." He put the machine pistol back in his bag and picked up the Bible as the sound of matter dripping from the window echoed through the room.

A putrid stickiness appeared at the window, as if long, thin, glutinous hands with distended fingers were tugging something through the glass behind them - something pale and grey, like wet ropes that had lain in slime and absorbed it into their inch-thick coils. Streaks of red, like lengths of thread, were woven amongst them. Slowly, the "ropes" were tugged through the glass. They flopped onto the floor with wet slaps that stirred their stomachs with a feeling of nausea. More hands stretched from the sludge that had already spread from beneath the window across the floor. They picked at the slimy "ropes", arranging them in intricate patterns that slowly took shape on

179

the floor like deformed letters, while more of the same repulsive matter was pulled through the glass.

Nevil stood to see what was being done with the "ropes". A horrible feeling that he knew what the "ropes" really were was coming to him as he studied them with horrified concentration.

"Something is being spelled out," Nevil cried out suddenly in disbelief. "The letters are hard to make out. The stuff's too rubbery to keep its shape. But there's something. See!"

Krakowsky asked Vivian to help him to his feet.

"See that," Nevil pointed at a jumbled mass of deformed, rudimentary fingers that plucked at the "ropes". "That's a "T", surely, at the beginning there? And those shapes after it, if I'm not mistaken, spell "*This*"."

""*This is*"," Krakowsky read as he studied them. ""*This is... your last warning*"."

More lengths of "rope" slapped the floor. Eagerly now the protoplasmic fingers grasped hold of them, writhing their segments across the floor like lengths of enormous worms.

"That one over there," Vivian said, "is that "*Persist*"?"

Krakowsky darkened his brows. ""*Persist and you will... die*"," he read as the letters took shape.

""*This is your last warning - persist and you will die*"," Marian repeated in a dull voice. She looked at the professor, uncertain.

Krakowsky cast a brief glance at her, then looked at Nevil. "Perhaps you would look after your wife for a moment. You know what that stuff is, don't you?"

Nevil held his wife's shoulders. "I think so." By the look on her face it was obvious that Marian knew as well. They knelt down as the lengths of "rope" came to an end and the message they'd left warped into a meaningless jumble of lines.

More lumps of matter were dribbling through the window, and the piles that had gathered beneath it heaved forwards like a couple of hundredweight of grey sludge. Huge, sinewy hands quivered upwards out of the heaving mass and reached for the glass. Something else was starting to squeeze through - something red. The thick fingers of the protoplasmic hands took hold of the sack-like object and pulled. There was a squelch, like a huge sponge being squeezed tight, and the thing came free. It hit the floor, bounced, then came to rest a foot from the pentacle. Marian jerked away from it and clutched hold of Nevil with a feeling of horror as she recognized the thing for what it was. It was a heart – a *human* heart, she was sure. Marian felt her stomach heave at last, as she realized her worst suspicions about the lengths of "rope" were confirmed. They were segments of intestine - human intestine - still hot and fresh - still not completely dead. She grunted as she emptied her stomach in the pentacle. There was no holding back now. Nevil gripped her shoulders as the convulsions passed through her.

Krakowsky's face had never looked grimmer as he clenched hold of Vivian's hand with an iron grip. He stared at the window as if challenging whoever it was who was sending this to them to do their worst. His thin lips were white, drawn tight against his teeth in a grimace of hate.

The smeared glass seemed to bend inwards as a greyish red blob began to emerge. Again the hands reached up and pulled, and a human head, flayed to the muscles, was pulled from the glass with a repulsive sucking sound that set Marian back on her knees, vomiting, though her throat felt dry. The head hit the floor with a dull thud. Despite the brutal disfigurements, Krakowsky recognized the few remaining features of the Reverend Quigley.

More remnants of the curate's dismembered body appeared at the window. With a huge bump the flayed ribcage of the clergyman, split open, crashed amongst the intestines. The room between the pentacle and the window was like an abattoir now, with bits and pieces of human body flung across it, blood and bile dripping from the furniture and walls.

Marian sobbed into Nevil's shoulder, too shaken to watch any more. Even Krakowsky had a look of horror on his face.

"Do something, for Christ's sake, can't you?" Nevil grated, close to hysteria. "If you can do something to end this filth, do it now."

Krakowsky looked at him regretfully, far from impervious to his plea. And tempted, too.

He shook his head.

"If I did, Tarradellas would know I have learnt something of the rituals he has been using to raise demons at his command. I dare not risk warning him. I dare not. We must bear what he sends. He cannot harm us physically. Not while we stay within the pentacle. The worst he can do is to break us mentally. We must resist."

"But he's succeeding, God damn it," Nevil said. He hugged

onto his wife. "He's damn near got us broken now."

"I wish I could do something, but I must not. It would reveal too much. Too much and too soon." The old man knelt on the floor and picked up the Bible. He touched Marian on the shoulder. "Let us pray," he told her. "Let us pray for the curate. It is what he would have wished."

Marian shuddered as she thought what had been done to the clergyman. Her face white - and close to fainting - Vivian reached for and held onto Marian, both of them comforting each other with their distress.

"We're strong enough to fight it," Vivian told her. "We won't let them beat us." She swallowed hard and tried to smile as the professor nodded encouragement. "Come on," Vivian said. "We'll beat that bastard - we'll beat the living shit out of him. And pay him back for what he's doing. Let's do as the professor says. Let's pray. It's what the curate would have wanted us to do. And we owe him that at least." She clenched her eyes shut against the tears that automatically started to flood as she remembered how Quigley had flung himself at Tarradellas and given them the chance they needed to escape from Elm Tree House.

"Our Father," Krakowsky roared with a look of defiance, "who art in Heaven."

Marian peeled her face from Nevil's shoulder and looked up, her eyes wet with tears. Her voice trembled as she joined the prayer. For a moment Nevil stared into her eyes, swallowed the rage that burned inside him at the abominations strewn about the room, then joined as well.

Their prayer seemed somehow to seal them in even more than the pentacle from the charnel house horror that had polluted the room around them. Black shapes skittered from the shadows to gesture in rage or with obscene movements of their misshapen bodies, but the four of them kept their eyes on each other as the professor read out prayer after prayer from the book. As the hours went by, their voices grew hoarse, but they prayed still, as if this alone could keep them sane.

By dawn they were exhausted, as the last grey shapes shrank and faded. When the first glint of sunlight hit the windows, only the body of the dead Satanist and the curate's remnants remained within the room as grim reminders of what their opponents could do. Krakowsky bowed his head with fatigue as he laid the

Bible down at last with a sigh and forced himself to his feet. Vivian gripped his arms, as weary as he was, and helped him up. The smell of the intestines and the other pieces of flesh - the liver, the kidneys, spleen and lungs - steamed into the air, and Nevil went to open the windows as wide as they would go to allow some fresh air into the room and cleanse it as much as it could.

He looked at the mess.

Krakowsky followed his gaze.

"We'll have to go out and buy some bin bags," the professor said, "and fill them with this. When we roll back the carpet no one will see the bloodstains soaked into the floorboards. We'll need a linen basket. The kind with wheels at each corner. We can place the bin bags inside it when they're full and wheel it out of the hotel to your car. You'll have to drive away with it." He nodded at the look on Nevil's face. "I know it seems to get worse, but the end is in sight, believe me. Tonight, we pay back those devils for what they've done."

"With luck and Providence on our side?" Nevil re-echoed from what the professor had said the night before. He smiled faintly, as if the fact the odds seemed stacked against them didn't matter anymore.

CHAPTER 30

"Are you sure you feel up to this?" Nevil said as he buckled the seat belt in the van they had hired.

Marian nodded, her face pale and drawn after the rigours of the night.

"I'm all right, Nevil." She reached for her seat belt, hesitated a moment, then pulled it tight.

All of them felt the strain of last night - and the nerve-racking chores of the morning as he, Krakowsky and Vivian Connors cleaned up the remains of the curate's body into bin bags. The smell, as the heat of the room got to it, especially the intestines, was appalling, and Krakowsky had felt obliged to order them a couple of bottles of vodka to help them complete their task. Once she had recovered from her nausea, Marian concentrated on making all the arrangements to dispose of the remains. She went out to buy the kind of wicker hamper Krakowsky had suggested, plus a padlock to hold its lid in place. Nevil and Vivian managed to manhandle the sealed bin bags into it. Then they pushed the body of the Satanist Krakowsky had shot on top of them and locked it shut. With the hamper finally secured in the back of the van, and the carpet rolled back into place in their hotel suite, heavily dosed with disinfectant, there was nothing to indicate what had happened there except a lingering smell which the professor said would have faded by nightfall. They booked the suite the rest of the week and, hopefully, it was unlikely that anyone would enter the place in time to suspect that anything had happened here.

After they had taken the hamper to the van, the professor insisted on a meal in the hotel restaurant while they checked over their plans, even though none of them, including Krakowsky, could do more than pick at their food.

"You're sure?" Nevil asked, concerned at the tremors that still persisted in shuddering through his wife's shoulders, as if she could still feel the unnatural cold that had chilled them through the night.

"Quite sure, Nevil," Marian insisted. "We can't give up now, can we? We've too much to lose. If we don't destroy them, they'll destroy us. They won't forgive us for how we've opposed them."

He reached for the ignition key and started the van. He still wasn't sure about having Marian with him, but she had insisted. And, he supposed, she was safer with him than with the professor and Vivian Connors, who had a much more dangerous part to play tonight.

Nevil drove out of the hotel car park and headed through the city streets for the motorway. It was still only early afternoon, and it was important they did not get back to the village before dusk, but Nevil wanted to get to within a half hour's drive of their destination, where they could park up and wait for the right time to complete their journey. Neither of them felt comfortable with the bundled remains in the back of the van, but Krakowsky had explained that these, if nothing else, would make the police act - and act fast - once they saw them. Nevil was certain they would. And he did not suppose, after what had happened, that Quigley would have objected to helping them bring about the destruction of Ramon Tarradellas and his Satanists, however undignified his role might be.

*

Joseph Krakowsky, you are a miserable, pathetic old fool, the professor told himself with characteristic scorn as he winced at the bandage he was trying to tie as tight as he could about his leg in the locked bathroom of their suite at the Kingsway Hotel. Twelve months had done more to heal the multiple fractures in his leg than either the doctors or he had ever hoped they would, but the stress and strains of the past few days had left his leg aching with agony, and he wondered if one or more of the breaks had fractured again. It hurt almost too much to bear his weight, and he took out a packet of painkillers from his pocket, swallowing two of them dry.

He leaned over the sink and turned on the cold water, splashing his face till he felt refreshed. It was late in the afternoon now, and he and Vivian would have to set off soon if they were to reach Elm Tree House by nightfall. He wished he was ten years younger, or at least escaped some of the injuries that had left his legs a ruined mess. He would feel more capable of fighting Tarradellas if he was. He clenched his fists. This was defeatist nonsense. He could - he *would* fight Tarradellas - and win. He stared at his face in the bathroom mirror, wishing he felt

185

as formidable as the image he stared at. At least, he supposed, what others saw - however little it mirrored reality - helped bolster their confidence. He knew that Nevil had felt his moral rebuilt by it this morning after they had cleared up the lounge. And that Marian had regained a semblance of her composure when he spoke to her. Perhaps only Vivian saw the real Krakowsky, the old man, crippled and tired and closer than he had ever been to utter exhaustion.

He raised himself up, clasped his walking sticks hard and unlocked the bathroom door. Vivian was waiting for him in the lounge. A warm breeze blew through the open windows, and most of the odour had gone.

"I've hired a car," she told him as he entered the room. "It's in the hotel car park. We've to collect the keys from reception."

"Good." He looked at her a moment with fatherly concern, though he had never had any children of his own - had never even married. "I wish you were not coming with me," he said.

"How far would you get, professor?" She smiled at his concern. She was twenty-five, though she looked nearer thirty, with a few grey hairs that would add even more years to her appearance soon. She hooked her thumbs into the belt of her jeans. "You need me, professor, and you know it. There's no question about whether I should go with you tonight. I must. You know it." A look of bitterness entered her eyes. "Ever since I lost the only man I've ever loved to the kind of bastards we're fighting here I told you I'd help you - anywhere, anytime. I don't intend backing out now. And I don't want you to ask me, professor. Okay?"

Krakowsky shook his head, defeated.

"I won't," he promised. "I can't."

They left Birmingham an hour later, taking the same route that Nevil and Marian had driven three hours before. The sky was sun-bleached blue and seemed to quiver with heat in a belated return to the kind of temperatures they'd been used to earlier in the month. Vivian drove carefully, conscious of the importance of avoiding any kind of accident on the busy roads. Krakowsky sat in silence, brooding on what he would have to do soon.

On their way they pulled up at a jewellers, where he bought Vivian a silver crucifix on a chain. Before giving it to her, he went into a nearby church, where he dipped it in the font.

"Wear it," he told her when they were in the car again. "You

186

saw how effective the curate's was. It won't protect you as much as I'd like. And if you are attacked from behind or by more than one demon, it won't help you much at all. But it will be better than nothing."

"Thank you, professor." She kissed him on the cheek. "I wish you were my father, instead of the drunken slob I had."

"I wish you were my daughter." He looked at her fondly, tenderly - and hating himself for the danger he was putting her in. If she had been his real daughter would he be risking her life like he was? "Come on," he added brusquely, as if embarrassed, "we'll be maudlin soon."

As she drove off, he felt inside his jacket for the heavy machine pistol. He pressed the lever onto automatic fire. This simple act seemed to prime his mind, ready for action. The time for sentiment was over. He glanced out of the window at the darkening mauve of the sky to the east with a feeling of anticipation. A signpost read FENLEY 10 MILES. Another twenty minutes and they would be at Elm Tree House.

CHAPTER 31

The village hall in Endon had become even more hectic since the motiveless murders of Inspector Dickinson's wife and son and the knife attack on Norman Goodspeed. Although the main centre for the search co-ordinated for Peter Dickinson was in the police station at Fenley, men had been seconded to the village as part of the operation. Since the murders last night nothing more had been seen of Dickinson, apart from a few eyewitness reports minutes after of a strange, half-naked figure seen skipping or leaping down the avenue from the scene of the attack on Goodspeed. What Chief Inspector Miller could not understand were the suggestions that a dark creature of some kind - possibly two - was seen holding onto Dickinson as he cavorted down the road, screaming his lungs out. Nor could he grasp the fact that his subordinate had gone berserk. Peter had loved his wife and child, God damn it! Anyone who knew him knew that. Miller's eyes surveyed the village hall from his desk. The sky outside the large windows was darkening now, and the lights that had been switched on looked yellow in the evening gloom. The voices of the policemen in the room were a meaningless drone that failed to penetrate the Chief Inspector's introspection. He had liked Peter Dickinson. The man had worked for him for more than three years, and there had been a bond of sorts between them. However much evidence was piled up against him, Miller could not believe that Peter had done it.

He looked up as a policewoman approached his desk with a note.

"We've had a telephone call that a package has been left for us by the Squire's Arms."

"Who sent the message?"

"It was anonymous, sir. We've sent a car to investigate. Should we warn them it might be booby trapped?"

"Tell them to leave it untouched if there's anything there. I'll go myself." He stood up and reached for his hat. He was tired of inactivity. Anything that could take his thoughts off brooding about Peter Dickinson was welcome now. He strode down the hall, waved an impatient hand at a constable and went towards his car, parked outside. He climbed into it as Constable Stubbins flung his half-smoked Woodbine into the grass and jumped in beside him.

"We're off to the Squire's Arms," Miller said, as he drove towards the road. The car's headlights dipped across deserted pavements. The village looked like an abandoned film set. Lost and lonely in the twilight, like the stage for an Agatha Christie movie when the cast and stagehands had gone home.

The Squire's Arms was only a couple of minutes drive away, and they arrived as a squad car pulled up beside it. Two uniforms exited the squad car and approached Miller when they recognised the burly figure moving towards them.

"Let's see where that package is," Miller said. "*If* there's anything here and we've not been the victims of a time-wasting hoax."

Somehow, though, he had a queasy feeling they weren't.

CHAPTER 32

Nevil pulled up a hundred yards down the road from the gates to Elm Tree House. He switched off the engine. In the sudden silence they both felt drained of energy after the tension of leaving the wicker basket by the public house a few minutes ago and telephoning the police from a call box. Nevil felt the reassuring weight of the gun Krakowsky had given him.

"Do you feel up to it?" he asked.

Marian turned to him in the gloom. "We've got to," she said. "We can't let them do it by themselves. It's too dangerous for two."

"It won't be all that safer for four," Nevil said with a nervous smile.

He opened his door and climbed out. Marian got out the other side and looked up the road. Silence surrounded them, except for the wind ululating through the upper branches of the trees that soared above them.

"Krakowsky should be here anytime now," Nevil said. He hoped the professor had not decided to change his plans at the last minute and approach the house from a different direction, leaving them waiting uselessly. According to what they had originally agreed, their part in tonight's activities was over, but they had decided they would cut back after leaving the curate's bagged remains by the pub and lend what help they could to the others. They had come to the conclusion that the professor was trying to keep them out of danger, but they knew this was nonsense. If Krakowsky failed they would still be in danger, wherever they were. And he would have a better chance of success the more of them there were with him.

Less than five minutes later they saw a car appear. It drew up slowly, then stopped. Krakowsky climbed out and hobbled towards them on his walking sticks.

"What the devil are you two doing here?" he demanded. "Has something gone wrong?"

Nevil said, "Everything's been done. We phoned a few minutes ago and came straight here. The police should be on their way to the Squire's Arms."

"Let's hope they won't waste much time before deciding to open the basket." The professor sighed, exasperated. Then grinned. "Well, my friends, since you're here you may as well help an old man over that wall. It won't take the police forever to get round to looking inside those bags."

He raised his arms as Nevil took hold of him, and with Vivian's help they pushed him over the tumbledown wall between the hedgerow and the woods on the far side. The elms swayed over them with a hushed rustling of their leaves. Once over the wall, they moved in a tight-knit group, alert for anything that might be prowling the woods.

"If you hear or see anything, leave it to me," Krakowsky said. "And spare the use of your guns for human targets, though I doubt we'll see any of them till we're inside the house now that it's dark."

An all too familiar cold filled the woods and it felt as if they had stepped outside the pentacle during one of the nightly attacks by Tarradellas. Used as they had become to cowering within the safety of its protection, they felt vulnerable without it surrounding them.

The wood was dense, with no path leading through it. The ground was thick with broken twigs and tangled briars that caught at their legs like unseen claws. Far ahead of them, up a slight incline, they could see, now and then through gaps between the trees, the dim lights of Elm Tree House.

"We must get there before the police arrive," Krakowsky said. His breath came in gasps as he forced his aching legs through the tangled undergrowth. "While they create a diversion for us we must get into the cellar."

Something crackled ahead of them, and a wall of cold air struck them.

"It's there," Marian gasped.

Something rustled through the trees. This, they knew, was what killed Merriman and half-maimed Teb all those years ago. The dimming light only partially revealed it. What showed looked white, leprous and thin between the blackened rags that hung from its shoulders.

Krakowsky stepped ahead of them. He braced his feet, let his walking sticks drop to the ground and held himself rigid, his hands outspread on either side.

"In the name of Solomon I grant you freedom from the chains and shackles with which you have been bound to this place. I

191

dismiss you - Abbé de Malmatre, François de Calabria. Go in peace. I command thee." He waved his right hand three times in front of his face in a strange gesture.

The approaching figure halted as he spoke. Its hesitancy changed as his words ended. There was a sigh, unbelievably deep, as if pent up for untold centuries - a sigh, like the drawn-out death held back for so long. And the cold striking them began to fade.

Nevil stared at what had been facing them, half hidden in the trees. For a moment he wondered if his eyes were misleading him. Then he saw there was nothing there, only a haphazard tangle of branches silhouetted in the gloom.

"Has it gone?" Marian whispered.

Krakowsky's shoulders sagged.

"Quickly!" he grunted.

Vivian caught hold of him as he swayed, while Nevil knelt for his walking sticks and pushed them into his hands. The old man's face looked strained and sick. Then he tightened his grip on the walking sticks and pulled himself straight.

"I'm all right," he told them, though his voice almost cracked. "I'm all right," he repeated. He turned to look at them, though his features were blurred in the darkness. "We know that some of what I learned in London is effective, at least," he said. "That is something. I had my doubts. Now, though, we must get to the house. And quick."

He grimaced at the pain in his legs as he turned and pushed his way through the trees.

CHAPTER 33

Chief Inspector Miller was appalled. In all his years as a police officer he had never seen anything like this before. For the first time since he was a raw recruit, faced with his first sight of a murder victim, his head battered in a drunken brawl with a cast iron poker, he was almost sick. Only the white faces of the three constables beside him gave Miller the grit to force back the vomit in his throat.

His fingers grasped hold of the handwritten note pinned to the top of the bin bag they'd opened, and he read it again:

"THIS MAN WAS MURDERED AT ELM TREE HOUSE"

A trick to put them off the trail of whatever maniac had done this? But why? Miller reached into his jacket for a handkerchief to wipe his face, while two of the policemen, less constrained by rank than their superior to maintain an image, retreated to the side of the pub and emptied their stomachs with groans onto the grass.

Miller cleared his eyes.

"Get onto base at once," he growled at the remaining officer. The man glanced at the others as they leaned against the pub, as if he would have to dart over and join them. "Get onto base for me at once," Miller repeated harshly, and he saw, with a dull feeling of satisfaction, that the man made an effort at self-control.

"Sir?"

"Tell them I want every available man at Elm Tree House. Straight away." He looked at the policemen by the pub. "Stubbins! Now you've got rid of your dinner, get back here and drive. You're a policeman, not a bloody schoolgirl who's found a frog in her soup!"

CHAPTER 34

They halted at the edge of the trees at the back of the house. A narrow stretch of tarmac separated them from it. The professor was breathing harshly now, and Vivian felt concerned that he was in far more pain than he would admit. He fumbled in his pocket and took out a packet of painkillers, and she saw him push one between his lips.

"How long do we wait?" Nevil asked. He'd pulled out his gun and was watching the house keenly. A light was on inside the kitchen and they could see through the uncurtained window that two women were washing dishes in the sink. "I wonder if they've been having a celebratory dinner," Nevil grunted.

"In anticipation?" Krakowsky asked. "I wouldn't be surprised. I wouldn't be surprised at all." He turned to peer at where the drive curved into sight, before extending through the trees towards the road. Car headlights flared through the elms. More headlights danced like searchlight beams behind them. "The police are here. We must get into the house as soon as their attention is diverted."

The lights went off in the kitchen. Instantly they dashed across the tarmac. When Nevil tried the kitchen door, he found it locked. Seeing his difficulties, Krakowsky reached inside his jacket and handed him a knife.

"Put its blade beside the lock and lever it. Dig the lock out if you must. But hurry. It won't take Tarradellas long to deal with the police."

Hearing the urgency in Krakowsky's voice, Nevil gripped the sheath knife hard and pushed. He levered it in further, sweating with anxiety at every second's delay.

CHAPTER 35

Miller stamped his feet impatiently as he waited for the door to be answered. A group of policemen, uncertain what they had been ordered here for, but ready to act at one word from their chief, stood behind him. Two cars blocked the drive, while more police officers stood in a line further back. If anyone tried to get away from here they wouldn't get far. If, Miller thought, *if* anyone wanted to get away from here anyway. *If* the note wasn't a grotesque hoax. If... *if!*

The door opened and Oliver Atcheson asked if he could help. The man's nervousness sent a warning signal to Miller's brain. He stepped towards the author, his greater height and far greater bulk giving him a façade of authority which he knew how to use when the time was right. As he sensed it was now.

"I'd like to ask you some questions," Miller said. "If you would invite me in," he added, shouldering the man out of his way as he stepped into the hallway. The policemen followed as Oliver stumbled in behind him.

"Certainly, certainly," Oliver stuttered. There was a look of confusion on his face, which did not escape Miller's attention as he stared around at the other people stood in the hallway. There were three men and a girl. They looked as startled as Oliver Atcheson at the sight of half a dozen uniformed policemen bustling in behind him. Guilt - that was what Miller saw when he looked at their faces - raw, unmitigated guilt.

What the hell had he stumbled on?

Miller turned to Oliver.

"How many people are staying here?" he asked.

"Ten of us," Oliver said. "Ten," he repeated. "Just ten."

"*Just* ten?" Miller pulled himself to his fill height. "Well, Mr Atcheson, I'd like all ten of you in one room for questioning. Now."

"What's the matter? What's happened? I don't understand."

Miller glared at him. "There's been another murder, Mr Atcheson. A brutal, savage, hideous murder. I almost threw up everything I've eaten today, and I'm not prepared to stand here bandying words with you when I've work to do. Get everybody in this house down here now. This instant." He turned to his men. "No one's to leave this house. Understand?"

"Can you get everyone to come here," Oliver said to the other people from the house. Then his face relaxed with a look of relief. Miller, noticing this, followed his eyes and saw a tall, bald-headed man enter the hallway from a door at the back.

"May I help?" the man asked. Unlike the others, he had an aura of self-possession, which even Miller found impressive, though there was something about his eyes he did not like - which he did not like at all. Miller pulled his gaze away from them with an effort of will, suddenly, unnervingly confused. It was as if, for an instant, he had been a schoolboy again, nearly forty years ago, hauled up before the headmaster. He glanced at his officers stood by the door, as if seeking reassurance of his authority.

"Could I help you?" The man's voice, with its foreign lilt, called to him again, and he had to look round. He had to look, even though he knew he shouldn't. "Perhaps you'd like to come in here for a moment so we can straighten out any misunderstandings that seem to have occurred," the man said.

Miller nodded, his head suddenly whirling with thoughts he could barely grasp hold of, as if he'd been given a drug that confused him. The man's eyes seemed to stare at and swallow his own. In that instant, as his feet took him out across the hall, he knew he was lost.

CHAPTER 36

The lock suddenly gave with a sharp crack and the door sprang open. Nevil halted it, then looked at his companions.

"Ready?"

Krakowsky nodded. "Now!"

Nevil pushed the door open and they slipped into the kitchen. Vivian brought up the rear. She carefully closed the door behind them, then followed them through to the door into the generator room. The dull hum of the huge machine was the only sound as they went inside. Nevil crept to the door into the hallway and inched it open to peer out.

"The police are in there," he whispered back. He watched the scene as a tall, heavily built police officer in plain clothes, obviously in charge, strode across the hallway. Tarradellas stood by the door into the lounge. He opened it to let the policeman in, then closed it after them.

Nevil told Krakowsky what he'd seen.

The professor nodded.

"It won't be long before the police will be gone," he said. "God alone knows what Tarradellas will put in the man's mind, but you can be sure it will be enough to clear all the police out of this place." He pivoted himself on his walking sticks to face the door into the cellar. "We must go down there now," he said. He looked at Nevil and added: "If any of Tarradellas's people see us down there shoot them dead. Instantly."

"And those others?" Marian asked. "Can you deal with them like you did that creature in the woods?"

"The creature in the woods was no demon, not like the thing we found down here" Krakowsky said. "Though vicious and brutal, the thing outside was nothing more than the trapped spirit of the old abbot of the monastery that stood on this site. Damned through the centuries, his monstrous spirit was only too willing to quit this place. What Tarradellas has raised here, though..." He shook his head.

They had to help Krakowsky down the steps, and it was obvious to each of them that his condition was worsening. Vivian saw him slip yet another painkiller between his lips and swallow it down with a grimace, but she said nothing. There was no point in raising objections now. They needed him, just as he needed them. And that was that, she told herself as they made their way down the steps to the cellar floor. Krakowsky pulled out a torch and shone it across the paving stones ahead of them. Absolute silence and absolute darkness surrounded them, as if they had stepped into the deepest disused pit in the world.

"Over there," Krakowsky grunted. He led the way, hurrying as much as the pain in his legs would allow. They paused for a moment at the stone altar they had seen before. "Past this, beyond the next few pillars, where the light from their candles won't reveal us to them," Krakowsky instructed. There was a note of urgency in his voice now. Like the rest of them he had noticed a sudden drop of the temperature in the cellar. As they moved past the altar, he fumbled in his pockets for a piece of chalk. "Help me," he said to Nevil. The librarian took one arm while Vivian took the other to aid the professor on. "Here - here will do," Krakowsky grunted. "Now, mark out a pentacle, quick, on this side of the pillar, away from the altar. You remember how we did it in the hotel." He directed Nevil in his task with urgent instructions, his voice clearly showing the danger he was sure they were in while the pentacle was being drawn. As if to emphasize the threat, the cold became worse. Much worse. Quickly now, Nevil finished the last of the lines, then sprinkled salt over them from a packet passed by Krakowsky. No sooner had he finished than Krakowsky snapped: "Everyone inside it, quickly." He clasped hold of his walking sticks as he stood within the pentacle, swaying slightly, his eyes shut tight as he fought back the pain. He did not dare take any more tablets, though. For what he had to do he had to keep his head clear - as clear as the pain would allow.

"Professor! *Look!*" Vivian pointed at something black a few yards from them. Krakowsky raised his torch towards it, and they saw the thin face that stared at them, part reptile, part insect, like something from a deranged nightmare. Its slanted eyes were narrow slits of red like unhealed wounds sliced deep into its head. Stiletto-like teeth, overlapping each other in a tangled chaos of spikes, filled its pointed jaws, as a tar-like tongue slid over them. It bent its back like a coiled spring and crouched, as if ready to leap and tear them apart. Retractable claws slid from the tips of its fingers as it peered at the lines of the pentacle surrounding them, then backed away from it, reluctantly, a hiss wheezing between its teeth.

"We are safe," Krakowsky said as he watched it go, to merge once more with the darkness. Till then he had been unsure if the hastily drawn pentacle would be exact enough. There had not been time for the kind of precision he would have normally employed in drawing it.

A noise at the distant cellar door alerted them, and Krakowsky snapped the torch off, plunging them into darkness. Marian cringed against her husband as she thought of the thing now hidden in the dark.

"We're safe," Nevil whispered to her. "Safe."

Krakowsky turned, touched his arm and whispered: "Silence! They must not discover us or we're finished."

A line of candles seemed to descend the steps. Only the cowled heads of the Satanists could be seen at this distance in the rippling light, like a wavering procession of disembodied heads, bobbing through the darkness. Krakowsky eased one arm over Vivian's shoulders and told her as quietly as he could to hold him steady. He pulled out the machine pistol from inside his jacket and felt to make sure it was ready for automatic fire, then waited. Even in the poor light from the candles they could tell that the Satanists were holding two of the people coming down the steps. Unlike the others they wore pale robes and their heads were bare. Nevil recognized Morgan and Winnie Davies, even though their faces were skeletally thin, each angle of their cheekbones jutting out painfully sharp through emaciated flesh.

"Will you shoot Tarradellas now?" Nevil asked.

Krakowsky shook his head impatiently.

"I cannot," he whispered back.

Nevil stared at him in the darkness, puzzled. *Cannot?* He would have questioned the professor more, but the Satanists were too near now as they filed between the pillars like a line of monks on their way to vespers. They stopped at the altar where they formed a circle about it. Morgan and Winnie were led forwards and made to kneel before the altar, while an antique-looking silver chalice and an inverted crucifix were placed with ceremonial care on top of it. Another of the Satanists, with well-practised precision, proceeded to draw a design about them, inscribing Cabbalistic signs inside it. The remaining Satanists hummed a rhythmic chant, almost hypnotic in its potency. More

199

candles were placed on the ground between them, and in the increased light the faces of the worshippers could be seen - Tom Paxley's ruddy features stood out as he leaned towards Morgan and sprinkled him with incense from an elaborate censer. A head taller than any of the others, Tarradellas stood before the altar. Despite the solemnity of the rites being performed in front of him, Nevil noticed that the man could not resist a smile of restrained contentment on his pockmarked face. On the other side from Paxley, Hazel Metcalfe stepped forward and, like the sculptor, sprinkled incense on the bowed head of Winifred Davies. Tarradellas motioned them back to join the rest of the Satanists as the chanting rose to a crescendo.

Nevil felt for his gun, as Krakowsky stood motionless in front of him. Surely at this range neither of them could miss Tarradellas? Nevil nudged the professor. With his machine pistol Krakowsky would be even surer of killing him. But when he saw what Nevil was doing Krakowsky pushed the Browning down.

"No," he whispered. "Not yet."

Not yet? Nevil stared at him in the darkness, unsure if he had heard him right.

"You saw what happened when I tried to shoot Tarradellas last time," Krakowsky whispered harshly. "Even though we are protected from his creatures in this pentacle, they would stop any bullets we fired at him now. If we failed to kill him, Tarradellas would have us at his mercy."

"When do we kill him?" Nevil whispered back.

But Krakowsky signalled for silence. His face turned away as he concentrated on what the Satanists were doing.

An odour of decay seeped into the atmosphere as Tarradellas raised his hands into the air before the bowed figures of the Davieses. Perspiration glistened in the candlelight on his narrow forehead as his eyes turned upwards till only the whites could be seen.

"*I call thee, Gods of the Underworld, Masters of the Cold between the Stars, I call thee to my summons. Rise as I call thee. By the blood of life I call thee.*"

One of the Satanists - it looked like Howard Brinsley in the brief glimpse Nevil caught of his face beneath his cowl as he stepped forwards - handed Tarradellas a cruelly curved sacrificial knife. Its jewelled hilt was encrusted with rubies that coruscated like burning coals in the candlelight. Tarradellas clasped it in both hands and raised it high above his head. Nevil saw the razor-sharp edge of its steel blade. However ornamental the hilt might be, there was nothing theatrical about that blade.

Tarradellas moved the knife from side to side as two of the Satanists reached in the darkness behind them and dragged out two objects. One, Nevil saw, was a black cockerel, while the other was a pure white hen. Both appeared to have been drugged, lying limply in their hands as the Satanists held them upside down before their leader, while Tarradellas, a sudden gleam in his eyes, reached out and pulled the head of the cockerel back. Nevil saw its neck feathers rise and fall as it breathed. Then the Spaniard moved the knife in an elaborate ritualistic arc, slicing the bird's throat open with a quick movement of his wrist. Blood, brighter than Nevil would have expected, suddenly pumped from the wound, gushing onto the floor before one of the other Satanists moved forwards with a chalice to collect it. Tarradellas moved on to the hen, where he repeated the sacrifice with ritualistic precision. Blood poured from the hen as the chalice was held beneath it, brimming to overflow.

"By the Blood of Life I call thee!" Tarradellas boomed.

The stench of decay seemed to coagulate in the air as an arctic chill froze the atmosphere. Now Tarradellas moved fast. He nodded at the Satanists in front of him and they threw the carcasses of the birds away. They turned, took hold of Morgan and Winnie and pulled them forward.

"I offer thee the souls of two who are pure as thy blood of obedience. You cannot refuse this gift that I offer. Nor may you relinquish the chains this offer will bind you with."

So that was it, Nevil thought. Two lives in exchange for obedience from whatever creature Tarradellas was raising from the Pits of Hell. The ground rumbled beneath them and darkness closed in, a darkness that seemed to force back the feeble light of the candles of the Satanists.

Tarradellas nodded once more, and the Satanist behind Morgan tugged back his prisoner's head. Tarradellas stepped forwards, raising his knife. Drops of blood still dripped from its blade.

"Kill him now!" Nevil whispered to Krakowsky, almost beside himself with agitation. "Kill him now, for Christ's sake, before he slaughters them like he did those birds." Nevil dug his fingers into the professor's arm as if to force him to act. Krakowsky tugged his sleeve free, then steadied himself on Vivian's arm, before stepping out from the protection of the pentacle. Before any of the others could react to this unexpected move, the old man raised the machine pistol, holding himself steady with an effort of will on his protesting legs. Sweat dripped down his face, staining his beard as, grey-faced with pain, he stared down the barrel of the gun at the Satanists. He cried suddenly:

"By the pledge I made thee I give you their lives, freely, to do with as you will, free from all bonds and promises - free from all chains that restrain and hold!"

Krakowsky pulled on the trigger and a hail of bullets ripped across the cellar. The first struck the back of the nearest Satanist, hurling him off his feet. The head of another exploded in a spray of blood and brains and chips of bone as he was flung, spinning like a shop-window dummy, across the floor. The rest of the bullets zeroed in on Winifred and Morgan Davies. Oblivious of what was happening, they were hit by the heavy calibre bullets. Blood drenched the torn rags of their robes as they were tossed from Tarradellas and thrown across the cellar into the horrified arms of the Satanists behind them. Krakowsky fired relentlessly. Those holding them were cut down and killed as round after round crashed into them. Someone screamed. Not believing what he saw, Nevil reached out, too late, to grab Krakowsky and drag him back. Vivian hit the librarian in the stomach. He felt the hard nose of her automatic pressed into his solar plexus.

"I'll use it," she warned, "if you try that again."

Krakowsky's machine pistol shut off suddenly. The silence, its depths reverberating with real or imagined echoes of the explosions, seemed false. Tarradellas, untouched by the bullets, stood as if mesmerized by the carnage. A third of the Satanists had been killed outright or lay moaning on the floor. Blood was splashed across the paving stones, trickling down the cracks between them.

Krakowsky lowered his arms. He was panting heavily. His legs trembled with effort as Vivian reached out to him as support, while she trained her pistol warningly at Nevil.

An electric expectancy pulsed through the air in the brief moment of silence. Krakowsky stared at Tarradellas. The

Spaniard's face was twisted with rage and he made as if to leap at Krakowsky when the silence was broken by a crackling sound, like finger bones breaking beneath heavy boots. Tarradellas paused, stepped back and stared into the darkness. Something was out there. Something large. Something old. Its age - its *enormous* age - seemed to radiate like a foul stench. And it moved. With slow, lethargic, unhurried movements it crawled across the floor. Scales scraped across the paving stones somewhere in the darkness. And more bones crackled, splintered and broke. Nevil felt his flesh cringe. Every nerve in his body seemed to tingle with instinctive revulsion. Krakowsky swayed, then took two faltering steps into the pentacle, all authority gone from his bowed shoulders as he let Vivian take hold of him, drawing him to her. She glanced at Nevil.

"He *had* to do it," she said.

Marian sobbed, shaking her head in disbelief, too stunned to react as Nevil, his anger overcome by revulsion at whatever was moving through the darkness, took hold of his wife and hugged her to him protectively.

Something thin skittered out of the air behind them. It landed on the paving stones between them and the Satanists, swept a glance at the four with its thin black face, then turned away and snatched at the nearest Satanist. Hazel Metcalfe's face was uncovered as her cowl was flung back by the violence with which the creature tugged at her. Its hard talons picked at her robe, before swinging her half-bared limbs above its head as if she was all but weightless. It thrust out a hand that looked more like a garden rake, a nightmarish fan of curved talons that disappeared into her. Her screams rose in a screech of agony as blood spun from her, and the creature, its hands shifting this way and that in lightning-like movements, tossed her torn, dismembered body at the altar.

Tarradellas looked shaken. Whatever moved in the darkness was coming towards him, while the demon, which Nevil recognized as the one that had threatened them earlier, stalked the Satanists with grim tenacity. They scattered before it, screaming in terror as its reddened claws struck out at them. It caught one man by the arm as he tried to outrun it back to the steps. It whipped him in front of it. Its head jerked forward and snapped at his shoulder. The man howled as the demon pulled

203

back its head, a huge lump of the Satanist's flesh clenched in its teeth. The man writhed in its grasp, unable to escape its clutches, all sense and reason gone from his eyes as he stared at its hideous, blood-splashed face. For a moment the demon chewed at the flesh in its mouth, then spat it, fixed the man with its eyes - then lunged. Nevil tensed with horror as the creature's jaws clamped with a stomach-wrenching crunch on either side of the Satanist's face. The splintering, grinding sounds went on with unbelievable relentlessness as the demon tightened its jaws and its teeth bit deeper... till they met. Dead now, the Satanist's faceless carcass was flung to one side as the demon swept its slit-like eyes from side to side at the Satanists, who scrambled before it in blind, unreasoning panic. Tom Paxley was already halfway up the cellar steps when the demon leapt. Its talons took hold of either side of his face. It hooked its thumbs; the claws jutting from them slid out even further, extending like scythes. Paxley screamed in inarticulate terror through his squashed lips as it paused for an instant, letting him see what it planned to do. Then its thumbs moved forwards, piercing his eyes. Even before the sculptor's insane, agonized screams had died, it split his head like an over-ripe melon, disgorging his brain on the steps between its feet, then trampled it.

Only Tarradellas seemed untouched by the panic of the others.

Oliver Atcheson, his face splattered with blood from his butchered comrades, stumbled in front of Nevil. He stared at the pentacle marked on the floor and a look of hope flashed pathetically across his face. Nevil raised his Browning.

"Try it," Nevil warned. "Just try it." He clenched his finger tight about the trigger.

Oliver shook his head. Sweat covered his face as he glanced across the cellar at the carnage behind him.

"Please," he pleaded. "Let me in."

Krakowsky turned his head and looked at him. His eyes, almost lifeless, stared at Nevil.

"Do it," Krakowsky whispered. "Shoot him."

Two shots hit Oliver's chest as Nevil's finger jerked on the trigger. The writer was thrown back, dead before he hit the ground, a dazed look frozen on his face. Somehow Nevil felt he had died too quickly - too cleanly. He felt sick.

Krakowsky reached for his arm, but Nevil recoiled from his

touch. Insistent, the professor said: "It's time we got out of this place." A look of tremendous tiredness filled the old man's face, which even the hardness that had been a sign of his will could not temper. He let Vivian take the brunt of his weight. "*Now!*"

Nevil pulled Marian behind him as Krakowsky, almost carried by the girl, led them out of the pentacle. The ground before the altar was slimy with blood from the dismembered bodies littered around it. For an instant Nevil wondered if to shoot Tarradellas as they passed. The Satanist seemed frozen before the altar. His eyes stared into the unfathomable darkness at the farthest extremes of the cellar with a look of paralytic horror. Sounds of movement grated towards them as they passed, and Nevil glanced back to see what it was that Tarradellas stared at, but the darkness was too dense for his eyes to penetrate. The sounds, though, were unmistakable - menacingly deliberate, they turned his stomach to water as Krakowsky led them towards the steps.

Its trail of death through the Satanists complete the demon turned its slit-like eyes upon the four. It took a step towards them from the disembowelled corpse of its latest victim, its arms red with blood. Nevil pushed his wife up the cellar steps ahead of him. Once they were through the doorway at the top they would be safe, he knew. But the creature was fast. Too fast, he realised. He aimed the Browning at it, even though the professor had told him it would be useless against creatures like this. He shouted to his wife to hurry while he held it back, then fired. His first shot hit the demon in its chest with a sound like a stick being punched through a paper bag. His second shot, higher, lifted the top of its cranium in one piece, like a large black skullcap. The only reaction from the creature was to grind its teeth as it took a step towards him. Its claws seemed to lengthen even further from its fingers. Black shapes, like worms, squirmed within the opened top of its head where its brain should have been. Nevil fired at it again, blasting a hole through one eye, but the creature didn't even falter as it moved towards him.

"Nevil! Get to one side. *Quickly!*"

It was Vivian.

Nevil looked back and saw she had propped the professor against the wall a few steps from the top of the stairs. She pulled Marian past her and took a few steps towards him. She clenched something tight in her fist. Warily, the demon shifted its unblinking gaze from Nevil to the girl, as if it sensed the potential menace of her actions.

"Get up those stairs now," Vivian ordered.

Nevil tried to protest, despite his terror, till he saw her pull back her arm to throw something past him. He ducked and ran forward. As he did so he glimpsed something flash above his head. Behind him the creature howled so loud that the noise seemed to scrape inside his eardrums. He looked back as he bumped into the girl and saw the demon writhe. A silver crucifix was embedded in its face. Two arms of the cross stuck out of the creature's putrefying flesh, as the rest of it sank inwards, puffing out jets of thick black smoke. But the demon's cries were drowned out an instant later by the roar that shook the cellar walls, sending clouds of plaster and chips of stone about Nevil's head. Across the cellar floor, almost hidden by the gloom, as candle after candle went out as if snuffed, a massive, arm-like shape reached out from the darkness. Long and grey, like withered, reptilian, leprous flesh, it was as thick as a man's torso, rippling with tendons that stood out from it like cables. The hand at the end was broad and scabrous, with talons that looked vaguely birdlike as they opened outwards, reaching towards Tarradellas. A thick breath, cold as death, poured over the Satanist. The voice that came with it was a hoarse cough, redolent with menace.

The fingers, their flesh pitted with sores and decay, closed in on him.

The voice, its source so obviously huge, sank into a whisper that made Nevil back, step by step, up the stairs, till he felt the door post behind him. The others had already retreated into the generator room. Conscious of the evil that whispered below in the darkness of the cellar, Nevil climbed out and joined them. Only then did he fully realize the extent of the fear filling him as his hands started to tremble and the Browning he'd been clenching so hard in his fingers fell from his grasp to clatter down the steps. A piercing scream of utter terror swept out of the darkness.

"Shut the door," Krakowsky said. His voice a travesty of its former self - an old man's voice - cracked with tension. Nevil flung the door shut and bolted it. He looked at Vivian. "Can you help the professor? We'll get out of here. We've done what we came here for." Nevil shot a look of accusation at Krakowsky. "All of us," he added, thickly.

EPILOGUE

In the weeks that followed the events at Elm Tree House that Midsummer Eve, Nevil and Marian tried their best to forget what occurred. The explosion that night, which resulted in the destruction of the house and the sinking-in of much of the grounds into a foul crater more than a hundred yards across, was overshadowed by the continuing search for Peter Dickinson and by the eccentric antics of his former boss, Chief Inspector Miller. Despite a nation-wide search and a close watch on all docks and airports, no trace was found of Dickinson, not even amongst the bewildering array of bodies unearthed by rescue teams sent in to search through the wreckage of Elm Tree House. Chief Inspector Miller was eventually given early retirement on medical grounds after disciplinary proceedings for the apparently motiveless search parties he launched throughout Fenley, blocking roads in and out of the eastern end of the town.

Nevil felt sorry for Miller when he recognized his photograph in the evening paper afterwards, but there was nothing he could do or say to anyone that would have helped.

Joseph Krakowsky, his health undermined by the rigors of the last twenty-four hours before Tarradellas's destruction beneath Elm Tree House, lapsed into what appeared to be a form of senility. Vivian took him away the next day to his home in London. A letter from her several days later said the professor's doctor had had him placed in a nursing home where, so far as Nevil knew, he still remained.

September had given way to October and the first frost of autumn was already in the air when a car pulled up outside their house in Endon. Nevil looked up from the plants he had been tending in their garden at the sound of a car door slamming shut and footsteps coming towards the gate. He waved when he recognized Vivian Connors. She wore a rust-coloured cardigan against the cold. Her hair was streaked with lengths of silver that made her face look even older now. Fine wrinkles radiated from her eyes as she shook hands with him, then pecked him with a kiss on the cheek.

Nevil greeted her as warmly as he could, though neither he nor his wife relished talking about what happened. Marian came out to see her and invited her in.

"I was preparing a cup of tea for Nevil," Marian said. "He's been out all morning with those plants."

"Thank you," Vivian said as she accompanied them inside.

"Sit down," Nevil told her. He waved at an armchair. "Marian will only be a minute, I'm sure. We can relax and have a drink." He took a seat opposite as the warmth from the open coal fire in the grate soaked into him.

Vivian was unsure of herself at first as she drank her tea. Marian's face looked so vulnerable after the events they shared only three months ago.

But it was Marian who opened the conversation though.

"How is the professor?" she asked.

Vivian stared at her tea, then met Nevil's eyes.

"As fine as can be expected," she said. "I go to see him once a week. I think, sometimes, he recognizes me." She paused, took a sip of her tea, which was still too hot for her, then went on: "There was never enough time afterwards to talk about what happened. I suppose we were too concerned about trying to evade having to answer questions from the police."

"For us it was fortunate," Nevil said, " they were in so much turmoil after what had been going on inside their own ranks."

"The Inspector and Chief Inspector? Yes," Vivian agreed. "From our point of view, you're right, of course. Completely." She blew on her tea, then sipped it again, her mouth dry. "I know you couldn't understand why the professor did what he did," she said a couple of minutes later, when she'd finally laid her cup to one side. "But he had no choice. You know that, don't you? He couldn't kill Tarradellas, not like you wanted him to, because he knew that *they* wouldn't let him, those creatures of his. He knew that after the first time he tried. Even the pentacle might not have protected us against the full fury of their attack if he'd tried. That was why he originally planned to have neither of you with us at the end."

"You knew what he planned?" Marian asked. "That he was going to kill Morgan and Winnie Davies and offer their souls to that thing?"

Vivian bowed her head and breathed a sigh.

"The professor told me what he was going to do, yes. He also told me why, Mrs Wilkes. That's the reason I've come here today. While he was in London the professor not only arranged to get the weapons he shared out amongst us, but made a pact of his own. This pact was what he fulfilled in the cellar. Two souls, freely offered, for the life of Tarradellas - and his destruction. It was an offer that could not be refused. Not only did the demon Tarradellas hoped to raise get the souls of the intended sacrifices, but those of Paxley and the other Satanists as well - and Tarradellas." She stared at Nevil earnestly as he met her eyes, trying to reconcile his feelings with the hideous necessity Krakowsky must have felt justified what he did. "Do you think the professor is like he is now because he took what he did lightly?" Vivian asked. "It broke him. Even though he knew he was right to do it, that he had no choice - it broke him, Mr Wilkes. It broke him and made him what he is today." Tears glistened in her eyes as she stood, wiping them away with impatient flicks of her handkerchief. "I'm sorry," she said. "I just had to let you know, that's all. I'll leave you now."

Later that day Nevil went for a walk by himself through the village. For the first time since the events in June he strolled past the Squire's Arms, notorious since the remains of the curate, the Reverend Quigley, were found nearby - then out along the road towards Elm Tree House - or what remained of it. The first elms he saw as he drew near still stood as tall and black as before, though they had lost their leaves even earlier than any of the other trees hereabouts. Their branches looked dead, and he wondered, as he walked by, whether buds would appear on them in spring. Somehow he doubted that they would.

Beyond the gates lay the huge crater within which the house had sunk. The trees that surrounded it had been ripped from the ground by the strength of the explosion that shook the building in its collapse. They lay on their sides, their upturned roots like thousands of arms that reached uselessly for the sky. The scars of caterpillar tracks still showed on the dark earth where bulldozers and mobile cranes, brought in by the rescue teams, had been driven during the search for survivors. Nevil stared at the mound that rose like a prehistoric earthwork around the crater's edge. Something black stood on top of it, silhouetted against the clouds. A tall, thin figure. For a moment Nevil felt his stomach muscles tighten with fear as memories of demons returned to his mind. Then the figure turned and looked towards him as the sun briefly showed through the clouds, and Nevil made out the lopsided features of Teb, the nearest he had ever seen to a smile on the old man's mouth. Nevil waved at him and Teb waved back.

Now, at last, Nevil knew it had gone. All of it. Perhaps that had been part of the pact.

Perhaps.

As he walked back home Nevil heard the raucous laugh of the old man behind him, a discordant litany that echoed triumphantly through the trees.

Also available from
Parallel Universe Publications

KITCHEN SINK GOTHIC
Selected by David and Linden Riley

**WILL ANYONE FIGURE OUT THAT THIS IS A REPACKAGED
FIRST COLLECTION?**
by Johnny Mains
ISBN: 978-0957453579

BLACK CEREMONIES
by Charles Black
ISBN-10: 0957453558

**HIS OWN MAD DEMONS:
DARK TALES FROM DAVID A. RILEY**
ISBN: 978-0-9574535-8-6

THEIR CRAMPED DARK WORLD AND OTHER TALES
by David A. Riley
ISBN: 978-0-9574535-9-3

THE HEAVEN MAKER AND OTHER GRUESOME TALES
by Craig Herbertson
ISBN: 978-0-9932888-2-1

GOBLIN MIRE
by David A. Riley
ISBN-10: 095745354X

THINGS THAT GO BUMP IN THE NIGHT:
A TREASURY OF CLASSIC WEIRD
edited by Douglas Draa and David A. Riley
ISBN-10: 0957453566

CLASSIC WEIRD
Selected David A. Riley
ISBN: 978-0-9574535-3-1

Check our website:
http://paralleluniversepublications.blogspot.co.uk/

www.ingramcontent.com/pod-product-compliance
Lightning Source LLC
Chambersburg PA
CBHW070006260626
47159CB00005B/1687